My Three Husbands

My Three Husbands

Swan Adamson

Strapless

KENSINGTON BOOKS
http://www.kensingtonbooks.com

KENSINGTON BOOKS are published by

Kensington Publishing Corp.
850 Third Avenue
New York, NY 10022

All Kensington titles, imprints and distributed lines are available at special quantity discounts for bulk purchases for sales promotion, premi-
ums, fund-raising, educational or institutional use.

Special book excerpts or customized printings can also be created to fit
specific needs. For details, write or phone the office of Kensington
Special Sales Manager: Kensington Publishing Corp., 850 Third Avenue, New York, NY 10022. Attn. Special Sales Department. Phone:
1-800-221-2647.

ISBN 0-7582-0447-7

First Kensington Trade Paperback Printing: June 2003
10   9   8   7   6   5   4   3   2   1

Printed in the United States of America

For the dads, together twenty-five years
And for Rachael Arthur, with love

Chapter

1

"How about a honeymoon *en famille?*"

I hate it when Dad Two uses foreign words.

"What does that mean, Whitman?" I asked.

He twirled spaghetti around his fork and smiled. "We'll go with you."

"You mean like chaperones?" I let out a choked-sounding laugh and looked over at Dad One, my other dad, my real dad, to see if he was in on the joke.

He wasn't. The expectant look on John's face as he gnawed on a piece of crusty Italian bread told me he hoped I'd say yes.

The old worrying fear that I was about to be trapped or tricked by the dads stirred in my gut. It was a side effect from childhood, from a time when I wasn't old enough to say no and the dads always overwhelmed me.

"Not chaperones," Whitman said. "More like guides."

"On my honeymoon." It sounded weird, even to me. "I don't think so." I smiled nervously, looking from one dad to the other. "I don't think Tremaynne would be comfortable with it."

"Darling, the man's been living in a *tree* for three months." Uh-oh. Dad Two was starting to get impatient. "I'll bet he'd jump at the chance for a free vacation in a luxury wilderness resort."

My ears perked up when I heard the words *free* and *luxury*.

"We could go on all sorts of off-road expeditions." Whitman raised a pee-colored pinot something or other to his lips. "I know, let's call Tremaynne and ask him right now."

I grabbed that cute little Finnish phone from his hand. "No!"

"Afraid he'll say yes?" Whitman held out his hand and twiddled his fingers until I returned the phone.

John the peacekeeper stepped in. "She doesn't want to, Whit. Let's just forget it."

"Why?" Whitman said, clearly befuddled.

"Because it's just too *weird!*" I couldn't think of a word that really expressed it. I tried to keep my voice low and the hot little-girl flush from rising to my cheeks.

Whitman, of course, wouldn't keep his voice down. He turned up the volume, the better to be heard by everyone around us. "What is so *weird* about two *fathers* joining their only *daughter* and her new *husband* on their *honeymoon?*"

The thin, sour, sauerkraut-blonde girl at the next table glanced disdainfully in our direction. She must have heard. Now she knew. *I was the daughter of these two men.* The bitch, all in Prada, flattened herself to table level and began whispering to her dot-com fiancé—or maybe she was talking to that huge diamond engagement ring he'd given her.

Tremaynne doesn't believe in rings. Rings, he said, are symbols of capitalism. (Since his bankruptcy, he's been very down on capitalism.) So instead of that beautiful platinum-and-diamond ring that appears regularly in my dreams, floating just out of reach like a helium balloon, I got one made out of ink, skin, and pain. I paid for the tattoo myself since Tremaynne doesn't have a paying job. When I showed it to him, he kind of freaked. "You had that done for me?" he said. I think he was scared of the commitment it represented. You can't take off a tattoo and hurl it in your husband-to-be's face or drop it accidentally down the toilet or lose it at the beach. It's there, like, forever.

Whitman pressed on. "If you weren't so glum and unimaginative about everything, a four-way honeymoon could be fun."

I rolled my eyes.

"You never *think*," he said. "All you do is *react*. Against anything I say or suggest."

"Parents. Don't. Go. On. Honeymoons. With. Their. Kids." I tore off a hunk of bread and eyed the big sweet slab of butter. My two perfect fathers, ever mindful of their trim waistlines and smooth-flowing arteries, never spread butter on their bread. Whitman always said butter was vulgar unless you were in northern Europe. My mother, on the other hand, always encouraged my slatherings.

"Is there a rule?" Whitman asked, raising his eyebrows and watching as I slid my knife into the butter. "Is there a law inscribed somewhere on the Holy Tablets of the Boring Middle Class that says, Thou shalt not accompany thy daughter on her honeymoon?"

"Whitman, drop it," said Dad One. I could tell he was nervous because he was compulsively realigning the silverware, dishes, and glasses, calibrating everything on the table to some orderly pattern in his head. Daddy's an architect.

"Yeah, drop it," I chimed in.

"Drop it? What am I, a dog?" Dad Two turned slowly from Dad One back to me. He spoke as though I were retarded. "Look, honey, I know it's difficult for you, but let's be practical here. You don't have a penny to your name. Am I correct?"

I sat tight-lipped, wishing with all my might that you could still smoke in restaurants.

"You've just declared bankruptcy. At age twenty-five. Am I correct?"

I refused to answer.

"You've been married twice—even though I happen to know you were happier as a lesbian—"

"Ha-ha."

"—and you've never been on a honeymoon." His voice softened. "That's something every girl should have at least once in her life.

Even if she's *not* married. So this time around we're offering it to you."

"But it's not a honeymoon if you two come along!"

"There's no honeymoon, period, if we don't." Whitman let out a sigh. "Look, honey, we'd love to send you off on a romantic trip to a luxury resort where you get fabulous spa treatments and pampered like royalty. But the truth is, I lost my shirt in the dot-com crash. We just can't afford it."

"Then how come you can go?" I asked.

"Because your dad is the architect and they've invited him out for the gala opening. And I snagged a juicy little assignment to write the place up for *Travel* magazine."

"So where do me and Tramaynne fit in?" I asked.

"Tremaynne and I," Whitman corrected. "Well, I knew this place would do anything to get in *Travel* magazine. So I pulled a prima donna."

"A what?"

"I said I needed to bring along my assistants, to help with the story."

"You demanded," Daddy said.

"I demanded," Whitman said, "and they agreed. So now you and Hubby Three can come along with us. I even got you your own suite." He let out a sudden snort of laughter. "You didn't think we'd all be staying in one room, did you?"

Oh, I loved that word—*suite*. "I don't know what I thought. This is the first I've heard about any of it."

"A free honeymoon," Whitman whispered emphatically. "Think of it. Free. All you have to do is pretend you're my assistants. Does that really sound so awful?"

"You mean we have to, like, carry your luggage?"

"No, you don't have to, like, do anything. Except pretend you're taking notes."

"It's a scam, in other words."

My comment took him aback. "It's a *present*," he said with wounded dignity. "For *you*."

"And there's the other part, too," Daddy reminded him.

"Yes, but I wouldn't *dream* of asking your darling ungrateful self-centered daughter to celebrate something with *us*. God forbid." He rose abruptly and strode off to the men's room, leaving us in the dust of his melodrama.

"Celebrate what?" I asked my dad guiltily.

Daddy took my hand and stroked it. "We're getting married, too."

"What?" Tears popped into my eyes. "Daddy!" It took me a minute to recover from my sentimentality and think clearly. "But how?"

"Well, it's not the same as being married married, but it's all we're allowed."

"That registry thing?"

He nodded. "It has no legal bearing on anything. But we thought it would be a nice idea to celebrate our twentieth anniversary by getting Dped."

"Dped?"

"Domestic partnershipped."

"I want to be there. When are you doing it?"

"The first day it's possible. July first."

"Oh." The timing made me suspicious. I wondered if Whitman had chosen that date in order to overshadow my ceremony on the Fourth of July. The dads were being remarkably cool about my upcoming wedding. They didn't talk about it and hadn't offered to help with the preparations.

"That date's all right, isn't it?" Daddy's always extra solicitous when Whitman isn't around.

"Sure. Why not?"

"Back-to-back ceremonies," he said. "Honeymoons together. Kind of fun."

I let him pull me close and kiss me on the cheek. I wanted to lie back right there in the restaurant in front of everyone and be cuddled in his arms. But I was as rigid as my old skateboard. The sauerkraut blonde couldn't keep her eyes away. She was confused. I can always tell when they're confused. She couldn't place me, peg me, pigeonhole me. Maybe Ms. Prada thought now that I was Daddy's girlfriend or his wife. I closed my eyes and let him cuddle me.

"Who all's going to be at your DP ceremony?" I asked.

"Just a few close friends."

"Are you going to invite Mom?"

He tensed. "I'll think about it."

A tall, handsome man with thick sandy-brown hair, sharp blue eyes, and a long, straight nose appeared at the far end of the dining room. Whitman. Daddy's lover and my faux pa. He smiled at us over the heads of the diners. It was only a naughty-little-girl fantasy, but I imagined him seething with jealousy. Wanting me for himself.

In actual fact, the one who was seething with jealousy was Ms. Prada at the next table. Don't ask me why. I didn't do anything to make her fiancé stare at me like that.

After my fancy-ass dinner with the dads, I drove my dying Toyota back over to the east side where my mom lives. I wanted to be with her, but I didn't know why.

It had something to do with the dads getting married. I felt kind of anxiously protective, as if I were the mom and Mom were the little girl, and I had to break some potentially traumatic news to her. If the dads didn't invite her to their DP ceremony, she'd find out about it and be devastated because she was left out. But if they did invite her, she would make up some excuse not to go because she'd feel humiliated in front of all their friends.

Twenty years the dads had been together. Which meant it had been twenty years since Dad left Mom. Which meant it had been twenty years since my own life had taken that fateful turn. A jumble of memories suddenly swelled up in front of me, like those wafer-thin sponges that expand in water. Whitman used to buy me one at Zabar's every time I visited them in New York.

Christmas and my birthday, those were always the big events. One of my earliest memories is being with Mom and Dad on Christmas morning in the big Victorian house with a fire roaring in the fireplace and what looked like hundreds of presents under the tree. It was the first time I understood the meaning of Christmas (toys, all for me) and the pretty stuff that went with it: the giant tree hung with glass balls and strung with white lights, vases of fresh-cut holly, cards, cookies, ribbon, the special incense that my mom would burn. Carolee just loved to decorate for Christmas. I was wild with excitement as Mom presented me with box after wrapped box, laughing as I tore off the paper and hauled out dolls, stuffed animals, games, clothes, candy and books. At some point in my rampage I was so idiotically, incandescently happy that I ran over and jumped into Daddy's arms. He held me the way I liked to be held, suffocatingly close, squeezed tight as a swaddled papoose. My mom stopped laughing and said tenderly, "Oh, look at all that lovin'. Can't I have just a little?" And I said, quite deliberately, as Daddy rocked me in his arms, "No. I hate you."

My first Christmas alone with Carolee was an unwanted memory, but I found myself reliving it as I drove east toward her house. It was during the Big Change, after Daddy moved out of the big beautiful Victorian house. For months nothing had been clear to me. Daddy still lived in Portland but was talking about moving to New York. Fear gnawed at me day and night. I couldn't figure out why he'd left us and I was terrified that he would move away forever. Mom went from being happy to being a sobbing wreck. Without Daddy the house felt disjointed, scary, empty. That Christmas, as I came down the wide oak stairs wearing my Big Bird slippers and Wonder Woman cape over flannel pajamas, it was not Daddy I saw but Mom's support group. I stopped dead in my tracks. The smell of coffee and pot wafted up to my nose. "Merry Christmas, sweetheart," Mom called out as I stood there staring down at them. "Santa's left lots of presents for you."

I could see the presents, but I knew she was lying about Santa. "Is Daddy here?"

One of her friends muttered, "No, your asshole daddy is not here."

"He's not an asshole," I shot back, hotly defensive, *"you* are."

They coaxed me downstairs with the lure of sweets and joys beyond measure. Only I felt dry and empty, like someone had pulled the plug and my bubble bath of happiness had drained away.

That Christmas, the first one without Daddy in the house, Mom's support group worked valiantly to cheer us up. They clapped and oohed and aahed as I opened my presents. Then they inducted me into a daddyless world of all women. One of them gave me a perm. One of them painted my toenails gold and my fingernails green with red stripes. I got to put on foundation, powder, lipstick and mascara. All day long they sucked on cigarettes and joints and sipped coffee and drank eggnog and munched cookies and took turns holding Mom, who spent most of the day sobbing on the sofa.

Then there was that birthday with Daddy. That's what he and Mom both told me it was going to be. But it wasn't just with Daddy. As Daddy pulled up to the big house, I saw Whitman in the front seat of the BMW. That had to mean something important, but I didn't want to know what it was. I was sick with tight-lipped apprehension as Daddy took my hand and led me down to the car. Whitman smiled out the open window. "You remember Whitman?" Daddy said, opening the *back* door of the BMW.

I shook my head. Whitman laughed. I felt panicky.

"Whitman's coming with us today. For your birthday."

"I don't want him," I whispered.

"Well, honey, he's going to be with us today," Daddy said in a low firm voice.

I started to squirm as Daddy buckled me into a seatbelt. In the backseat. I *always* rode in front, next to him. "No!"

"Venus—" That tone. I hated that "you have no choice" tone.

I looked anxiously back toward the big house, but it seemed to mock me, mock my fear. I saw Mom standing upstairs, in the front turret, her arms crossed. Then she disappeared.

Whitman turned around and smiled at me. "Happy birthday, Venus. I brought you a present."

I calmed myself sufficiently to snatch the beautifully wrapped package he held out.

"What do you say, honey?" Daddy prompted.

I thought for a moment before answering. "Fuck you," I said.

I didn't know what the words meant, but I'd heard Mom's support group using them. And they seemed to have some magic effect because Whitman's eyes opened so wide I could see his contact lenses. He stared at me for a moment, then said, "You're welcome," and turned back around.

Birthdays in Portland were for little girls who lived at home with their overloving lesbian moms. Birthdays in New York were for "The Fabulous Miss Venus Gilroy" (as Whitman called me) who flew off all by herself four times a year to spend a week with her handsome dad and his handsome lover in their cramped Manhattan apartment. When I was in New York, I rarely let on that I was having a good time, but fun did seep into those always-too-short visitations. One birthday they took me to the Rainbow Room, where I drank Shirley Temples and danced with Daddy on the revolving dance floor and Whitman never once butted in. Another time they took me to lunch at Windows on the World and we all had foie gras on toast. I could always count on a Broadway show, usually a musical with some big star. It never ceased to amaze me that people I'd seen on television or in movies with my mom were there, alive, on a stage. New York birthdays were one big, new, scary, shivery delight after another: an opera, a concert at Lincoln Center, a show at Radio City Music Hall. A new dress from Bloomingdale's, shoes from Bergdorf, a winter coat from Saks. And when I'd get back to Portland with all my shopping bags and looked at the stuff my mom had given me for the same event, I could barely suppress my disdain. Sometimes it actually seemed like the dads knew me better than my mom did.

I pulled up in front of my mom's dinky little house ("Early Crackerbox," I once heard Whitman describe it) and sat there, smoking and listening to my old Black Garters tape. Black Garters was this awesome all-girl garage band that lasted about a year. JD, lead singer and lead guitar, gave me the band's one and only demo

tape when we were lovers. Her singing voice was a hoarse, croaky
rasp of anger.

Mommy! Daddy! Where are you?
I'm fucked up, man, but you are too!
You say you love me.
You say you care.
You say all kindsa shit,
But you ain't really there.

I just sat there in my incredibly messy car (Whitman had once
likened it to a hamster's nest) thinking about my mom, my dads,
and me. If you eventually turn into your parents, no matter how
hard you try not to, which one of the three was I doomed to become?

Long ago, back in the mists of the '80s, even before my dad left
us, I realized that I could twist Carolee, my mom, around my little
finger. I could get her to do anything I wanted.

It's kind of horrifying, in a way, to realize how much power you
can have over another person. What intrigues me about Whitman,
for instance, is that I have zero power over him. Back when I was
five, and Dad was just starting to date him, Whitman and I would
get into stupid fights over things like who got to sit next to Daddy in
the front seat of the BMW. I always won. But it was because
Whitman let me. He could afford to because he had the real power,
and we both knew it. He had Daddy.

And Carolee didn't. Not anymore.

When Dad left, all Carolee had was her "support group"—this
huge congregation of women bitching and bawling their way
through the pain, pain, pain of wrecked dreams and fractured lives.
My mom was the focal point, the earth mother, the good witch
doomed to stir the cauldron of unconditional love until she keeled
over from the fumes.

She was a size eight back then. She was my size, and my age,
which is too freaky to think about.

They came, all those women, because Carolee had the biggest heart and the nicest house and the largest alimony check. Back then we lived in a huge old Victorian that Daddy had turned into a showplace. Some of Mom's endless women friends hung out there so much they had their own rooms. "You could almost call 'em boarders," my grandma sourly observed, "if they ever paid any rent."

During the year they were separated, Daddy continued to pay the mortgage and all the bills. And after the divorce, Mom had alimony for three years and child support until I was eighteen. So she didn't have to work back then, except to take care of every freeloading sob sister who showed up at our door.

I took advantage of her like everyone else. I got everything I wanted because my own mother was afraid of me. If I didn't get my way I turned into Linda Blair in *The Exorcist*. It worked every time.

Until one day I made the mistake of calling my mom a "fucking bitch" in front of my grandma. Mom let out a weird noise and started to cry. But Grandma's hand shot out and slapped me so hard I went blank with terror. And in that moment of shocked blankness, Grandma, furious in a way I'd never seen before, leaned down and said through her new dentures, "Don't you *ever* call your mother that again, young lady. Do you understand?"

I nodded dumbly. It was the first time in my life that I'd been disciplined, and it was overwhelming.

"When you say that, it means you have no respect," Grandma hissed. "You should always respect your mother because she does her best for you."

Mom, of course, got furious with her mom for slapping me because I'd never been spanked or physically mistreated in my life. I played it up for all it was worth, loving the way Carolee's dark eyes glowed with fiery maternal indignation and concern. It meant I'd be getting more presents than usual.

But I have to say: Grandma's smack and admonition did work. I heard what she said. I remembered. Her slap sent me flying into a new phase of understanding, or trying to, anyway.

Respect. Like that old Aretha Franklin song. Mom with her big hair deserved R-E-S-P-E-C-T.

But then the dynamic changed and Mom began sucking me into her confidence. Every night she drank a bottle of red wine, drew me close, and told me all the scary non-fairy tales that turn bratty little girls into fucked-up women. What she didn't know was that her life was territory I didn't want to explore. It was dark and scary and lonely in that forest. There were horrible monsters hiding behind every tree.

Daddy had been her one fairy tale come true. A young hot-shit ar-chitect, he plucked her from the receptionist's desk, married her, and introduced her to a world of high-flying affluence that just about wrecked them both. Mom had just divorced her first husband, a Sixties radical who got busted for selling LSD at UCLA. Dad had just been divorced by a mysterious Italian woman who ran off after she became an American citizen.

John gave Carolee this short, fabulous life. Then he took it away. She wasn't Cinderella after all. The glass slippers shattered into sliv-ers that pierced her feet and made them bleed. That wasn't a dia-mond tiara perched high atop her big red hair; it was a dunce cap.

Mom never blames anyone for anything. She's chronically unable to express hatred and anger. She tried to understand where her hus-band was coming from. She even tried to support his decision to leave her for a man. But other betrayed women in her support group kept telling her how awful Daddy was, how selfish. I heard what they said. Daddy was just another incomplete, incompetent, insensi-tive man, and she was a wimp if she didn't take him for all he was worth. Under their influence, Mom began ragging Daddy con-stantly. Never to his face, because she was afraid of him. She did it in private, to me.

I began to see Daddy in a very different light, one that made me resent him for what he was doing to us. His side of the story didn't matter because he was the one who fractured our fairy tale.

Then Carolee got into this weird competition thing. If Daddy was gay, and dating a person of the same sex, then she would, too. God knows there were enough lesbians in the nonstop cotillion passing through our beautiful old house.

Only Mom didn't get a Whitman. She didn't get a rich handsome younger man who spoke foreign languages and wrote travel books. She got Jerri. A possessive, alcoholic dyke who spent her life spinning the same ugly brown clay mug over and over on her potter's wheel. I never could see what the attraction was. Mom was so pretty. Jerri was thirty years older, with short-cropped gray hair and false teeth that looked too big for her mouth. They met at one of the endless garage sales Mom and her friends were always throwing.

Their affair lasted about two years. Jerri was subtly abusive when sober, insanely jealous and violent when drunk. One night she hauled off and belted my mom across the face. It was true-blue black-and-blue physical abuse. One woman smacking another. I saw it with my own two eyes.

Saw that shocked look on Mom's face before it crumpled into tears. She probably felt like I did that one time Grandma slapped me.

But Mom didn't even have the balls to order Jerri out of the house. All she could do was politely ask the cunt to leave. But of course, as I know all too well, the sick sweetness behind abusive behavior comes afterward, when the abuser is contrite and the abused is forgiving. The puke of souped-up emotions between Mom and Jerri made me sick and fearful.

It was so different when I was with Daddy and Whitman. They had this breezy affability with one another. They were full of secret looks and jokes. I resented their happiness because I knew it didn't include me. And I couldn't figure out why they were so happy. There was no sign of physical affection between them, no terms of endearment spoken. Whitman wouldn't allow it. When my eagle eyes caught Daddy trying to stroke Whitman's ass or pull him into an embrace, Whitman always cut it short. Once I heard him whisper, "Not in front of her."

Her.

That was me.

For five years I was shuttled back and forth between the big beautiful house where Mom lived with her female support group (and more and more junk and clutter), and the austere apartments where Daddy and Whitman lived with just a few sticks of designer furniture.

It was all very complicated. But it was what I knew.

It was my life.

Mom, the former receptionist, doesn't answer the phone much anymore. She can't say no to anyone, no matter what they're selling, so she filters calls. I pulled out my old cell phone, so outdated and clunky that nobody even wants to steal it, and called her from my car. I said what I always say: "It's me. Pick up if you're in there."

She was on the line instantly. "Where are you, sweetheart?"

"Outside."

She drew back the curtain. We waved at one another. "Lock your car if you're coming in, sweetheart. There's been a lot of gang activity lately."

A moment later she unlocked the three locks, drew me in, and quickly relocked the door. "I heard gunshots last night," she said.

Mom was wearing black polyester lounging pants with an elastic waistband and a long, flowing, floor-length robe with a pattern of silvery lines in the weave. Thanks to some really bad fashion advice she had new glasses with white, laptop computer-size frames. The one thing she never gave up was her big hair, still piled high atop her head and dyed a shade of red you only see in early Technicolor.

The house was stuffy because she'd had the windows painted shut. One of her doctors told her she might be allergic to dust, so now air filters and deionizers hummed in all four rooms.

She muted the old black-and-white movie playing on her VCR. Bette Davis, with big gluey tears in her eyes, was pleading with some guy for something or other. Mom's a real Bette Davis freak. Back when she smoked and drank, she used to do bad Bette Davis imitations at parties.

She gingerly embraced me, afraid to pull me too close because I smelled like cigarette smoke. One of Mom's doctors told her she might be allergic to it. This was after years of smoking two packs a day and inhaling down to her toenails.

"Well, to what do I owe the honor of this visit?" she asked, using her gentle "what did you do in day care today" voice.

I shrugged and collapsed onto her overstuffed sofa.

"Is something wrong?" she asked warily.

I shook my head.

"Do you need money?" She started for her purse.

"That's not why I came over."

"You're all dolled up, sweetheart. High heels and everything. You look bee-you-ti-ful. Did you just come from someplace fun?"

I kicked off the red stilettos that were killing my feet. "The dads took me out to dinner."

"Oh?" She moved closer. I was her only source of information about the glamorous private lives of the dads. "Where?"

"Gianicolo."

"Oh? I haven't heard of that. Is it new?"

"It's this fabulous new Italian restaurant over in the west hills. Everything's gray and black-and-white marble. Except for this blue wall of water."

"Was it expensive? How much was the bill?"

"A hundred and fifty-four with tip. For three entrées and three Caesars. I had a dessert and we all had espresso. And wine."

"Who paid?"

"They split it."

"Was the food good?"

"They were raving."

"The dads were?"

"*Mm-hm.*" I waited a second. "They're getting married."

"The dads are?" She didn't so much sit down as drop into the chair beside me. "You mean like a commitment ceremony?"

"That county registry thing. Domestic partnership."

"Well," she said, "isn't that nice."

"Did you know they've been together for *twenty* years?"

"Yes, sweetheart, I'm aware of that."

"That's longer than anyone I know. Straight or gay."

Her eyes stole over to the television screen.

"They invited me and Tremaynne to go on our honeymoon with them."

Mom cocked her head, like a bird who's just heard a worm, and slowly rose from her chair. "Would you like some passionflower tea, sweetheart?"

"Ick, no."

"I'm afraid I can't offer you very much. I'm off coffee, pop, wine, off everything but natural herb teas and pure spring water. Carla"— her nutritionist—"thinks I might be allergic to wheat. Gluten. And of course I'm lactose-intolerant."

I didn't want details but dutifully asked if she was feeling any better.

"Well, sweetheart, I've been ill for a very long time, you know. I just didn't know it. And nobody's been able to figure out exactly what it is."

Lose a hundred pounds, turn off the Bette Davis movies, and get out of this house once in a while, I wanted to shout. But didn't. "Should we go on a honeymoon with the dads?" I asked.

"Well, sweetheart, it depends on what you want."

Out of the blue I just blew up. "Can't you ever just give me one solid piece of advice? My whole life it's always been up to me to decide everything. And it's like I never make the right decision."

Mom was on the verge of tears. Breathing hard to fight down her panicky agitation. "Well, we learn from our mistakes," she said wobbly.

"Then why do I keep doing the same stupid things over and over again?"

"I don't know where you're coming from, sweetheart. Did you have a fight with Tremaynne?"

"No, but it pissed me off that he wouldn't even go out to dinner with me and the dads. They invited *us*. It was supposed to be a kind of special prewedding kind of dinner thingie for *us*. For me *and* Tremaynne."

"A celebration."

"Yeah. But he wouldn't dress up, so I just told him to stay at home."

"Are you having second thoughts about marrying Tremaynne?" Mom asked.

"Well, the first two turned out to be duds, didn't they?"

"Maybe three will be your lucky number."

To smoke, I had to stand outside on her teeny front porch. Mom stayed inside, behind the screen door, seated and listening like a priest in a confessional.

"Sometimes I think I have, like, absolutely no ability to judge character," I said, trying to blow my smoke away. The breeze blew it right into the house. Mom coughed. "It's, like, I'll believe anything a guy tells me."

"Well, you essentially trust people, sweetheart. You assume they're always telling the truth."

"They act one way when they want to fuck you and then turn into something else afterward."

"Tremaynne seems more . . . *intelligent* than either Sean or Peter," Mom observed. "Or JD for that matter. But he seems shy. He doesn't share a lot."

"He doesn't trust people."

"Oh. Well, when you lose your trust—" Mom said vaguely.

I flicked my cigarette out toward the street and lit another. The caffeine from that last double espresso at the restaurant zoomed through my veins. I wanted to be out on a dance floor. I wanted to be happy. I wanted never to end up like Mom.

Tremaynne was sleeping when I got home. He'd left all the candles burning, which meant he wanted to make love.

Once he came down from that tree, after spending three months in it, it's like that's all he wanted to do. It never got boring. Tremaynne said he loved my body, and he proved it every time we fucked. I faked orgasms with my first two husbands. I didn't fake them with Tremaynne. I never fantasized that he was Ethan Hawke or Leonardo DiCaprio.

But tonight I was still pissed off with him for not going out to dinner with me and the dads. I crouched down beside the futon and looked at his sleeping face, the wispy goatee, the long eyelashes, the oh-so-kissable lips. His warm, earthy smell seeped up from the tangled bedclothes.

I thought: This man will always tell the truth. This man will never compromise his principles. This man will never wear cologne (maybe not even deodorant). This man is dedicated to being natural.

All that was good.

Then, suddenly, I had a glimpse of the future. Our future. I thought: I will never see this man dressed up in a drop-dead suit. This man will never shine at one of the dads' big parties. This man will never take me out to a hip restaurant or on a trip to Venice. This man will never play the status game, so we'll never have a pretty house or a cool car or stainless-steel appliances. This man is part Teflon: He won't let my middle-class fantasies stick to him.

Tremaynne was an alternative media star when I met him. He was famous because he'd spent three months living in a tree in the Siskiyou Mountains of southern Oregon. It was a grove of old-growth redwoods that some lumber company wanted to cut down.

He joined a group called Arbor Vitae. This group did everything it could to stop the logging. They spiked trees, damaged equipment, and chained themselves to tree trunks. Then Tremaynne volunteered to actually live in one of the oldest and largest of the threatened redwoods. The lumber people were so pissed off with Arbor Vitae they wanted to kill everyone in the group. Especially Tremaynne.

Living 180 feet up in a tree was the kind of publicity stunt that Tremaynne knew would draw attention to the cause. He looked like a movie star when he was on the news. Like Brad Pitt without the jaw line. A local station covered the story and I just happened to see it one night when I was at my mom's. Then a local indie rock station started a weekly "Tremaynne in the Tree" story, asking him how he was doing and what was new. His life was, like, totally surreal and fascinating.

When his tree-sit was over, the tree-man who called himself Tremaynne came to Portland. He got more publicity when he joined an Animal Liberation Front demonstration in front of a big animal research facility. Tremaynne Woods, movie-star-cute hero of environmental causes and animal rights, was in the news again. You listened to his stories of animal cruelty because he was so incredibly sexy.

But he still had to go through the bankruptcy thing because he'd been living on plastic for two years and his creditors were hunting him down.

There are so many bankrupts that the proceedings are held with groups of ten at a time. Tremaynne and I met as my group was coming out of the bankruptcy courtroom and his group was going in. It was, like, ordained. The minute I recognized him I knew I'd marry him. We weren't shy with each other at all. It was, like, we both instantly understood that we wanted to be together.

The one thing I wasn't quite prepared for was how short he was. He looked a lot taller on TV.

"How was the judge?" he asked. "Did he sentence you to debtor's prison for the rest of your life?"

"No. It went just like the lawyer said."

"I don't have a lawyer," he said. "I'm doing it all myself." He held up a copy of *Bankruptcy for Dummies*.

"I used a kit for my recent divorce," I said, all smiley, making sure he saw I wasn't wearing a wedding ring.

He looked me up and down, slowly, his eyes licking me up. I felt a hot stirring in my crotch.

"What did the judge let you keep?" he asked.

"My car. I suppose because it's not worth anything."

"I don't own a car," he said. "I don't want to contribute to global warming."

"You're Tremaynne Woods, aren't you?" I had to make sure.

He smiled and cocked his head, pleased that I'd recognized him. "And who are you?"

"Venus Gilroy."

"The goddess of love. Here in bankruptcy court."

"I hate money," I said.

"But you have such beautiful assets."

A warm shudder ran through me. "Not anymore."

"Oh yeah?" he said quietly. "I don't believe you."

"The judge wiped out my debt, but he wiped out my credit, too. It's cash-only for the next seven years."

"Those weren't the kind of assets I was talking about, Venus." He kept his voice low, intimate, like he was sharing a secret with me.

In the hot, focused beam of his eyes I felt like kindling just starting to catch fire. My clothes were burning away. "If you're interested," I said, "I could show you my spreadsheet."

He looked me up and down again. He came as close as a whisper. "Do you know how they kill foxes to make fur coats?"

"I don't wear fur," I said.

"They stick an electric rod up their asshole and electrocute them."

"That's horrible."

"I worked in one of those places. Undercover. I got pictures." He gently took hold of my wrist, looked into my eyes, then glanced at my watch. "I gotta go. Destitution beckons."

We both stood there, staring at one another, not wanting to break the magic bubble.

Someone should write a book about what it feels like to fall in love at first sight. It's a weird, almost dangerous feeling. Nothing and no one else matters. It's like looking into a wild river. You know that it's there, just waiting to suck you away in its dark, powerful current. All you have to do is jump.

I would have run away with Tremaynne Woods that minute if he'd asked me to.

"They like it when you sound contrite," I said. "In court. Like you've learned your lesson."

"I learned my lesson all right," Tremaynne said. "Too bad it was the wrong one." There was a kind of mocking defiance in his voice and cocky manner.

"You don't think we're supposed to learn from our mistakes?"

"I don't make mistakes," he said.

"Everybody makes mistakes."

"Everything I do, I do for a reason," he said. "Where's your car parked?"

"Not far."

"You want to drive me to the homeless shelter when I'm out of here?"

I didn't know if he was joking or not. "You don't live in a homeless shelter."

"Are you inviting me to move in with you?"

The river was waiting. I closed my eyes and jumped in.

The fact that we'd met in bankruptcy court always seemed kind of crazily romantic to me. Now an irritating little voice whispered: "This man has no money and no credit cards. Like you, he doesn't know how to make money or keep money. He'll never be able to support you; you'll probably end up supporting him."

And did I really want a life committed to environmental activism? A life dedicated to saving trees instead of roaring around in a gas-guzzling SUV?

I looked down at my tattooed engagement ring, wondering why I'd even asked him to marry me. Because if I was brutally brutally honest, Tremaynne Woods had nothing to offer except the best sex I'd ever had in my life. He staked a claim on my body the first time we made love. When sex is that good, it has to mean something.

As I crouched there, petting him and wondering about our future, he opened one nut-colored eye and stared at me. Brushed his fingers along my cheek. "Why you crying, babe?"

I shook my head. I really didn't know why I was blubbering. Sometimes life and who you are and what you want and what you end up with just seems like too much. Or too little.

Confusing.

Underneath all my doubts I did love him. The question was, why? He was strong but tender, with a secret vulnerability that made me want to take care of him. He was committed to something in a way I never had been. He seemed to exist in a larger picture, a larger world than mine.

"Come to bed." He sat up and slowly began to undress me.

The futon was all warm and ready, just waiting for me to slide in between the sheets.

"How was dinner with your dads?" Tremaynne asked as he slowly unbuttoned my blouse.

"I wish you'd been there."

He pulled off my blouse and rested his head on my breasts. "Mmmm. So warm. This is my dinner."

"They were so disappointed," I said. And let out a sigh as he moved up and began nuzzling my neck. "It was supposed to be a celebration."

"I hope you had a good time," he said, squatting behind me. He brushed my hair to one side and gave the back of my neck little love bites.

"I may as well tell you now," I panted.

He reached around and popped my breasts out of the sexy little black French bra I'd found on sale at Victoria's Secret. "Let's not talk. Let's just suck."

He pulled me down to the bed and slid his tongue into my mouth. I had a sudden fear that my breath stank of coffee and cigarettes and the meat that I told him I didn't eat anymore. "You'll laugh," I said, pulling away.

"Okay." His lips slid up into an anticipatory smile.

"They want us to go on our honeymoon with them."

Tremaynne scratched his chin.

"To some wilderness resort. My dad was the architect. Whitman's writing about it. It would all be free."

"What resort?"

"I think it's called Pine Mountain."

"Pine Mountain Lodge?" He propped himself up on an elbow. "Your dad was the architect for that?"

"You've heard of it?"

"Yeah. It sounds familiar."

"We'd have our own luxury suite," I said. "There's a spa. It would all be free."

Tremaynne suddenly leapt off the futon and headed for the computer. He was completely naked. I had a flash of his hard, tight little buns. I could hear the mouse clicking, the sound of the keyboard being tapped, the hushed shrieks and boings as he connected to the Internet.

He was always doing that. Sometimes in the middle of a conversation he'd raise a hand and say, "Wait a minute, I've got to check something out." Sometimes I'd wake up in the middle of the night and see him sitting there in the dark, his body washed by the gray light of the computer screen.

"So I'll tell them no," I said.

He was clicking away, reading something. "Who?"

"The dads. I knew it was a crazy idea. Whoever heard of going on a honeymoon with your fathers?"

He stopped clicking, read a little more, and then looked at me. "Call them right now," he said. He pointed to the telephone. "Tell them we'd love to go to Pine Mountain Lodge."

Chapter
2

Remember when my dad told me that "just a few friends" would be at his and Whitman's DP ceremony?

Yeah, right.

What really happened was so typical of how they operate. Or how Whitman operates, I should say.

"We're just letting a few close friends in on this," he insisted. "If they *want* to show up, they can."

"Aren't you sending out invitations?" I asked.

"Oh God, no. There's no ceremony of any kind. Nothing romantic. It's like registering a dog. You sign a paper and give them a check for sixty-five dollars. That's it."

"Doesn't anybody pronounce you husband and husband or something?"

"No, sweetheart. Nobody speaks through the entire procedure except to ask how you're paying. It takes place in this really ugly office building in need of major feng shui."

I felt sorry for them. They're both so into making their surroundings so perfect. This was a big deal for them, but there was no way they could make it romantic or special.

They couldn't get legally married because according to state law only a man and a woman could do that. They weren't allowed any kind of civil union that gave them any legal rights or status as a couple. All they had, as Whitman pointed out, was this local registry thing. It had no legal bearing outside the county and gave the signers no privileges within.

"It's the crumb they've thrown us so we won't revolt," he said.

But the dads were determined to be there the first day the registry opened. And that just happened to be July first, three days before Tremaynne and I were getting married. So I had a lot on my mind as I ransacked my messy apartment trying to find the only show-offy dress that I owned.

Tremaynne doesn't worry about clothes because he doesn't own any. All he owns is what'll fit into his backpack.

He didn't own a car either, so I had to drive us to the registry office. By the time we arrived, about a hundred people were already gathered outside and more were arriving every minute. These were the dads' "few close friends." I saw so many familiar faces that at first I thought it was a humongous party. Then I saw a large, angry-looking man holding up a sign that read "Adam and Eve, not Adam and Steve."

Then I saw a local television news truck.

"Oh shit."

"What's going on?" Tremaynne asked.

My adrenaline kicked in hard and fast. "It's the first day of the registry. So they're protesting."

"Who is?"

"Who do you think?" I snapped. It just made me so mad I wanted to start swinging. "I'm not going to let those assholes ruin this for the dads!"

"You're beautiful when you're pissed off," Tremaynne said. "Come on, let's get into the action."

I had to park my junky old Toyota blocks away, amidst a shining sea of Mercedes, BMWs, and forty-thousand-dollar SUVs. We walked fast. Easy for Tremaynne in his blue jeans and hiking boots, murder for me in my heels and tight evening dress. I wobbled down the uneven sidewalks, wishing Tremaynne would slow down and give me his arm.

"There's Venus!" someone shouted as we turned the corner and approached the registry office. Everyone looked in my direction. Some of my friends whistled. I waved, feeling like a five-second movie star. I'd never forgotten that Sylphide, the dads' pretzel-thin yoga teacher, once said I looked like Marilyn Monroe in my tight red dress.

Everyone I'd ever seen at one of the dads' parties was hanging out in front of this nondescript office building. Most of my best friends were there, too, because the dads were like their dads, too. Everyone was dressed up, but I was the only one showing a bit of skin.

It was a bright, windy day. Mount Hood was glowing in the distance.

As a seasoned party girl I can usually gauge the mood of a gathering pretty fast. Everyone who'd come to celebrate the dads' DP was excited, but they didn't quite know what to do. They wanted to be happy, the way you're supposed to be happy at weddings. But there wasn't any sort of ceremony to look forward to, or a church where you could sit down. And there were seven people hanging off to one side like an ominous storm cloud.

"God hates homos!" they chanted.

I could feel my bare skin turning really hot.

Ed and Thisbe Nesbitt were serving champagne from the back of their Lexus SUV. In crystal glasses, very classy. Thisbe airkissed me and whispered: "It was all so nice until those unpleasant people showed up."

"Nobody told them that dinosaurs are extinct." It was Marielle, the gorgeous six-foot-two Dutch woman who was Whitman's best friend. She'd set up a table on the sidewalk next to Ed and Thisbe, laid it with a white cloth, and was serving sushi canapés.

"Are my dads here yet?" I asked her.

"No, but they're due any minute."

"I wish we could do something," Thisbe said anxiously. "This is such an important event. Those extremists shouldn't be allowed to spoil it."

Fokke, Marielle's venture-capitalist Dutch husband, angrily bulldozed his way through the crowd. "Muricans," he grumbled, shaking his head. "Ya, I told doze bastards to go but dey-dey-dey want a fight."

"Ya, all they want is the publicity," Marielle said.

"Okay," I said, feeling reckless and insanely protective of the dads, "I'll give the fuckers some publicity."

"Nay," Marielle scolded. "You can't fight in that pretty dress."

"Watch me." As I sized up my targets, Tremaynne slipped his hand into mine.

"At least have some sushi and champagne before you attack," Marielle said.

Tremaynne shook his head. "None for me, thanks."

"What?" Marielle looked offended. "You don't like sushi?"

"Fish," Tremaynne said. "I don't eat anything that has eyes."

Marielle squinted, puzzled, then shrugged and looked at me. "You, Venus, you love my sushi."

"I sure do."

I stared at her jewelry as she quickly served me pieces of raw, liver-red tuna with wasabi and soy sauce. Marielle always wore huge handmade pieces of platinum and gold inset with the jewels her husband bought for her in South Africa. A yellow diamond the size of an elf's eye winked in her ring. Something I would never have. I wouldn't even come close. Tall beautiful Marielle and her short pushy husband (pretending not to eyeball my cleavage) lived in a world beyond my dreams. The world of millionaires.

Tremaynne and I were paupers. We'd never even been rich before we went bankrupt, just bogged down with credit-card debt.

I had a sudden sinking feeling that it was always going to be like that. Tremaynne wasn't interested in making tons of money and I hated to work. I floated from one boring, dead-end job to the next, much to the dads' dismay.

Thisbe handed us flutes of champagne. "I hear you're getting married on the Fourth of July and then you're all going off together on a family honeymoon. I just think that's so . . . *unusual.*"

"Is dis the guy you're going to marry?" Fokke wanted to know. He didn't give me time to answer. "What do you do?" he demanded of Tremaynne.

"I work for the earth," said my fiancé.

"Ya," Fokke the developer said, "what does that mean? What does the earth pay you?"

While they were talking, Lorenzo Lopez passed by with a tiny cell phone held daintily to his ear. He was an interior decorator from a rich Argentinian family. "Venus, darling." He airkissed me. "Congratulations!"

I thought he was referring to my impending marriage. "Thanks."

"When is it due?" Lorenzo asked.

"When is what due?"

He pointed his cell phone at my stomach. "The baby!"

Mortified, I sucked in my belly. "I'm not pregnant, Lorenzo."

"Oh, darling, I am so sorry." He smiled, showing a mouthful of teeth so bright you could read by them at night. "I truly didn't mean to humiliate you."

"Come on," I said, pulling Tremaynne away from Fokke's harangue. "Let's go kick some ass."

As the seven homophobes brayed their slogans, Wendell Tuttle from the symphony sat playing his huge gold harp near a rhododendron bush. It was so weird: a party and a protest in one. Like some new kind of performance art. Love and hate, hand in hand.

My old girlfriend, JD, provocative as ever, stepped in front of me with her arms spread. She was wearing the teeniest miniskirt I'd ever seen and huge platforms, like those tottering Japanese girls in Tokyo. "Hey Venus," she said, ignoring Tremaynne and pulling me into a kissy embrace. "Let's get hitched like your dads."

"Isn't it kind of early in the morning for Ecstasy?" It had to be drugs talking because JD undrugged was terrified of intimacy. That's why I had to break up with her. It was like making love to a Popsicle.

She caught sight of a news-cam pointed at us and pulled me closer, posing like it was a photo op. "I'm JD, and I used to be with Black Garters, but now I'm lead singer with Go-Go Girls. And this lovely girl next to me is Venus Gilroy. She's the daughter of the dads."

"Daughter of the Dads?" The newsman was confused. "Is that a band?"

JD laughed. "No, stupid, the dads are her dads. You know, like her male parents. They're coming here today to get married."

"Not married," I corrected, "domestic partnershipped."

"What do you think of the demonstrators?" the newsman asked me.

"They have their rights, but if they don't shut up I think there's going to be trouble."

Of course they didn't shut up. They got louder. And the dads' friends started to get angry, like me. Nobody wanted to get violent, but we all wanted them to shut the fuck up.

It was Whitman who taught me how to heckle. When I was about twelve and visiting the dads in New York, he dragged me along to a big political rally down by City Hall. Something to do with AIDS. There were hundreds of angry gay men. I'd never seen such a sight. I watched Whitman jeering and making fun of the politicians. It shocked and excited me because in Portland everybody is always so nice. At least on the surface.

Even now, faced with fanatics, the dads' friends were exhibiting the kind of polite self-control that's always eluded me. "You god-damn gay-bashers!" I shouted at the fundamentalists. "You don't know anything about God or love!"

Horribly, everything got real quiet. Everyone looked at me. I stood there in my low-cut red dress and red high heels, a cigarette in one hand, and felt like I'd stepped into a dream.

"Go, girl," JD murmured.

"Give 'em hell, Venus," Tremaynne urged. "Right now. While everyone's listening."

One of the protestors, a man with scary glistening eyes, took advantage of the momentary lull to shriek, "Homosexuals recruit children! That's why they try to adopt them!"

When I heard that, I just went ballistic. Someone tried to hold me back, but I charged into the homophobes' picket line and grabbed one of their signs. The man holding it wouldn't let go. Tremaynne joined me. I heard a "Wheee!" and looked over to see JD applying her Bic lighter to another sign.

Then others moved in and started to grab at the signs. The funny thing was, people were trying to do this without mussing their beautiful clothes. It was the politest fight I'd ever seen. The protestors looked scared but hung on. You could see they wanted to be martyrs. They wanted it to be rougher than it really was.

A perspiring official from the registry office came rushing out and threatened to have us all arrested for trespassing and creating a civil disturbance. Someone threw a handful of rice in his face as he was speaking. In that moment, one of the protestors swung his sign and hit me broadside. It didn't hurt but threw me off balance. One of my heels buckled and I went down with a scream of surprise. As I fell, my evening dress somehow got yanked up to my underpants and one of the spaghetti straps tore.

The whole crowd surged forward. The registry official scurried back inside, brushing rice out of his hair and saying he was going to call the police.

Tremaynne whisked me to my feet. His face had that excited glow it gets when he confronts authorities. I was a little dazed but could hear angry taunts and snapping branches as the 'phobes were pushed back into the rhododendron bushes in front of the building. Then, suddenly, there was harp music again and JD shouted: "They're here! The dads are here!"

My heart just melted when I caught my first glimpse of them. Dad One was driving. He stopped the car and I ran over to them.

My dress was all grass-stained and wrinkled and I had to hold the bodice up to keep my left boob from plopping out. I don't know what happened to my shoes.

Whitman's window came down. He gave me a puzzled stare, quickly surveyed the brawling crowd, then opened the car door and pulled me inside, onto his lap, into his arms. "Are you hurt?"

My dad kissed me and brushed my hair with his fingers. "What happened?"

They were both wearing black tuxedos. Whitman was wearing what looked like a little black pillbox hat. They listened, peering out the window and stroking me as I breathlessly rattled off the events. "Venus, calm down," Daddy said. "Everything's all right."

"No, it's not!" I cried. "I wanted you to have such a special day. Everyone did. And those goddamned assholes ruined it!"

"Nobody's ruined anything," Whitman said. He was supernaturally calm, the way he always is in the midst of an emergency. "We're still going to do it." He turned to my dad. "Aren't we?"

"We can come back another time," my dad said.

"No." Whitman straightened his hat. "I refuse to be inconvenienced by ignorance." He pointed to the parking lot. "We'll begin by taking advantage of that free parking spot for customers only."

Daddy spun their sleek black Acura into the parking lot. I made an awkward exit. I must have looked like a real slut with my wrinkly ruined dress that I was trying to hold up, and my hair all messed, and mascara and lipstick smeared all over my face.

The dads took care of me. I felt like a five-year-old before a pageant. Daddy One wiped my face with his perfect white hanky as Daddy Two twitched my dress straight. "We have to fix this," Whitman said. He unpinned a small orchid corsage from his buttonhole and used the pin to repair my torn strap. Then he tucked the orchid in my hair. "There. But where are your shoes?"

I shrugged. I was so embarrassed and ashamed that I couldn't speak. Embarrassed because of the way I looked, and ashamed because I hadn't been able to do one single thing to make their day special.

"You'll have to pretend you're in Hawaii," Whitman said. "Barefoot among the orchids. Unless you want your dad to pull out his size-ten sneakers from his gym bag in the trunk."

I shook my head.

"Okay then, but your nylons are ripped to shreds so better slip out of them." He and Daddy closed rank like bodyguards. They turned around and made a protective wall so I could slip off my black fishnets. I remembered how the dads used to do this on road trips, so I'd have some privacy when I had to pee beside the road.

"Okay," Whitman said, "everybody ready? Should we all walk together, side by side?"

"Let me be, like, the flowergirl," I whispered.

Whitman plucked the orchid from my hair and tucked it in my hand. "Then you should walk a couple of steps in front of us."

By then everyone was pretty quiet and you could hear Wendell Tuttle's harp. He swooped his fingers back and forth, doing that harp thing, then picked out a melody I didn't recognize. Whitman sucked in his breath.

"I don't want anyone to get sentimental," he hissed, his voice catching in his throat. "Understand?"

By now we'd progressed from the parking lot to the front sidewalk. I walked a couple of steps ahead, holding Whitman's orchid (I'd *thought* of bringing flowers but was low on cash). The dads walked behind, arm-in-arm. Their friends stopped fighting with the Jesus freaks and lined the sidewalk and lawn, applauding and whistling. The news crews trained their minicams on us. Behind them, the 'phobes regrouped and renewed their attack.

"God hates queers!" they chanted.

I froze. Their hate was like a roadblock, an evil spell. They stood so close to the front door of the registry office that the dads would have to confront them. The faces of those five men and two women were so livid. You just had to wonder where that anger came from.

"Take a deep breath," I heard Whitman say behind me. "Keep moving forward."

I nodded. Scanned the crowd but couldn't see Tremaynne anywhere. One of those videocams was right in my face. A woman newscaster stepped around me and held her microphone up to the dads.

"Would you care to explain to our viewers just what it is you're doing today?"

"We came here today because it's our twentieth anniversary and we wanted to sign the domestic partner registry," my dad said.

"Why?" the newswoman prodded.

She looked slightly taken aback when Whitman said, simply, "Because we love one another."

"And this is our daughter, Venus," Daddy said.

The newswoman stepped back and looked me up and down. "Were you an *adopted* child?"

"No, I lived with my mom and my dads."

"And is your mother here as well?" she asked me.

Before I could answer there were two loud honks from one of those horns that have a big rubber ball on the end. I looked over and felt my knees go weak.

There was my mom.

Dressed in a clown suit.

Her face was made up like a clown's, with those big hideous up-turned lips and a round red ball for a nose.

"Heaven strike me dead," Whitman whispered.

I turned around to see how Daddy was taking it. He looked like a balloon had just been popped in his face.

Carolee, my suddenly *ex*-mother, pushed her way up to us. I wanted the earth to open up and swallow her, or me. My dads and I stood paralyzed as she honked her horn at each of us in turn. When Whitman said, "Hello, Carolee," and leaned over to airkiss her, she squirted him with water from the fake flower on her lapel. Then, feigning surprise, she disciplined the flower with a tap of her hand, pulled out an enormous checkered cloth, and mopped Whitman's face.

The dads' friends began to whisper amongst themselves.

"And who are you?" asked the newswoman.

Mom honked her horn in my direction. "Her mother."

"And would you care to tell our viewers why you're here dressed as a clown?"

"Because I just started clown therapy," my mother the clown said. She peered at the ranting Jesus freaks through her windshield-size glasses. "They don't look very happy, do they?" With that she laboriously made her way toward them, hardly able to walk in her oversized shoes. Her costume, bright and ridiculously exaggerated as anything you'd see at the circus, was topped by a snarled yellow fright wig I recognized from Halloweens past.

I stared at my dads, so embarrassed I wanted to die. *It was all my fault.* Mom was my responsibility. Nobody else wanted her. And now, obviously, she was insane. And there I stood, the nut's daughter, barefoot, dress ruined, more like a ten-year-old tomboy than a mature woman who'd gone through bankruptcy and was about to get married for the third time. It was Mom and me against them—against the dads and all their rich friends. We were the ones who would never fit in, no matter how hard we tried.

I was afraid my dad was going to explode. His face was mottled and his fists clenched tight. He was staring at *me,* his eyes as blue and cold as ice. "Who asked her to come?" he squeezed out.

I shook my head, unable to speak.

"I did," Whitman said. He patted my dad's shoulder and suddenly left our side.

My dad and I just stood there, like everyone else, watching to see what would happen next. "I'm sorry, Daddy," I whispered. Daddy put his arm around me.

Whitman made his way up to Carolee. Honking her horn and throwing confetti, she had managed to force the protesters back and away from the office door. They looked more frightened of her than they had earlier during the melee. "Carolee, darling, you're brilliant," Whitman said. "Thank you so much."

Mom kept throwing confetti and shooting water from her lapel. "Maybe now's a good time to go in," she said.

"Adam and Eve," one of the women protestors squawked, "not Adam and Steve!"

Whitman turned on her. "Thank you, my dear, but I'm gay. I already know *All About Eve*." He then motioned for us to join him. Daddy took my elbow and we moved down the front sidewalk. Everyone was watching. My body felt really stiff. When we reached Whitman, he smiled and made a mime-like show of dusting us off and straightening our clothes. For a second it was like he and my mom were part of the same act. Then he turned me around, took Daddy's arm, and shouted, "For-ward, march!"

And that's how we finally got into the registry office.

Lorenzo Lopez pulled open one door, Fokke the other, and we swept in with about a hundred people, a clown, and a news team trailing behind. Outside, Wendell Tuttle bravely played his harp as the protestors shouted and did their best to spoil the dads' special day.

Chapter

3

After the DP signing, the dads invited everyone over to their house. They just happened to have a caterer on hand and enough champagne, coffee, and dessert for a hundred people. Even Mom, wearing her idiotic clown getup, was invited. I heard Whitman breathe a sigh of relief when she said she couldn't make it.

"Well, my dear, we'll meet again *very* soon," he promised, giving Carolee a hug. "When you're feeling a little less passive-aggressive."

"You'll be coming to Venus's wedding," she said. "At my house."

"Of course."

Carolee the Clown started to cry in his arms. "Oh Whitman, I want you to know that I'm not angry with you. I want you and John to be happy."

"We are," he assured her.

"I know Venus thinks of you as family. And so do I."

"Come on, Bette Davis." I dragged her away, like a mom dragging a kid away from a costume party. I put her in her car, slammed the door, and whispered ominously, "I'll deal with you later."

Tremaynne and I raced home so I could change clothes. I drove so fast that all the warning lights in my junky old Toyota started blinking. "Damn car," I scolded. "Don't you dare break down on me today." I could smell burning oil.

"That Acura your dads drive must have cost a shitload," Tremaynne said.

"The dads always drive beautiful cars." I kept praying they'd give one of their cast-offs to me.

A party at the dads' is a big deal. And I had nothing cool to wear. I mean nothing. All I could dredge up was an old bustier with a long black skirt and red cowboy boots from my days as an exotic dancer. The bustier showed off the body art on my chest and back, but it was so tight I felt like my head might blow off.

"It's like a museum," Tremaynne whispered when I ushered him into the dads' house an hour later. He'd never been there before.

Tremaynne had been living with me for three months, but the dads had only met him twice, once at my apartment and one time at a vegan restaurant Tremaynne had chosen. The restaurant had Formica tables, fluorescent lights, and steamy windows full of spiderplants sending out long tentacles with babies on the ends. Definitely not the sort of place the dads would ever go to on their own. Whitman was amazed that you could get an entire meal for under five dollars. "Don't they have a profit margin?" he asked.

Which made Tremaynne suspicious because he hates capitalism. He hates the whole idea of wealth.

The dads' house is up in the West Hills of Portland, in what Tremaynne calls "Snobtown." It's this modern thing that Daddy designed, all steel and glass and wood. It's set up high on a hillside with a view toward downtown and Mt. Hood. When you're inside you feel like you're floating, and then outside there are these suspended terraces that hang out over a canyon and give me vertigo.

There are no soft, round, or curvy shapes anywhere in the dads' house. Everything has a razor-sharp edge. There's no "fluff and filler" as Whitman contemptuously calls knickknacks, photos, and throw pillows. The furniture is hard so your body doesn't sink into it. You could never lounge around in an old robe with a bowl of Sugar Pops watching Saturday morning cartoons in the dads' house. Anything that's displayed must be of the highest quality and meet the dads' exacting design standards. Nothing is ever out of place. Nothing is ever dusty or dirty. There's never a dirty plate or fast-food carton left out. Mom still hasn't figured out where they hide their TV.

"I wonder how many trees they had to cut down to build this place," Tremaynne said.

"Don't ask until after we're married, okay?"

"Why?"

"I don't want you to hold it against me."

"Well, obviously this isn't *your* lifestyle," Tremaynne said.

"I can't help it if my dads are rich." In fact, until I met Tremaynne I'd always regarded this as a selling point, believing the dads' wealth made me more desirable to the guys I was dating. "They're nice people, Tremaynne. Not all rich people are assholes."

"How come they're so rich and you're so poor?" my fiancé bluntly asked.

A question I couldn't answer. Except to say that I was too old to leech off the dads. I did, of course, whenever things got really desperate, but I always promised to pay them back. Pay Daddy back, I should say. I never dared borrow money from Whitman. He's the one with the fortune. I don't know how much he's worth, but I did peek once at a bank statement and saw a balance of $197,843.59. I've never forgotten that figure. That's why it's such a joke when he talks about how "poor" they are. Whitman isn't poor except when he needs to be.

Tremaynne kept close to my side as the guests swirled around us, chattering to me and appraising him. Nobody seemed to recognize him as an alternative media star.

Trying to steer clear of that old society-column bitch Lordie Mallory was impossible. She actually came up to us, her face frozen into a permanent smile from one too many lifts, and said to me in a loud, wine-slurred voice: "Is this the new one, Venus?"

I introduced her to Tremaynne. "Venus is such a popular girl," she said, extending her gnarled hand to Tremaynne. "Every time I see her, she's with a new man."

I gave her an inane smile and dragged Tremaynne off for some champagne.

There was a lot of posing as guests with expensive cameras drew people into glamorous, grinning groups and snapped their digital photos.

"Come on, honey, smile," Whitman urged during one sudden photo op. "Open your mouth and show your pearly whites."

But I wouldn't. You'll never see a photo of me showing off the bad teeth I inherited from my mom. That's why I quit modeling school: They couldn't get me to open my mouth. When I finally did, they told me I needed ten thousand dollars' worth of orthodontic work.

It was pretty clear that Tremaynne wasn't comfortable with the dads' friends. He has no rich-people skills. But rich people aren't anything special, really. Rich people are just poor people with money. Of course, I knew most of the guests and had my own secret network of friendships and flirtations with them. If I didn't know a person, all I had to say was that I was John and Whitman's daughter. As their kid, I was immediately accepted. But as we walked around, mingling, Tremaynne looked terrified, like a boy who'd been thrown into deep water and couldn't swim. He clung to me like a barnacle, wouldn't let go of my hand.

I tried to imagine Tremaynne moving through a crowd the way my dads did. No way. He's got charisma but, like, no social graces. He's the way I used to be before the dads moved to New York. When I started visiting them in Manhattan, they forced me to meet all their friends and took me around to parties and openings. Every time I'm with a large group of people I can still hear Whitman saying to me: "Work the crowd, honey. There's nothing to be afraid of. Talk to people. *Mingle.*"

The bustier was killing me, but at least no one could mistake my few extra pounds for pregnancy. At one point I left Tremaynne to go to the upstairs bathroom (the giant one in the dads' bedroom) for a breather. I unbuttoned the bustier and let everything hang out. It felt soft, mooshy, wonderful.

I was just coming out of the bathroom when Whitman came into the bedroom. "Oh, there you are," he said. "I've been looking for you." He closed the bedroom door and undid his belt.

I wondered what it would be like to be married to him. Daddy never revealed a thing about their sex life, but I know it's intense because I listened in once when they were having phone sex while Dad was visiting me in Portland and Whitman was out in New York.

Dad Two looked so handsome in his tuxedo. His blue eyes sparkled, partly because he was wearing color-enhanced contacts. He smiled, flashing his perfect white teeth, recently bleached and bonded, as he unbuttoned and unzipped his pants.

"Ahhh." He let out a deep orgasmic breath. "My pants were killing me." He said he was wearing the same size 32-inch waist trousers he had on when he met my dad twenty years earlier. "I suppose it's like squeezing into an old wedding dress or army uniform."

If he could, I could, so I undid the lower buttons of my bustier. "Ahhh," I sighed.

We laughed.

"All right," he said, "I know I'm just your old faux pa so I can't object to anything you do. But I want you to tell me what it is you see in Tremaynne."

I was used to Whitman's sudden interrogations. He keeps his questions to a minimum when he's with Daddy and then pounces whenever he catches me alone. "Tremaynne's committed to something," I said. "He's smart."

"But sweetheart, he has no money. You met him in a bankruptcy court, for God's sake! Don't take umbrage—"

"What does that mean?"

"It's a literary way of saying don't be pissed off. Just talk to me about it. Allay my fears."

"Well, I can't, because he doesn't have any money. The work he does is always for free. For a bigger cause."

Whitman sighed. "Yes, I'm sure he's very noble. As long as someone else is paying the bills. Are you going to support him?"

My voice rose defensively. "For now."

"On what you make at that video store?"

He meant Phantastic Phantasy, where I work. "I pay my rent. It doesn't cost that much more for two to eat."

"Yes, but—" He turned away, agitated, rubbing his long hands together. "What about the bigger picture?"

"What bigger picture?"

"Going back to school. Doing something with your life. Sweetheart, you're a smart person but you don't act like one. Don't you want something more?"

"Like what?"

"I don't know. When I was your age I wanted so much."

"And you got it."

"I *worked* for it," he said sharply. "Damned hard, too, because my family cut me off without a dime. And even so, even working as hard as I did, I only got some of what I wanted."

"Only some?" I chided him. "You got my dad, didn't you?"

"I was lucky to meet your father," he admitted. "He wanted many of the same things I did. That's how true partnerships work."

"Are you saying I'm incapable of forming a true partnership?"

His voice turned steely. "Don't get angry with me just because I'm being frank with you. Your biological parents accept everything you do. I don't, but I always feel like I have to keep my mouth shut."

"You generally get your point across," I said.

"Okay, the point is this: You've made two mistakes already. You've chosen major losers. In both cases, you said that you loved them."

"I did love them. They just turned out not to be right for me."

"And then, bang, you're divorced as fast as you were married. Why can't you just live with Tremaynne for a while? Why do you have to marry him?"

"Because that's what we want to do."

"Why?" he asked sharply. "It can't be for the tax benefit."

"Because we want to be together. We love one another."

"You can be together without marriage. You can love each other without marriage. That's what your father and I have done for twenty years."

"Only because you couldn't get married."

"Try it out for a year or two," Whitman suggested. "Maybe it's nothing more than sex."

"It's more than sex," I said.

"He doesn't look like he's any good at it anyway," Whitman said.

I let out a squawk of boy-are-you-wrong laughter. "If you don't like him," I said, "why are you so gung-ho for us to go on our honeymoon with you and Daddy?"

"I didn't say I didn't like him. I know nothing about him. Except that he seems extremely ill at ease in my presence."

"You intimidate him."

"I've never intimidated anyone in my life," Whitman scoffed. "I'm one of the nicest people I've ever met."

"I know that," I said, "but Tremaynne doesn't. His dad used to beat him. So he's, like, wary of authority figures."

"Sweetheart, don't, like, hold this against me. I'm just asking, okay? But what income level does Tremaynne come from? Is he from the lower-middle-class like your other husbands?"

"I don't know. I don't judge people that way."

"I'm not judging him. I know nothing about him. I'm trying to place him in some kind of socioeconomic milieu that might help me to understand him better."

"You'll just have to get to know him. You're a lot alike. You both have strong opinions about things."

Whitman opened my purse and extracted my cigarettes. He shook one out for himself and then one for me. He hadn't smoked in five years, so it had the feeling of a special ceremony. Like a drug ritual. Holding his pants up, he went into the bathroom and came back with a glass of water. Opened the sliding glass doors to the balcony. Threw back one corner of the slippery yellow silk duvet and motioned for me to sit down beside him on the enormous bed he shared with my dad.

Whitman looked at me before putting the cigarette between his lips. "Promise you won't tell your father?"

"Promise." I gave the oath, then lit our cigarettes. Whitman closed his eyes and inhaled, coughing softly.

"Venus," he said, "your dad and I have lived together for twenty years. We can't get married. We're not considered morally or psychologically fit to control our own destinies." Another inhale. "Now I want you to think for a moment about what it's like to be in our position and to see you, our daughter, going through marriage after marriage."

"Are you pissed off with me because I can get married and you can't?"

He thought about it. "Maybe. A little. Because you don't seem to know or value permanence."

I flicked my ashes into the glass he was holding. "Maybe that's because I never had much when I was growing up."

"Get over it! You had your mother and you saw your father at least twelve times a year."

"Wow, twelve times a year," I said, remembering how simultaneously excited and angry ten-year-old me would be when I was about to see my dad again.

That anger was my worst enemy. It was evil. It lay in wait like a big black boiling-mad monster that would just suddenly rear up and grab me. All sorts of things set it off. Resentment was a big part of it. Daddy *claimed* to love me, but he didn't love me *enough*. I wanted him to think of nothing and no one but me, and he didn't. When he wasn't there, I felt like I was being punished somehow. The punishment was his absence. And the time we had was so short. We saw each other every month. Either Daddy flew out to Portland for a long weekend or I flew out to New York for a week. In Portland I had him all to myself, for three paltry days. In New York I had to share him with Whitman, and I had to spend my days with Whitman in the apartment while Daddy was at work.

Three days or a week, it was never enough. The world was an entirely different place when I was with Daddy. He plucked me out of the cruddy garage-sale life I lived with Carolee, that world of used but "perfectly good" clothes that never quite fit and toys that were always missing one critical part so you couldn't play with them.

I wanted to savor every moment with Daddy. But the monster wouldn't let me. I'd be in some wonderful spot with Daddy, having fun, and suddenly Carolee's bitter, wine-slurred voice would echo in my ears. I'd hear her cursing and complaining about *him*, about how rich *he* was, or *they* were, and how poor *we* were. And then my own music-box of resentments would start to play. The terrible public school that I had to go to. A school where I learned nothing, was afraid for my life, and had no one to protect me. There was no one who understood what I was going through, or cared enough to do something about it. There was no one who gave a shit about what happened to me day after terrifying day as I eluded gangs of girls out to rob and beat me up and boys who threatened that they were going to "get" me. Daddy was the only one who could save me from all that, but he didn't. He *wouldn't*. Instead, he lived a *fun life* with Whitman in New York.

The monster would grab me by the toes and yank me down to his lair. From a sunny moment of having fun with Daddy, I'd suddenly disappear into a black hole of rage. I'd spend hours stewing in the dark stinking sludge with the monster, thinking up ways to punish Daddy, or Whitman, or both of them, and Carolee, too. Someone had to pay for my misery. Otherwise I'd have to accept it as an everyday part of my life.

I wasn't that angry ten-year-old girl anymore, but every now and then I felt her kicking, like a baby, wanting out. She was there now, wanting to scream at Whitman, but I clamped a hand over her mouth.

"Your dad and I lived like paupers in New York," Whitman was saying, "so we could fly you out there, and have your dad fly back here, and pay Carolee alimony and child support."

"I'm sorry I was such a financial burden," I said.

"I don't want to get into a blame game here," Whitman said. "I just want some assurance that you know what you're doing. That you've actually thought about it. That you aren't just rushing into this marriage because you can't live without having a man around."

"It doesn't matter what I say, Whitman, you won't believe me."

"Venus," he said, "I've been watching you since you were five years old. I've seen how you behave. I've seen how you make your decisions and present them to your parents as *faits accomplis.*"

"What does that mean?"

"You don't ask for approval or advice; you just tell them what it is you're going to do. Quit school. Become a model. Get married. Get divorced. Join the army. Be a lesbian. Get married. File for bankruptcy. You're an only child, so they give in to you. They've never put any limits on you because they want to believe that you know what you're doing."

"This time I *do* know." I got up and paced around the big bedroom. "Tremaynne and I love one another. We want to be together."

"Okay." Whitman held up his hand. "The next question is, what are you going to do for a ceremony this time?"

"It's about time you asked," I said. "We're writing our own."

"Well, don't forget there's a grammar and a spell check on that computer I gave you. Next question: Where is it going to take place?"

"At my mom's. I told you. She told you. At two in the afternoon."

"Her place is awfully tiny," Whitman said. "How about if we did it here? It could be very pretty. What are you wearing by the way?"

"It's a surprise."

"Doesn't Donna Karan have some simple white dresses this season? Jackie Kennedy sort of nineteen-sixties A-lines. Maybe we should go down to Saks and find something that covers at least some of your tattoos."

"I don't want a suck-ass dress from Donna Karan," I lied. "I've got everything all planned out. *My way.*"

"Okay. Next question. This event is to take place on July Fourth. Doesn't that seem a tad inappropriate?"

"Why?"

"Well, it's such a patriotic day."

"Carolee had a chart done. The astrologer said the Fourth is auspicious for me."

"Is this going to be one of Carolee's pagan ceremonies?" he asked cautiously.

"Sort of. We're planning everything, me and Tremaynne."

"Tremaynne and I. And what about the reception?"

"A big costume party."

"What about Tremaynne's family?"

"He doesn't want anything to do with them."

"Oh." Whitman dipped his cigarette into the glass of water and watched it fizzle out. He stared out the glass doors. He didn't say anything. I thought maybe I'd pissed him off.

"What's the matter?" I asked.

"Nothing. I was just wondering what I would do if I could get married to your dad. I mean really married." He turned to me. "I was raised so differently from the way you were."

By which he meant his family was rich and had come over with the *Mayflower*—the ship, not the moving company. Daddy said the Whittlesleys were one of the oldest families in Boston. That's about all I knew. Whitman rarely talked about his family.

"You know, I used to get into huge fights with your dad about you," Whitman said.

I waited for more, always eager to slurp up any emotional crumb he might toss my way.

"I'll tell you a secret," he said. "I'm the only person I know who identified with Joan Crawford in *Mommie, Dearest*. Not the coathanger thing. No. Her strict sense of order and discipline. Everything you didn't have when you were growing up. I worry that you're just going to drift through life. Like a jellyfish."

I put my arms around him and kissed him on the lips. He obliged with his usual chaste pucker. "Don't worry, Daddy dearest," I said. "I'm a big girl now."

"Okay, time to suck in the guts."

He was zipping up his pants and I was buttoning my bustier when the bedroom door opened and Tremaynne walked in.

Later that night I barged like a mobster into my mom's house and screamed: "Just what the fuck did you think you were doing showing up in a fucking clown suit?"

Her face had that wincing, please-don't-hit-me look that makes me even madder.

"A clown suit!" I raged. "Did you think it was funny or were you trying to humiliate the dads and me or what?"

"Sweetheart, it was part of my clown therapy," she whimpered. "I *had* to do it."

I rolled my eyes. "Clown therapy? What the *fuck*, pray tell, is that?"

Mom told me all about it, trying to calm me down and defending herself at one and the same time.

Clown therapy was Carolee's latest attempt to put some meaning into her life. The astrology charts and psychic forecasts weren't yielding any results. The ten thousand affirmations she taped to the fridge ("Today I will rejoice in my hunger between meals") and bathroom mirror ("I honor the goddess within every time I look at my body without shame") just weren't doing the trick. Clown therapy was the newest of the endless alternative therapies she was forever trying out. None of them ever did any good that I could see. They perked her up for awhile, like a new boyfriend, and then she'd get tired of them and her spirits would droop and the whole cycle would begin again.

"It was my initiation," she said. "The first time has to be the hardest. You have to choose the group you fear most."

"Let me get this straight. You choose the group you fear most and then make yourself into a fool in front of them? And that's supposed to help you?"

"It helps you to externalize your fear," she said.

"You looked like a fucking idiot!" I shouted. "And you made me, your daughter, look like an idiot. And the dads, what do you think they felt like?"

"Whitman *thanked* me," she shot back. "He said I was brilliant."

"He was being nice."

"Well, it all worked out in the end, didn't it? I'm the one who got those Jesus freaks to back off so the dads could get inside."

I stomped outside so I could light up. "So what do you do," I sneered, "go to a clown college or something?"

"Not yet. First you do a course on video." She waved a cassette at me from the other side of the door. It was the first in a series of ten videos that she was supposed to buy, along with "approved" clown merchandise, as she moved up the ladder toward clown mastery.

"It's a pyramid scheme!" I shrieked. I knew because I'd been suckered into quite a few of them myself, before bankruptcy. "Oh Mom, how could you be so stupid?"

"I know that's what it looks like," she said, "but it's not. Really, honey. This is something I've felt all my life. It's about releasing the little girl within. It's about turning grief into joy."

I didn't want to hear about her grief so I kept my yap shut.

"I don't like to talk about it," she said in a confiding tone, "because I don't want you to worry, but my nutritionist says I am seriously depressed."

"That's because you're horny, Mom."

"No it's not, honey. I talked to Corinna my psychic about it. It's all because of past-life experiences. Evidently I was a child laborer in Victorian England. I never got to play and have fun."

"That may be, Mom, but you're also a forty-five-year-old woman living today. You need to go out and have some fun. Now, before your hormones go on permanent disability."

"And who, pray tell, am I supposed to go out with?" she asked.

"Men. Guys."

"And where, pray tell, am I supposed to meet these guys?"

"I don't know. Be creative."

She sighed. "Sweetheart, I'm not young and bee-you-ti-ful like you. As Dorothy Parker said, 'Men don't make passes at women with fat asses.' "

"Then maybe you should try a woman again."

"Maybe I should." She gave her clown horn a couple of forlorn honks.

"Just promise me—*promise* me—that you won't turn up at my wedding in that clown suit. Promise. Because if you do, I won't let you in. I mean it."

"But I thought you wanted to have the ceremony here." She sounded nervous, as if she was afraid I was going to rob her of an opportunity to serve me.

"Whitman said I could have it at their house."

Her voice rose a notch. "He never told me that. Oh, sweetheart. I've been planning all the pretty decorations."

"We don't want any decorations," I informed her.

"No decorations?" She couldn't believe her ears.

You have to understand: My mom uses any excuse to decorate. She loves balloons, party favors, cute little hats, funny cards, and most of all, presents. She just can't resist giving things to me, although sometimes she does have to be nudged in the right direction. For instance, I knew if I played my cards right I'd get a couple hundred prewedding bucks out of her.

"He's never, like, done anything to you, has he?" Tremaynne asked, slowly untying the laces on my bustier.

"Are you kidding?" I sucked in my breath as he tugged it free, his hand brushing against my breasts. "He's always been like a stepfather to me."

"Yeah, but stepfathers abuse their kids all the time," Tremaynne said, kissing the rose tattoo above my heart.

"Not Whitman," I said. "Never."

"When I came in the bedroom and saw him zipping up his pants," Tremaynne whispered, sucking my earlobe into his mouth, "I thought—You know." His tongue moved up to probe my ear. "You didn't look upset or anything. But I wondered."

I threw my head back so he could give my throat a good swab with his overactive tongue. "Yeah," I sighed, lightheaded with delight, "I've wondered myself."

"You have?" He pulled me closer, breathing hard, kneading my butt like it was bread dough. "What?"

"What it would be like."

"What d'you think?"

"I don't know. He seems to make my dad happy." I sucked my lover's tongue deep into my mouth, then moved down to pluck at his little raisiny nipples with my teeth. "I know they have sex almost every day."

"So do we," Tremaynne panted.

"Yeah, but they've been together twenty years." I did some quick math, the one thing I'm good at. "That's like over seven thousand times."

"Wow." Tremaynne reared back, looking at me. Those dark eyes with the long black lashes had the power to melt me. "What do they do?"

"I don't know. That's always been another fantasy."

"What?"

"Watching two handsome guys make it."

"Watching your dads, or, like, watching two handsome guys?"

"My dads are two handsome guys."

"So, watching them."

"It's just a fantasy."

I could feel Tremaynne's hard stubby dick against my thigh. He eased me onto my back, cupped my breasts, and stared at my nipples as if they were two luscious desserts. His tongue flicked out, delicately licking first one, then the other, like a boy with an ice-cream cone in each hand.

"Oh, Venus," he sighed, tenderly laying his head against my heart.

"What, babe?" I played with his hair.

"Am I doing the right thing?"

I assumed he meant getting married. "Yes," I whispered.

"I'm afraid I'll hurt you."

"You won't hurt me," I said.

"You don't know who I am. Not really."

"Do you know who I am? Really?"

He was silent for a moment. "Yeah," he said finally. "I think I do."

Chapter

4

I kept giving Tremaynne chances to get out of going on our honeymoon with the dads, but he was like, "No, I really want to go."

"We'll be in the car with them for hours," I warned.

"So?"

"You'll have to talk."

"I can talk when I want to."

"You're not homophobic, are you? You'd better tell me now if that's a problem."

"There is something I should probably tell you." He cleared his throat and smoothed down his already smooth goatee. His eyes, usually so bold, grew shy. "I've had a couple of things with guys. Nothing serious. Just like you've had with women."

His confession confirmed something I'd been wondering about.

Suddenly it was kind of a dilemma. Because I didn't want to make the mistake of marrying a gay man, like my mom did. Gay men make great dads, but, as Whitman once said, you wouldn't want your daughter to marry one.

"I guess you could say I'm sort of bisexual," Tremaynne said. "Like you."

"So, do two bisexuals make one straight couple?" I asked.

"I'll never be totally straight," he said. "Not, like, totally."

We looked at each other. It was Truth Time.

"You do want to marry me, don't you?" I tried to keep neediness out of my voice.

For a moment he didn't say anything, just frowned and looked deep into my eyes. It was one of those moments when everything's on the line. You either move on together, or back off forever.

"It's been, like, really intense with you," he said. "But I've told you, and I'll say it one last time: Marriage for me isn't about sitting around in a little house with a picket fence and a baby on my knee and a nine-to-five job. You've got to understand that."

"Did you ever hear me say that's what I wanted?"

"No, but it's what a lot of women want. Stability. Nothing wrong with it, but it's not, like, on my agenda."

"It's boring," I agreed.

He pulled in his lips and chewed on the bottom one, like he was thinking something through. "Even when we're married, Venus, I have to be free to go off and do my thing. My conscience demands it."

"Can't I go with you?" I asked.

"It's not an easy life. I never know how long I'm going to be away, or what I'm going to be doing. There's never any money." He took me by the hands and gently pulled me over to sit beside him. He was being really tender. "Venus, maybe we should call it off."

"No!"

"Can you really accept me as I am?" he asked. "Not like you want me to be, but like I really am?"

"Will you—" I had to stop and frame the question as delicately as possible. "Will you, like, fuck other people when you're away?"

"There's no one to fuck when you're hanging eighty feet up in a tree," Tremaynne said with a laugh.

"Tell me the truth."

He nodded. "I'll always come back to you, Venus. As long as it works out for both of us."

"Jeez." I laughed and flicked away some excess moisture from my eyes. "You sound like a terrorist in a Tom Clancy novel."

He looked at me, his face stern. "I'm part of a movement," he said.

There I was with my wedding two days away and a free three-day honeymoon planned and I hadn't even asked for time off work. I was afraid Bruce would fire me if I did. I always worked weekends.

In the past, if I got sick of a job, I just stopped going. As a result, I had no references to show employers. On job applications I couldn't put down stints in the army and modeling school because I'd dropped out of both within a month. I couldn't type and working at a computer bored me, except for the chat rooms. In my fantasies I saw myself as a model or the star of my own TV series, but in real life it was like I had no aptitude for anything. When you're in that position, all that's left are the jobs in fast food, fast coffee, telemarketing, taking care of young kids, taking care of old people, or some version of scanning barcodes and stocking shelves.

Or you can work in the sex industry.

My job at Phantastic Phantasy was a last-ditch effort to remain independent after my bankruptcy. Otherwise there were only two alternatives: move back in with my mother or become a baglady. Living with the dads was not an option because I couldn't deal with all their rules and regulations. We tried it once, when I was sixteen and they'd just moved back from New York. I got the distinct impression that I was not welcome unless I made my bed every morning, hung up all my clothes, studied for hours every day, and stopped bringing my boyfriends back to the house after the clubs closed.

"Sweetheart," Whitman said one morning, "we love you, so you'd better leave now, before we kill you."

My overachieving dads just hate it that I work at Phantastic Phantasy. Just like they hated it when I was an exotic dancer (I never told them about my stint as a lingerie model). I don't know why they get so worked up about it.

Just because you work in the sex sector doesn't mean you're a whore or a slut. I kept telling the dads that. Tremaynne didn't mind.

He was, like, totally cool with it. He thought it was like a form of anarchy from everything middle class and repressive.

To me, it's just a job. It's what I do because I have to pay rent and my phone bill and keep my half-dead car running and buy food. I have to do all this with cash, baby, cash, because bankruptcy comes in like a tsunami and wipes out all your once-available lines of credit.

Credit cards were my worst addiction. Before I went Chapter Seven, I'd racked up $18,000 worth of debt that I couldn't pay off. For the next seven years, I can't buy anything that I can't pay for with cash.

When you work in the sex industry, you're part of a secret inner world that the larger outer world frowns on. You have to accept that, and accept the creatures you meet. You all share the same environment.

Most of our business at Phantastic Phantasy is video rental. We carry over a thousand titles, from nostalgic hits like *Thanks for the Mammaries* to patriotic offerings like *Yank My Doodle, It's a Dandy*. Our gay collection is the best in Portland and features all the current superstuds, including Ricky Ramrod, Carl LaCoque, and the Falcon stable of sexual athletes. Yes, there is lesbian porn, but only straight men rent it.

The front part of the store is video rentals and merchandise. All the street-facing windows are polarized because the people inside don't want to be seen by the people outside. It's like working behind a giant pair of sunglasses. The outside world is just a bunch of dark moving shadows that you can ignore.

Bruce renovated the store last year, putting in red and purple carpeting and different colored lights. He lets people smoke in designated areas, so there's always that nice comforting stale cigarette-smoke smell, like in my apartment. It's a smell I grew up with because my mom and both dads used to be heavy smokers.

In the back of the store, separated from the front by more racks of videos, there are twenty private viewing booths. There's an assortment of gay and straight movies available in every booth. You choose your own selection from a computerized menu. It's all very up-to-date.

I sell people the one-dollar tokens that operate the movies for five minutes. I don't go back in that area unless I absolutely have to. From up front I can see everything that's going on because Bruce installed surveillance cameras after the city tried to shut him down for prostitution.

It's like watching some weird kind of avant-garde TV show where the set is nothing but a hallway and twenty doors and the action is people going in and coming out. It's better than a lot of the video installations I used to watch in those art galleries the dads would drag me to in New York.

Gay guys have sex back there, but I can't see that because it takes place in the booths. There are also these side-by-side "buddy booths." One guy goes into one booth, another guy into the booth next door. While they're watching the movies, they can press a button and raise a screen between the two rooms. Then, I guess, they watch each other j.o. But the screen is not clear glass, so it's kind of like peering at a shadow. Straight guys and other gay guys j.o. in their own private booths.

But here's the rub. On a little monitor up front, we can see which booths are occupied and tell whether they're watching movies. No one can be in a booth unless they're putting in dollar tokens. If they aren't, I have to go back there, rap sharply on the door, and say in a loud stern voice, "You have to be spending money in there!" Tremaynne thinks that's the funniest part of my job.

Ever since the city tried to close him down for some health ordinance violation, Bruce keeps it very clean back there. Every booth has a roll of paper towels. Every time someone leaves a booth, Hosario or one of the cleaning boys goes in to mop the floor and wipe down the walls with this disinfectant that smells like pineapple and vomit. The bathroom is kept locked, so you have to ask for a key. That way we can keep it clean and stop people from going in there to have sex.

I've learned that nothing can stop people from wanting, hoping, or trying to have sex. Even on September 11, people came in to get their rocks off. Like Bruce says, "You can't put a lid on libido."

So we're open 24/7. People flit in and out of that shadowy back area all day and all night. Sometimes drag queens with big feet and their balls strapped between their legs come in, trying not to look obvious in their wigs and makeup. Sometimes they're transexuals on the road to gender reassignment. Real cute students, real ugly middle-aged guys, men of eighty wearing bib overalls and cowboy hats—I've seen them all. People who look like professors and people who look retarded. We are totally wheelchair accessible, so sometimes guys drive their chairs in.

Every morning my first task is to make sure all the video boxes are properly arranged in alphabetical order on their racks. I wear disposable plastic gloves when I do this because sometimes the customers aren't able to control themselves while browsing. I told Bruce I would *not* wipe up wet or dried sperm from the floor, the walls, or the boxes. Hosario or one of the cleaning boys does that.

Have you ever alphabetized porn movies? That's part of my job. *Anal Olympics* goes before *Ass Class* but after *A Touch of Ass*.

Those cover shots on the porn videos are really something. Lipsticked mouths with cum flying into them *(Saucy Suckers)* or running down cheeks like gobs of white snot *(Cum As You Are)*. Heavily made up women holding up their beachball-size tits and winking *(Big Hot Mamas)*. Rearends plugged by impossibly humongous pricks *(Ass You Like It)*. Shaved pussies held wide open, like mouths singing in a church choir *(Clitty Clitty Bang Bang)*.

The fetish sections are alphabetized by fetish and by title. *Bestiality* comes before *Bondage*. The bondage covers are the ones I can't stand to look at. I mean the ones where it's the woman who's being abused. It's kind of hot when she's the one with the whip and lace-up stilettos. You can tell that the bondage video covers are fake, though, because the models don't look like they're really in pain. They just look startled. Don't ask me to describe the ones with animals. Someone should call the ASPCA about those.

Of course we sell magazines, too. *Chicks & Dicks, 48 Plus, Open Wide, Cross Dressers Quarterly, Pussy Sandwich, Hanky Spanky.* They're all plastic-wrapped and electronically coded. If someone slips a copy of *Blowjob* under his jacket and tries to sneak out with it, the scan alarm at the door goes off. That's really a drag because then one of the assistant managers has to stop the guy and it's, like, really embarrassing to hear their lame excuses. Sometimes they go off into this belligerent denial, even when the proof's right there in front of them. You've got to be careful with shoplifters, though, because they might sue.

Phantastic Phantasy is usually as quiet as a library. It's like the reverse of the outside world. Nobody talks but the staff. I always keep the indie rock station cranked up so people won't feel so lonely and obsessive.

After arranging the videos, I check the merchandise. One of my jobs is to keep the display cases clean and to reorder items when we're low. There's a general sex merchandise warehouse I call down in San Francisco when we need stuff. There's this girl named Jamey I talk to down there.

It's not like we're good friends or anything, but I just had to tell her that I was getting married.

"Wow," Jamey said. "Congratulations. Was it like hard to get the fucker to commit?"

Before I could answer, Bruce came in. He owns three Phantasy stores and runs around from one to the other and then to the bank. I never knew when he'd be around so I figured I'd better snag him about the honeymoon. First I wanted to impress him with my professionalism, though, so I whispered to Jamey that I couldn't laugh or talk anymore.

"Cough if your boss just walked in," she said.

I coughed and flipped through my inventory checklist. "And let's see, I need four dildos."

"Small, medium, large, or impossible?" Jamey asked.

"That Jeff Stryker one. We sell a lot of those."

"I'm glad my boyfriend's not built like that," Jamey said, clicking the order into her computer. I pictured her with long nails and a headset. "I got enough size problems with him as it is. I'm four foot eight and he's six foot ten."

"Wow." I pictured a little piece of chicken stuck on the end of a long skewer. "Okay, I also need three of that new Wonderdong. The one that vibrates and shoots water." I covered the phone and said, "Hi, Bruce," real sweet, as he hurried toward the registers with his empty cash bags. "I'm doing the reordering, but I need to talk to you before you go."

He nodded.

"Okay, Jamey, you got that so far? I also need eleven buttplugs—the one called Rearender."

"The one with the little sticky-outy things in it?"

"Correct. Four dildos. Three Wonderdongs. Seven cockrings."

"And a partridge in a pear tree," she sang.

I turned away and tried to keep from cackling. "Right. Three cockrings of the adjustable leather kind with silver studs, two of that new Velcro model, and two of the rubber."

I saw Bruce surreptitiously strum his crotch. He was staring up at the surveillance monitors.

"A dozen of the crotchless edible panties," I continued.

"*Eeuuh,*" Jamey groaned. "You think anyone actually eats those things? I mean, what are they made of?"

"Some, like, kind of flavored vegetable fiber. They really itch, too."

"I wouldn't want to see my boyfriend eating a pair of my panties. Would you? Like, gross. Like, what are you, a dog? Like, eat me but leave my panties alone." She clicked in the order and verified all the price and shipping information.

Before I hung up with Jamey she said, "So you having a tradi-tional church wedding? White gown and bridesmaids and all that pretty shit?"

"No," I murmured. "We can't afford that."

"What can't we afford?" Bruce asked. He opened the first register and stared into the cash drawer like a glutton eyeing a smorgasbord.

"Not Federal Express," I said. "Just send the order UPS surface."

Bruce nodded approvingly.

"Gotcha," Jamey said. "Happy honeymoon."

Bruce's face is pitted with acne scars but his salt-and-pepper hair is always perfect, swept back and up in a kind of hairsprayed semi-pompadour that jiggles when he walks. His rabbitlike front teeth don't fit behind his lips so he always looks like he's about to start gnawing on something. Of late he's taken to wearing Porsche wrap-around sunglasses and overdosing on cologne. Bruce is a denim and leather kind of guy. He's a baby boomer, around fifty, and really starting to paunch out. His pants and shirts are always like a size too tight. He's about four inches shorter than me.

Trying to butter him up, I sniffed and said, "Mm, what's that sexy cologne you're wearing, Bruce?"

He puffed himself up a little. "Adonis Poor Oms."

"I'll bet your girlfriend loves it."

"We split," he said. "I'm single again. You wanna go out to dinner?"

"Bruce," I said, "listen, I haven't told you yet, but I'm getting married."

"When's your last day?" Suddenly he wouldn't look at me. His attention was fixed on the cash in the register.

"My last day?"

"You're quitting, right?"

"I wasn't planning on it," I said.

"Everybody quits. Why should you be any different?" He licked his thumb and began counting out twenty-dollar bills.

"I thought maybe I could just take a few days off. For my honeymoon."

He gave me a startled glance. I could see the shadows of his eyes behind the dark glasses. "A honeymoon?"

"Yeah. We're going to Pine Mountain Lodge."

"Whoa-ho-ho. Is your husband loaded or what? That place costs a fortune. I just seen a story on it in the paper."

"My dads are taking us. Free."

"Wait a minute. You're going on your honeymoon with your father?"

"Fathers. My dad and my stepdad."

"I thought I'd heard of everything." Bruce was so puzzled that he stopped counting out money. "You mean, these guys were both married to your mother and now they're going on a honeymoon with you?"

"No, my stepdad is my dad's partner," I explained. "They're lovers."

"Oh." He nodded. "The one named Whitman, is he your real father or your stepfather?"

"How do you know Whitman?"

"He called me."

I felt panicky, like a hand was clamping down on the back of my neck. "Whitman did? When?"

"When you started working here. He identified himself as your father."

My mouth went dry. "He did?"

"He made me promise I'd never have you work at night. And that someone would always watch to make sure you got out to your car safe." He lowered his voice. "I wasn't supposed to tell you."

My cheeks were burning. I was so embarrassed. It was like being a teenager and having your overprotective mom pick you up at school.

I couldn't believe Whitman would meddle in my life that way.

Bruce took off his glasses. His eyes looked bloodshot, tired. "Why do you want to work here at all, babe? You're not a sleazy girl. You could be a nice secretary somewhere. Or a nurse."

"I've been a good employee, haven't I? I haven't asked you for a raise or health benefits. I haven't missed a day of work."

"You've only been here a month."

"All I want is four days off. From the fourth. That's all I'm asking for. I'll be back next Monday."

He pointed with his chin toward the rack of Phantastic Phantasy lingerie. "Go pick out one of them Patty Cakes Baby Doll Negligees," he said.

I didn't know what Bruce was after but did as I was told. The lingerie we sold was the kind of stuff I used to model. It's the kind of stuff men buy for girlfriends and wives who are usually too ashamed of their bodies to wear it. Patty Cakes (designed and made by a drag queen in Taiwan) was a line that was supposed to make you look like a sexy little girl. The set included a pair of satin-crotched panties and a little see-through bed jacket edged with soft downy feathers and tied at the throat with a satin ribbon.

"Hold it up, babe," Bruce said. "Lemme see."

He sounded like one of the guys I used to model for. I held up the Baby Doll negligee. It was supposed to be light and delicate as gossamer but it was made out of some stiff synthetic material that felt like a Halloween costume and crackled with static. I blew on the feathers and twirled around.

Bruce's eyes were glued on me. He held a wadful of twenty-dollar bills in one hand. I couldn't see what the other hand was doing. "It's yours," he said, turning back to the cash drawer. "Wear it on your honeymoon and think of me."

Chapter
5

How do you end up with the people you end up with, that's what I'd like to know. Out of all the billions of people you could possibly meet, why them? Is it, like, destiny?

In that final countdown of hours before my marriage to Tremaynne, I found myself flashing back to my first two husbands and my relationship with JD. While a Vietnamese girl gave me a manicure and a pedicure, one of my mom's wedding presents, I reflected on my life up to now. It was July 3. The nail salon was decorated with flags and crepe-paper foldout rifles. Everyone was super-patriotic about July 4 now. It was an entirely different holiday from what it used to be before terrorists blew up the World Trade Center.

"Whucullanail?" the girl asked, showing me her tray of polishes.

"Black."

"Oh, you go funeral?"

"No," I said, "I'm getting married tomorrow."

The first guy I married was Sean Kowalski. Sean was a convicted felon. I don't know why I married him. Yes, I do. I wanted to get away from my mom.

I was nineteen and ready for whatever came next. I tried the army, thinking the discipline would be good for me. (Maybe it was, but I never stuck around to find out.) Then I enrolled in modeling school, where they told me to lose weight and get my teeth fixed. I didn't want to go to college and I didn't want to work and most of all I didn't want to live at home anymore. That's when I met Sean.

He drove a souped-up royal blue Grand Prix. He drove fast. He smoked. He drank. He scared me, but I kept seeing him because I liked the fizz of excitement, never knowing what he'd do next. He had a job selling used trucks out in Gresham.

When Sean asked me to marry him, I couldn't see any reason why I shouldn't. Mom was supportive but the dads weren't. "Your future husband uses double negatives, says *ain't*, and called me *dude*," Whitman said bluntly after meeting him. "He's ten years older than you, wears cheap cologne, and sells used cars. Would you please tell me what you see in this man?"

What I saw was my escape from my mother. But of course I didn't tell the dads that. If I had, they would have made a counter-proposal that I move in with them. And we'd already tried that three years before.

I didn't tell the dads or Mom about Sean's background as a felon (forgery and embezzlement). That part of his life didn't matter to me. If anything, it added a bit of luster to his otherwise bleak background as a child of foster homes and juvenile detention centers. He said he'd made a couple of mistakes and paid for them. I felt sorry for him, the way you do for dogs in the pound.

We got married in the apartment Mom and I were living in at the time. The wedding felt like a funeral. There was no real joy in me, my mom, the grim-faced dads, or any of my four guests. When I realized what was happening, I lost my nerve. I was upstairs getting dressed. "I can't do it," I squeaked to my mom. "My legs aren't, like, working."

"We can call it off," my mom said eagerly. "If you're not ready, sweetheart, don't do it. I'm not afraid to march down there and tell everyone it's not going to happen."

"What do you really think of him, Mom?"

"What I think doesn't matter," she said. "You're the one who has to live with him."

Trust her never to give me a prejudiced opinion of anybody. "What did the dads say to you about him?"

"Well, Whitman's not shy about giving his opinions. He said Sean was a sleazeball loser."

My stomach churned. "What about Daddy?"

"Your father doesn't like him either. He thinks you could do much better. He's sick that you're doing this instead of going to school."

I felt really fatalistic, like a convict who knows she can't escape but has to try anyway. I made it all happen, almost like a game, and now a husband-to-be was waiting for me at the foot of the stairs. I went to the window and looked into the branches of the big elm tree outside. When I was a minor drug addict in middle school, I used to escape from the house by climbing down that tree at night. I stood there thinking maybe I should shinny down right now.

But I didn't.

I went through with the wedding.

I had to show them that I knew what I was doing. And I had to get out of my mom's house.

We stayed married for nine months. (Whitman calls it my "starter marriage.") In the beginning, Sean was tender. But he drank so much that I could never count on him for anything. His real love was Wild Turkey. He'd drink until he passed out.

I felt like I was supposed to make a home for him. But it was like a game of make-believe. I didn't have a clue about living with a man. I tried to do those wifely things I'd seen on reruns of *The Brady Bunch* and *Bewitched*, but I quickly realized that what looked fun on TV was a big fat bore in real life. It just didn't give me a thrill to clean the cardboard-walled apartment we lived in, overlooking I-405, or to cook dinner by heating up frozen meals in the old microwave Mom had given us.

In bed Sean was a Johnny-Come-Quickly. Foreplay was a dirty word to him. And he had this weird thing about my rear end that I just couldn't get into. I was on birth control so he refused to wear a rubber. Looking back, it's a miracle that I didn't catch some STD.

I just couldn't feel like a grownup, no matter how I tried. Most of the time I was bored out of my gourd. I got Daddy to pay for my tuition at a junior college and started hanging out with some girls I met in Women's Lit night classes. After class discussions of *Jane Eyre* or *The Country of the Pointed Firs*, we'd go out to clubs so the single girls could meet guys and the married ones could pretend they were single again.

I never cheated on Sean with a guy. But I did meet JD and fall in love with her while I was still married to him. She was up on stage, singing "Stay Away, Bitch," when I first saw her.

Funny, all the things you don't see or want to see before you get married. It turned out that Sean had a violent temper. Weird things would suddenly set him off. He'd smash stuff and make threats and bellow about how he was going to fix So-and-So, who'd cheated him. Then he started getting jealous. He hated it that I was going to school. "What're you learnin' there in Women's Clit?" he'd mock. He accused me of flirting. He'd say things like, "I saw you shaking your tits at that asshole in the gas station."

Half the time he was right. I was always on the lookout for someone better. I was ready to bail, but I didn't know how to get myself out of what I'd gotten myself into.

I never asked the dads over. I was too embarrassed. The freeway noise was so loud you practically had to shout. Everything we had was mismatched, cast-off, hand-me-down. And Sean was really homophobic.

"Them dudes are sick motherfuckers," he said once.

That pissed me off. "Are you talking about my dads?"

"I'm talkin' about queers."

"You're talking about my dads," I said. And he was talking about me, too, because by that time I'd had my first lesbian experience with JD.

"I seen their house that one time you took me over there," Sean said. "You'd get all their shit if they croaked, right? How much you think they're worth?"

That scared me.

Sometimes I'd go over to Mom's and we'd cry together. Sometimes Grandma would come over and cry with us. She'd been through four husbands, "each one worse than the last."

"Sometimes, honey, it's better to divorce right away," Grandma advised me, "before he drags you down any further." Grandma hated all men, but especially the ones she'd married. She didn't trust a single one of them. She'd actually needlepointed a sampler that said, "If it has a prick, it is a prick."

One night Sean accused me of making eyes at some guy in Pizza Hut. He slapped me. I flashed on Mom getting belted by Jerri. No way. I was not going to take physical abuse. I packed my stuff and moved in with JD.

Sean wheedled me back a couple of times. I was too weak-willed to say no. Then he'd drink, blow up, and whack! It enraged him that I was living with JD. "Are you my fucking wife or a fucking dyke?" he'd scream. "Did you catch it from those sick motherfucking dads of yours?"

Every time I left him, JD would take me back in. For a while, it was very dramatic. They fought over me. I liked that.

There was no property to settle, so finally I got Sean to agree to a cheap do-it-yourself divorce. It's this kit you buy, with all the necessary papers and instructions. But I made sure the dads were with me when I went over there for his signature. They acted like bodyguards.

The last I heard of Sean was through Mom. One day she got a phone bill for eight hundred bucks. Most of the calls had been made to phone-sex lines and charged to her number. The phone company traced the calls to Sean Kowalski, only by that time my first husband had completely disappeared. For all I knew, he was on the lam.

What do lesbians do on their second date?
They rent a moving van.

It's an old joke, but there's some truth in it.

After Sean came the period of living with JD. Mom approved. The dads were flabbergasted but supportive.

"My dear," Whitman said, "you don't *have* to be a lesbian, you know. You don't have to feel obligated."

"I don't."

"It wasn't because of us, was it?" Whitman asked, all concerned. "I mean, your father and I never encouraged you to be a dyke, did we?"

"No, Whitman."

"I mean, you've always seemed so relentlessly heterosexual. Ever since you were twelve and the men used to whistle at you in New York."

"Just because men whistle at you doesn't mean you're straight," I pointed out.

He turned to my dad. "Maybe she takes after you and she's bisexual."

"I'm not bisexual," Daddy said.

"Well, you were married," Whitman said. "Twice. And you did sire a child. I'm the only virgin in this family."

"Mom's bisexual, Dad's gay, you're a virgin, so what? That doesn't have anything to do with my sexual choices."

"Of course it does," Whitman insisted. "You've been surrounded by deviants since you were five years old. You weren't raised with any kind of religion, so you never developed a disapproving attitude. You just accepted it all. I'll bet you don't even feel guilty when you lick JD's pussy, do you?"

My cheeks flamed. I was shocked that he could be so vulgar. "No! Why should I?"

"You shouldn't," Whitman said. "But just because everyone around you is queer, don't think your life as a lesbian is going to be easy."

But why shouldn't it be easy? I'd met this really cool woman and we had this instantaneous attraction. I didn't have to worry about hiding it from any of my parents. I didn't have to worry about getting pregnant.

JD was riding the crest of a wave, so she was exciting to be around. For a while, it looked like her band, Black Garters, was going to make it big. She had a cult following among Portland's huge dyke population and played gigs in most of the straight clubs, too. Her band even played the coveted ten o'clock spot during the Rose Festival down at Waterfront Park.

I loved being her Primary Groupie. I loved her creativity. I loved being in on the endless drama of a band. They were always yakking about *producers* and *labels* and potential *contracts* and *moving down to L.A.* I floated along, as JD's girlfriend, and felt like I was a part of it all.

I was there in the studio when they made their one demo tape. I'm the one who arranged the photographer for their CD cover. That cover, my idea, was so cool. The band members all had their bare legs in the air with their high heels touching. *Black Garters*, it said, *Hoseless*. Too bad the demo never got a commercial release.

Being a lesbian didn't present any weird psychic shocks for me. It seemed completely natural. Comforting, even, after the boring terrors of trying to be Sean's wife. Living with JD was so much more exciting. JD's house reminded me of my mom's when I was growing up. There were always women hanging around. I guess as a first-time lesbian, I was kind of naive. Only slowly did it dawn on me that half of them were in love with JD. JD didn't discourage adoration. She accessorized with women.

And she'd slept with most of them. The air was thick with simmering melodrama and jealous intrigue. I floated above it all because I was the undisputed number-one concubine in the harem.

In public everything was crazy, fun, exciting. In private it was another story. JD was messing around with heroin. So was just about everyone in Black Garters. I wouldn't touch the stuff. I'd enrolled in Junior AA when I was fifteen and sneaking around to get high with my friends. JD insisted heroin was nonaddictive. As long as you used a clean needle, she said, smack was okay.

Yeah, right.

In public, she couldn't keep her hands off me. She wanted everyone to know that we were girlfriends. I was like a trophy to her powers of seduction because I'd been straight and married.

JD has an outgoing personality. She's short, cute in an androgynous, punky sort of way, and has a perennially hoarse voice. Everyone loved her. Even the dads fell under her spell.

"I can't tell you how much fun it is to have Venus be a lesbian," Whitman confided to JD one night when JD and I went over to the dads' house for dinner. "You're just such a relief, darling, after that boring straight man she was married to."

"That's supposed to be a compliment," I told JD.

"Now that she's a lesbian," Whitman went on, "I can be so much freeer and more open with her."

Daddy caught my eye. "Haven't you noticed?" he said drily.

Whitman's attention was fixed on JD. "I always held myself back in front of Venus when she was growing up," he told her. "I didn't want her to feel pressured or influenced to be gay. I never used sexually explicit language. And I *never* allowed John to kiss or fondle me in front of her."

"I knew what was going on," I said.

"No, you didn't."

"Yes, I did."

"How?" he wanted to know.

"Well, you've slept together in the same bed since I was five."

"Why would you infer from that that we had sex?"

"Yeah," JD said, "they could have just been good friends who slept together."

We all laughed. But I realized that I had this whole cache of secrets about the dads that I'd never shared with anyone. Little scenes that I'd witnessed, things I'd overheard, private moments that I'd stumbled into.

Whitman was telling the truth when he said he never allowed my dad to touch or kiss him in front of me. But that apartment in New York was pretty small and I was a good spy. I'd seen them in bed,

Daddy with his legs in the air. I'd heard them panting and whispering, and seen how they contrived to secretly touch each other in public. I was always watching to see how they behaved with one another because they were the only long-term couple I knew. They never seemed to get bored with one another.

"JD," Whitman said, pouring wine, "Venus mentioned that your father's a doctor." We were sitting out on one of their suspended terraces overlooking the city. "Does your mother have a profession?"

"Yeah," JD said, "she's a professional bitch."

"Well, then, I'm sure we'll get along just fine." Whitman passed some dried spicy Japanese peas. "When were you first aware that you were a lesbian?"

"When I was about fifteen," JD said.

"I knew I was gay when I was twelve," Whitman said, munching on the dried peas.

"How did you know?" JD asked.

"I hated sports but wanted to be a cheerleader. John here didn't figure it out until he was thirty."

"Slow learner," said JD, looking at my dad.

"Yes," Whitman said, "but those are the best kind. They're always trying to make up for lost time. And they're so grateful."

"I knew long before I was thirty," Daddy said. "I just didn't know what to do with what I knew. My parents were missionaries, for God's sake."

Whitman stroked Daddy's cheek. The gesture sent a shiver of delight through me. I squeezed JD's hand. "I taught him everything he knows," Whitman said.

"You sound like a stage mom," JD said.

Laughing with the dads. I loved *that* part of being with JD. We could go to the dads any time. There was this kind of easygoing acceptance of us as a couple. I felt so grownup and so included in their lives. They'd cook for us. Well, Daddy would. He's a fabulous cook. Whitman is in charge of appearances and hygiene. He sets the table, serves, and cleans up. He praised JD's table manners. "Always a good sign when someone knows which fork to use," he whispered.

"She can eat with chopsticks, too," I said.

"Excellent." He gave me an impulsive hug. "You finally look happy."

I was. I honestly was. Both my dads were playful and fun to be around. I felt closer to Whitman than I ever really had before. It was like I was finally allowed into their secret inner circle.

The four of us would sit around and yak, or play Scrabble, or go to the theater, like we used to do in New York. It was the most normal, relaxed time I'd ever spent with the dads. They invited us to go to the beach with them. They even came to a couple of Black Garters gigs.

But it didn't work the other way around. JD never invited me to visit her folks. She said she despised them, but that never stopped her from cashing their monthly check. I wasn't working, so that check and what she made from her Black Garter gigs kept the household going. When Whitman hinted that it would be nice to meet her parents, JD freaked. It turned out she wasn't even out to them.

We kept it going for about a year and a half.

On stage JD was dynamite, but if I had to rate her performance in bed, I'd say she was about a 2. Sexually, it wasn't much better than being with Sean-Come-Quickly. Only with JD, I always had to be the aggressor. It was not a role I was used to or that I particularly liked. When we were alone together she'd, like, turn off. Nothing I did would arouse her. But in public, with the other women around, she'd act like my girlfriend.

I couldn't figure it out. It got to be really frustrating.

"Maybe she's afraid of intimacy," Mom suggested when I made the mistake of confiding in her. "Jerri was like that."

I was incredulous. "You're comparing JD to that dyke who socked you in the jaw? No way!"

Mom used her Glenda-the-Good-Witch voice. "Well, sweetheart, I found Jerri attractive."

"We're not talking about you and Jerri," I said sharply. "We're talking about me and JD."

"I am merely suggesting that JD may have intimacy issues, as Jerri did." Mom's eyes grew moist. She put down her wineglass. "Well, I had some unresolved self-esteem issues, too."

"How do you know when you've actually found the right person?" I asked my mom.

She shrugged. "I thought your dad was the right person."

I didn't want to bail, but I couldn't see any real future with JD. The band's problems grew steadily worse. Personalities didn't mesh. As a business, Black Garters was total chaos. Gigs were canceled. People had to be paid. JD didn't want to deal with any of the day-to-day shit. She kept shooting up. Everyone acted like smack was way cool. I didn't use it so I was the boring straight girl.

JD didn't want me to go. She didn't want to lose me, she said. But I just couldn't envision myself hanging around, like one of her other women, watching from the sidelines as she picked up new hearts to break and turned into a junkie.

After I split from JD, Mom offered to let me move in with her. But I couldn't go back home. She was always sick with some mysterious ailment or another, and I didn't want to take care of her. So she lent me enough money for a month's rent on a closet-size apartment and I started to look for work. I had no job experience of any kind.

Daddy was just starting his new firm in Portland, so he couldn't support me. Whitman never offered. He was working freelance as a travel writer, so half the time he was in Europe or out on the road.

The dads did say I could live for free with them, but *only* if I went to school and worked part time. I said I'd rather just work. What I didn't say was that my credit-card debt was rising like the fare in a taxi to hell.

"What kind of a job are you looking for?" Daddy asked.

"I'm thinking of being a topless dancer."

Whitman let out a strangled cry and threw up his hands.

"The tips are good," I said. "And it can be artistic."

"It's not artistic!" Whitman shouted. "Don't give me that bullshit! Tits are not talent." He turned angrily to my dad. "John, tell her she can't do it. Tell her there are some lines that cannot be crossed. Stripping, for Christ's sake!"

"If it's so awful, why did you take me to see *Gypsy?*" I asked defiantly. "She was a stripper."

"Yes, but she was not my daughter," Whitman shouted, red in the face.

"I'm not your daughter either!" I snapped.

"That's very true," he shot back. "If you were *my* daughter, you'd be at Smith or Wellesley with a full scholarship."

"I'm sorry if I can't measure up to your expectations," I cried.

"So am I." He tried to calm down by sucking in his deep yoga breaths. Buddha breaths, he called them.

"Right now," I said, trying to sound reasonable instead of desperate, "I just need to earn money. I don't have anything to live on."
I hoped they'd feel sorry for me.

Whitman was completely unsympathetic. He turned to my dad and said, "I have no authority here. You have to tell her she can't do it."

"I'm twenty-one," I reminded them. "I can do whatever I want."

"Live here with us," Daddy said, his voice calm, "and go back to school. I'll pay your tuition."

"Higher education is what separates topless dancers from corporate executives," Whitman said.

"I don't want to be a corporate executive!"

Whitman turned away as if he couldn't bear to look at me.

"Without an education," Daddy warned, "you're going to be stuck in this rut for the rest of your life."

"Is that what you want?" Whitman looked at me over his shoulder. "What do you do when your tits start to sag?"

"I'm not talking about a lifetime career," I said. "I'm talking about earning some money now."

"I thought you were a lesbian," Whitman said. "My dear, lesbians do not dance in topless bars."

"I'm bisexual," I announced. "I fall in love with the person, not the gender."

"Well, you're going to be seeing a whole lot of gender if you start throwing your tits around in a topless club, and it's all going to be male. Is that what you want? To be a sex object?"

"What's wrong with that?"

Whitman shook his head and turned to my dad. "Tell her," he said.

"Tell me what? I'm twenty-one years old! I don't have to listen to you."

It blew up into one of our larger fights and finally I ran out because I couldn't deal with the dads' hostile disapproval.

What was so bad about exotic dancing? You danced for fifteen minutes once an hour. Darlene, who worked at Terry's Topless, told me she made over two hundred bucks in tips on weekends. The men poked tens and twenties into her G-string.

"All you gotta do is lettem cop a feel," Darlene explained. She was a single mom saving up for dental hygienist school. "Can you handle a bunch of men pawing you?"

It sounded better than putting on a dorky polyester uniform and flipping burgers at Wendy's. Or calling strangers and asking them if they wanted their windshields replaced.

And who doesn't fantasize about being on stage? Being the center of attention. Being the star everyone looks at and wants?

So I did it. Just to show the dads that I wasn't their fantasy little girl anymore. And because I needed money fast and bad. I applied for and got every credit card that was offered. I charged everything. I was getting credit-card bills for hundreds of dollars.

The first night I was so scared it made me puke. Dancing in a club with your friends and a warm hit of Ecstasy in your brain is one thing. Dancing half-nude, by yourself, on a stage, in front of a bunch of gaping strangers, is something way different. I'm not really graceful. I'm not in really good shape. But there is something about me that men like. "It's called sex appeal," Darlene told me. "You gotta translate that into tips."

Tips were what you worked for at Terry's Topless because the salary was below minimum wage.

Mom wasn't overjoyed with my decision, but she wasn't negative like the dads. I made the mistake of asking her how to strip. "Well, honey, I don't really know. I suppose you—" She got up and tried to demonstrate.

"You look like an old lady on her way to the chiropractor," I said. "Didn't you ever strip for Daddy?"

"No, honey. I always hid under the bedcovers. I was so ashamed of my body."

I wasn't ashamed of mine. But if I was going to show off my charms, I wanted to do it in a way that was graceful and romantic. For my number I played "You Make Me Feel Like a Natural Woman" and stiffly paraded around the raised wooden runway wearing long gloves, high heels, and lacy satin lingerie that cost a fortune at Victoria's Secret. When it came time to shed the bra and reveal my luscious porcelain treasures, I couldn't undo the hook in back. It took me like five minutes of struggling. When I finished my number and teetered offstage, I didn't hear a single clap. I was so flustered that I'd forgotten the whole point was to get tips poked into my underpants.

I stood there panting, shaking, covered with sweat. "Was I terrible?" I asked Darlene.

"This isn't a fashion runway," Darlene said. "You gotta cut to the chase. Shake the components. Make it hot or you'll go home hungry."

Together we dreamed up this rockabilly cowgirl outfit. I wore a fringed rawhide G-string, a little fringed leather vest with Velcro that I could easily pop open for a boob flash, and a big Stetson. Instead of high heels I wore red snakeskin boots ($450 at Saks). Around my hips I had a leather holster with two squirt guns. I didn't go for graceful; I went for down-home heehaw.

That seemed to work. The first night I made forty-five bucks. The second night I made ninety. The one after that, a Saturday, I made a hundred and twenty.

I couldn't believe the number of propositions I got.

"Just don't ever date them," Darlene warned.

"Why not?" There was this one really cute guy who'd become a regular at my sets. I could tell he was interested.

"Just don't." Darlene brushed back her hair and showed me a long white scar neatly incised in the side of her neck.

One night Big Bill pulled a box from behind the bar and handed it to me. Inside were a dozen beautiful red roses and a card. "I want you," is all it said. Big Bill didn't know who'd sent them.

I thought I knew. Every night he was sitting there at a table, by himself, staring at me with glazed eyes and a dreamy smile. He never came up to stick money into my G-string. He was a little older than me, but not much. Cute. Clean-cut and sort of rumpled. Like a Banana Republic ad.

Weeks went by. More flowers arrived. They always came with short, unsigned messages. "You light my fire." "To the tattooed tigress." "In my dreams you're all mine."

No man had ever been, like, romantic with me before. I was filled with this glowing sense of mystery. Someone thought I was beautiful! I found myself daydreaming about my secret admirer. I called him Bud Light because that's all he ever drank.

But Mr. Light never made a move. I figured he was deathly shy. So one night, just for fun, I squirted him with my squirt guns, as part of my topless cowgirl routine. Instead of laughing, he looked at me with this stricken, heart-rending expression, stood up, and left the bar. He never came back. I felt terrible.

But fate works in really weird ways. Three months later I married him.

One night my mother's old calico cat died. Crookedy was my cat, too. I'd grown up with her. She went back as far as the big Victorian house I'd lived in with Mom and Dad. After we left there, because Mom wasn't working and couldn't afford the mortgage payments anymore, I lugged Crookedy around from apartment to apartment and house to house.

Anyway, one morning Mom found Crookedy lying on her special

catnip-laced pillow, stiff as a board. She called me and I rushed over and we cried and talked about Crookedy and then Mom said, "What do we do with her body?"

Neither one of us wanted to touch Crookedy. Her eyes were half-closed and her mouth was open and pulled back so you could see her crusty brown fangs. We couldn't bury her because there was no yard. In the Yellow Pages, I found Pet Away, a service that picked up deceased pets and disposed of them. I called the number and a guy said someone would be right over.

Mom and I were going through waves of shared grief over Crookedy. We'd be okay for a while, then burst into sobs. A part of my life was gone. I was so upset I didn't even look up when Mom opened the door for the Pet Away man. I just sat on the sofa sniveling and half-watching Bette Davis in *Of Human Bondage*.

I heard his deep, sincere-sounding voice tell Mom how much it would cost to dispose of Crookedy. It would cost more if she wanted the ashes returned. She had to pay in cash; no checks or credit cards accepted. Mom didn't have the bread, so I peeled sixty-five from the wad of tip money I carried around.

The Pet Away man picked up Crookedy and laid her in a nice cardboard box. "Would you like to say good-bye to your pet one last time?" he asked.

Sobbing, we went over and peered into the box he was holding. Then I looked up into the Pet Away man's eyes. It was Bud Light.

His real name was Peter Pringle. The same day we met over my mom's dead cat I invited him over to my place.

Pete was very romantic. "You're so beautiful you could star in one of them slasher movies," he panted as we made love.

"As the slasher?"

"No, as one of the beautiful girls who gets slashed."

I'm highly susceptible to praise. I asked him if he wanted to move into my apartment. I didn't want to live alone and neither did he.

Well, this time I really thought I'd found Mr. Right. Pete was clean-cut and had a steady job. All day long he drove around the city collecting dead dogs, cats, birds, snakes, hamsters, turtles, iguanas, monkeys, geckos, squirrels, bats—every kind of creature that you can imagine. He called himself an Animal Disposal Specialist.

A couple of times I went on his rounds with him. His van had a weird sweetish smell that could make you puke if you paid too much attention to it. It smelled like that roach spray the exterminator used in the dads' apartment in New York. Pete was always respectful to the pet owner's face. But then, when he got back to Pet Away, he'd flip the dead animal into the incinerator with a comical whistle. Sometimes he'd toss it in with an underhand lob, sometimes he'd slam dunk it in like a basketball. It all depended on the size of the animal.

He said the job didn't get to him. "You can't take it personally," he said, "or you go crazy."

I admired his orderly ways. "Neat Pete," I called him. Everything had to be in its proper place. He said he couldn't stand messes and asked if he could reorganize the apartment. Fine with me. I was still used to having my mom clean up after me. Once a week she'd come over to vacuum, pick up clothes, and scrub out the tub, sinks, and toilet. She didn't have to be my cleaning lady once Neat Pete moved in.

Pete wanted to get a degree in mortuary science and eventually have his own funeral home. But, like me, he had a problem with plastic. He owed thousands in school loans already, and he couldn't get out from under his debt load with the money he made at Pet Away.

He kept pointing out these programs advertised on TV that told you how to buy houses with no money down. "If you do it right, you can be a millionaire in a year," he claimed. His credit line was maxed out, so I charged the program for him.

Pete didn't want me to continue working at Terry's Topless. I was sick of it myself, but I didn't know what else to do. "What about cosmetics?" Pete said. "You see those ads all the time for Lorrie Ann Cosmetics. Those Lorrie Ann Ladies drive around in white Mercedes convertibles."

The trip to hell always starts with a toll-free number.

It all sounded reasonable enough. I liked the idea of being my own boss. And as a former model and exotic dancer, I knew the importance of makeup.

What could be simpler? The more Lorrie Ann I sold, the richer I'd become. There were "Commitment Tiers" that you pledged yourself to: You agreed to order a certain amount of merchandise each month. It was nonreturnable, but your discount increased proportionately to the amount of merchandise you ordered. If you brought in other Lorrie Ann Ladies, you got extra credits toward that white Mercedes convertible or bigger discounts on your merchandise. And best of all, your monthly or yearly stock of Lorrie Ann cosmetics could be paid for with a credit card. You got an even bigger discount if you joined and paid for a year in advance. That's what I did.

Pete, meanwhile, was trying to figure out how to buy real estate with no money down. We never went out to the movies. All we did was watch the No Money Down Real Estate System videos over and over again. All those people giving testimonials sounded just like us. They'd been bogged down in debt . . . they'd been sick of working for others . . . they were getting nowhere fast . . . and now they were millionaires!

But you were supposed to read this handbook, too. And I noticed that Pete never read it. Later on, I found out that he was dyslexic. Reading was a torment.

I pledged at one of the highest commitment tiers at Lorrie Ann. Before I knew it, boxes of shit were arriving. I freaked. Who was I going to sell it to?

My mom rounded up some of her girlfriends, and Grandma rounded up some of hers. I did my first Lorrie Ann Lady presentation to them. There was, like, no enthusiasm. One lady winced when she smelled the Midnight Lace perfume. "Smells like vanilla Clorox," she said. Mom and Grandma said they'd buy the expensive Night Time Hydration Formula, and someone else bought a lipstick. That was it.

Then I got a bunch of my girlfriends together. We were jammed in my tiny apartment and I was trying to be the Lorrie Ann Lady while my friends smoked pot and drank beer. We started laughing and playing with the makeup samples until we all looked insane, and then we went to *The Rocky Horror Picture Show* at midnight. It's been playing at the same theater for over thirty years. It's so old that my mom went to it when she was young.

The next day I tried to cancel my membership in Lorrie Ann. No way, they said. I was in it for a year. I was committed. The Lorrie Ann merchandise would arrive every month as per my *signed contract.*

I didn't tell the dads about any of this. Mom kept doling out money. She was working as a secretary-receptionist for a big corporation.

One day Pete looked up from the toilet he was scrubbing and said, "Let's get married."

I didn't say anything, just looked at him. I tried on the name: Venus Pringle.

"We could consolidate our debts," he said, "and apply for new credit cards as a married couple. With the new cards we could pay off all the old cards and maybe still have enough credit line left to buy a house. I mean, if we charged the down payment."

I was kind of dubious, but after a certain point in a relationship what do you do? You commit. You get married. Or you bail.

I loved Pete because he was so in love with me. All those flowers he'd sent to me when I was at Terry's Topless; they must have cost a fortune. Pete adored me. He was so sweet. He kept saying he couldn't believe he was having sex with someone as beautiful as I was. I was his queen. He did whatever I told him to. Half the time I didn't have to say anything: He *anticipated* my desires. It was like having a mother, a waiter, and a boyfriend rolled up in one.

We did the civil ceremony thing. We drove to the courthouse in the Pet Away van because my car needed a new carburetor. When I told Mom, she was like, "Oh, sweetheart, why didn't you tell me?" and started bawling. Right away she started in about having a party for us.

When I called to tell the dads, there was a long silence on the other end of the line. They were on separate extensions. Finally Daddy said, "Do we get to meet him?"

"Obviously she's ashamed of us," Whitman said.

"No!" I said, caught off-guard by the hurt in his voice.

Daddy suggested I bring Pete over for dinner. Whitman, ominously, said nothing.

The interrogation began the moment we walked in the front door. "I apologize in advance for being inquisitive," Whitman said to Pete, "but our daughter didn't even have the courtesy to tell us she was getting married, so I don't know a goddamn thing about you." He motioned for us to sit down on the new Italian leather sofa. "What do you do?"

"I'm an animal disposal specialist," Pete said.

"Is that a euphemism for exterminator?" Whitman flicked his eyes in my direction.

Pete was confused. He turned to me. "What's a euphemism?" he asked.

I racked my brains. "I think it's something that means something else. Like 'little girls' room' instead of 'bathroom'."

"I was asking if you're an exterminator," Whitman clarified.

"Oh. No, sir, I'm not. The animals are already dead when I get to them."

Silence.

"Do you have a degree?" Whitman asked.

Pete shook his head. "No, sir, not yet."

"But you're working toward one?"

"Sort of. Sir."

"Sort of?"

Daddy brought in a beautiful tray of canapés: olive tapenade, crusty Italian bread, smoked salmon. He smiled. I stood up so he could hug me.

"Daddy, this is my husband, Peter Pringle."

Daddy shook Pete's hand.

"Pringle," Whitman said, pouring drinks. "You're not from the potato chip family, are you?"

Pete shook his head. "No, sir. I'm from Boring."

"Boring?" Whitman said, a puzzled look on his face.

"Boring," Daddy said to Whitman. "We've passed it on the way to Mount Hood."

Whitman winced. "The place with all those little cabins and trailer homes?"

"That's Boring," Pete said.

"It certainly is," agreed Whitman.

It wasn't a successful evening.

We thought we were going to be yachting around as millionaires, but within six months we were drowning in credit-card debt. Every day, every night, there were threatening letters and phone calls from all the credit-card companies that had been so welcoming just months earlier.

As our dreams collapsed, Pete became more and more obsessive. There was always this trapped look in his eyes. It was kind of scary. He insisted that the dishes and glasses had to be arranged in a certain pattern on the shelf. The bed had to be made in a certain way. Our clothes had to be hung or folded just so. Every time I stubbed out a cigarette, Pete grabbed the ashtray and cleaned it. He showered in the morning and came home at noon to shower again, and then showered a third time when he got home from work and a fourth time before gong to bed. He kept complaining of strange odors.

I had to find some kind of job. Pete didn't want me to go back to Terry's Topless. He couldn't stand the idea of having his wife dance in front of other men. I called Darlene. She'd left Terry's Topless and was now doing lingerie modeling.

There are all these secret worlds out there. Worlds you never knew about as a kid. Worlds your parents hoped you'd never discover. Worlds you don't know about unless you're poor and looking for a job.

Like the world of lingerie modeling.

It worked like this. There was a dark, stuffy, windowless room with a bed and a chair in the center. It was like a theater set, surrounded on three sides by creaking chairs taken from an old movie house. Men paid to come in and furtively jerk off as you strolled around and posed provocatively in lingerie.

The goal was to get them to hire you for private modeling sessions. If you agreed, you got thirty bucks guaranteed plus whatever tip they gave you. For fifteen minutes of work.

The private modeling rooms contained a bed and a chair. The owner didn't want his business to be raided as a house of prostitution so there were strict rules. The client had to sit on the chair while you posed on the bed or stuck out your rear end for him to drool over. They could j.o. but you couldn't touch them. And you didn't want to. In fact, you didn't even want to look at most of them.

Except there was this one guy. An older gentleman, about my dad's age, beautifully tanned, with thick silver hair and a hawklike nose. He was always impeccably dressed, as if he'd just come from a board meeting. Dark suit, white or pale blue shirt with French cuffs, an expensive-looking tie, and Italian shoes. Every week he'd hire me for a private modeling session. He always gave me a fifty-dollar tip.

He wanted to get friendly, so I let him talk. He told me his name was Marcello. "Like Mastroianni," he said, but I didn't know what he was talking about. He had a deep voice with a foreign accent. Italian, I guess.

He was so polite in his requests for poses that I never minded. It was like working for a cameraless photographer. "Could you just pout a little bit more?" he'd say. "Good. Ohh, *buonissimo*. Now, cross your beautiful legs and lean back. Look impatient! Now pout. Now look angry."

All the while he'd be pumping his dick and dabbing at his face with a white linen handkerchief. With an agonized sigh, staring into my eyes, he'd ejaculate into the hanky. He'd sit for a postcoital moment, eyes closed, breathing deeply. Then get up, toss the hanky into the wastebasket, and leave.

I wouldn't date him. Wouldn't even meet him for a coffee. "I'm married," I said.

"Married?" He looked surprised.

Every week he pried out a little bit more. "Why is a beautiful young woman like you working in a place like this? Why isn't your *marito*, your husband, supporting you?"

"He can't. And he doesn't know that I'm working here."

"What does he think you do all day long?"

"He thinks I'm out selling cosmetics."

"So you do this because you love him. You want to help him. You're a very noble girl." He was silent for a moment. "Why don't you become my mistress?"

No, I didn't become Marcello's mistress. But I was really losing it with Pete. One of us had to do something to get us out of the credit-card quagmire, and it wasn't going to be him. He spent all his free time arranging and cleaning and trying to please me.

"You must be the top-grossing Lorrie Ann Lady in Portland," he said, watching like a hungry kid as I counted out my tip money.

I felt kind of guilty for fooling him. But when I said I was "selling Lorrie Ann," it was sort of true. "Laurie Ann" was the alias I used for lingerie modeling.

I don't know how he found out. Maybe he always knew. Maybe he was just too shy to say anything. One afternoon while I was modeling, I looked up and saw him staring at me from the last row.

Some people split their assets when they divorce. Pete and I split our debts. There was no rancor between us. On the day the decree came through I was feeling kind of sentimental, so I called Pete and we reminisced a little.

"I'll always remember those beautiful flowers you sent me at Terry's Topless," I said. "I think that's what made me fall in love with you."

"What flowers?" Pete said. "I never sent you any flowers."

* * *

So that's how I finally ended up in bankruptcy court. And it was in bankruptcy court that I met Tremaynne Woods, the man I was going to marry tomorrow.

"Okay, you like?" the Vietnamese girl asked.

I held up my hands and gazed at my black nails. "Perfect."

Chapter
6

The wedding ceremony took place in Carolee's hot, tiny living room. The temperature had shot up to a broiling 95 degrees, so we kept the front door open and Mom's big electric fan turned on full blast. The colorful streamers Mom tied on to the front snapped and buzzed as the fan swished hot stale air back and forth.

I waited nervously in Mom's bathroom, unable to sit down, while all the guests gathered in the living room. I'd chosen my wedding attire with special care, knowing that I had to stand out and make an indelible impression on Tremaynne. I had to dress like a memory that he'd carry around with him for the rest of his life. No one knew what I was wearing, not even Mom. It was going to be a huge surprise.

Tremaynne and I had worked out a short ceremony with one of my old club friends, Pastor Lucifer of the Church of Now. I'd done all the planning because Tremaynne had never been married before and didn't know the basics.

For an altar, I dragged out my mom's computer table and decorated it with two red roses and four black candles. Pastor Lucifer and Tremaynne were going to wait for me there, at the altar, right in front of the TV. The CD player was all set up and ready to play "Raging Hearts," the music I'd come out to, walking down the hall-

way from the bathroom to the altar in the living room. All Carolee
had to do was press one simple button. I showed her a million times.

Of course she fucked it up. A violent rap number came blasting
out of the CD player. Everyone stopped talking. I had to stick my
head out and call for her.

"That's not the right song!" I hissed.

She looked frightened. "I pressed the button you showed me."

"It's supposed to be 'Raging Hearts.' Track six!"

"What should I do?" Mom asked.

"Turn it off. Tell Daddy to play track six if you can't figure it out."
I pulled my head back into the bathroom and shut the door in her
face.

A few minutes later the right song came on. When I heard those
woozy guitars, I opened the bathroom door and started down the
hallway, walking slowly, carrying two red roses.

I was all in black, feet bare, my toenails and fingernails painted
black. My dress was a cross between a tight, low-cut gown and a
voluptuous satin negligee. It showed off the tattoos on my chest and
back.

I thought I looked beautiful. I thought I looked stunning. I
thought I looked hot. I thought I looked totally original, unlike any
bride I'd ever seen in any magazine.

But the first face I saw, when I entered the living room, happened
to be Whitman's. And he looked so shocked that it shook me. I
quickly turned away, toward Tremaynne, waiting at the altar.

My husband-to-be was wearing what he always wears: blue jeans,
cotton shirt, hiking boots. I approached him, smiling, and handed
him one of my two red roses. He was so nervous he didn't know
what to do. Just stared at me with a frozen smile. "Take it," I whispered.

Pastor Lucifer kind of fluffed out his long black cape. While he
gave his short spiel about why we were all gathered there, etcetera,
I secretly checked out my audience in the mirror beside the TV.
Mom was dressed like she was going to a garden party. She wore a
billowing floral-print muu muu with various diaphanous scarves and

a large, weird hat. Grandma was in a lime green polyester pants suit with white running shoes. Daddy wore his lightweight Armani summer suit and Ferragamo dress shoes. He looked incredibly handsome.

Whitman was in Kenzo and Kenneth Cole. Very tailored and up-to-date. He couldn't see me looking at him. He stood very erect, next to Daddy, and seemed to be staring down at my bare feet, unable to hide the appalled expression on his face.

His horrified disapproval sliced right through me. For a second it was like I knew *exactly* what was going through his mind. How shocking it must have been for him to see me not in a chic, white, Donna Karan A-line but a tight black negligee with bare feet and black nails. In his eyes I probably looked ridiculous.

It suddenly dawned on me: Whitman came from a completely different social class, and because of that he had a completely different set of values and expectations for me.

But I wasn't from his class. I was from *this*, from a tiny house in a crummy neighborhood. A house with interior decor that centered around an enormous TV set and a Felix the Cat clock with ticking eyes and tail. That's who I was. I wasn't a girl who'd gone to finishing school. I was a girl who'd gone to the worst public schools in Portland, where I was constantly afraid for my life and never fit in. My tastes and values were probably more like my mom's than I ever dared to admit to myself, because she was the one who'd raised me most of the time.

Whitman was brought up in a world where weddings were held in big churches, with organ music and ushers and bridesmaids and flowergirls. Everything was proper, traditional, done in a certain way.

And that's why nothing I did *my* way would ever please him.

Well, fuck you, Whitman, I said to myself, working myself up into a lather of defensiveness. *You can disapprove all you want to, but it's not going to change a single thing in my life. I'm not you, and I've never even met your rich family, and you don't see them anymore yourself, so how important can they and their old traditions really be?*

Pastor Lucifer brought me back to myself when he bound my

wrist to Tremaynne's with a leather thong. I'd come across the idea in a fantasy novel.

We spoke our vows.

The Church of Now has no special prayers or anything. In the Church of Now, you can believe in whatever you want. So in our ceremony there was no reference to an Almighty, and no request for supernatural blessings. Instead, we simply promised to love, trust, and cherish each other.

"I'll make my home in you," I said in a soft, nervous voice, looking into Tremaynne's dark eyes, trying to remember the words he'd written, "and I promise I won't stand in the way of your personal fulfillment."

Tremaynne spoke of "celebrating how we feel now, as two unique people in an evolving world in need of radical change."

"Venus and Tremaynne, by the power vested in me by the State of Oregon, I pronounce you man and wife."

On cue, we threw our roses, clasped one another, and kissed.

My eyes strayed from my husband's face just long enough to see Whitman take a deep Buddha breath. It was kind of a relief to see that both dads were crying.

Chapter
7

Tremaynne's bloodshot eyes were full of longing, a kind of wild sexual yearning. I felt it too. We both wanted to fuck like crazy.

But the dads were paying for our honeymoon, so there we were, holding hands and yawning in the backseat of their SUV, barreling east along I-84 through the Columbia Gorge.

Dad One was driving, which meant we were going faster than the speed limit. Dad Two was talking back to NPR as he flipped through a stack of CDs.

It was the fifth of July, the morning after my wedding. Tremaynne and I didn't get any sleep and the dads were there to pick us up at seven. We were both so tired and hung over we could barely lift giant lattes (thoughtfully provided by the dads) to our lips.

Outside, it was Oregon. We plunged into thick soupy fogs one minute and then came out into hot bright sunshine the next. Ribbons of gauzy white vapor snaked along the tops and sides of the mountains looming above us. Waterfalls squirted out from black cliffs.

"Wake up back there!" Whitman clapped his hands and pretended to be a tour guide talking into a microphone. "You are now entering the Columbia Gorge National Scenic Area. Notice the magnificent basaltic rock formations rearing up two thousand feet on either side of you. The explorers Meriwether Lewis and William Clark were the first white men to explore this area in eighteen oh five. But Native Americans used this mighty river for salmon fishing thousands of years before whitey arrived. Radiocarbon dating has established that Kennewick Man, the skeleton of a male found on the banks of this river, was—would anyone care to guess how old?"

"Nine thousand three hundred years old," Daddy said. "He was in his forties when he died."

"Correct. Now does anyone know what makes this skeleton so controversial?" Whitman asked.

"Some paleontologists have suggested that Kennewick Man had European or Polynesian features," Daddy said.

"Correct again. Nine thousand three hundred years ago a forty-something male with possible European or Polynesian features was ambushed on the banks of the Columbia River."

"Why do you say ambushed?" Tremaynne asked.

Whitman turned around as far as his seatbelt would allow. "Because they found arrowheads embedded in his chest and thigh."

I yawned and cuddled up next to my handsome new husband. I tried to put my head on his shoulder but it wasn't easy. I'm almost a foot taller than Tremaynne. I sort of rested my cheek on his black hair and zoned out.

"Anyone want to stop at Multnomah Falls?" Whitman asked a few minutes later. "Sixth-highest waterfall in the United States."

"Not really," I said.

"Yes, really."

"I meant, I don't really want to stop at Multnomah Falls."

"Just asking."

We drove on in silence for another fifteen minutes.

"Don't you kids take any interest in your surroundings?" Whitman asked. "Look, there's Bonneville Dam. National Historic Landmark. Franklin Delano Roosevelt came out for the opening in nineteen thirty-seven."

"They should blow it up," Tremaynne said.

Whitman ignored the remark. "Your father," he said to me, "designed the Visitors Center."

"You designed it, Daddy?" The old surge of pride every time I saw one of his buildings. I nudged Tremaynne and we both peered out, trying to figure out what we were looking at. The dam was this big ugly concrete sucker. "When?"

"Back when I was not my own boss," he said.

"Let's go visit the Visitors Center," Whitman suggested. "I've never been inside."

"I think they call it an 'interpretive center' now," Daddy said.

"You mean it'll *interpret* how this dam kills millions of salmon every year?" Tremaynne said. "Or how the dam's raised the temperature of the river and poisoned the water with PCBs?"

"I don't know," Whitman shrugged, "let's go see."

"We're *tired*, Whitman," I grumbled.

His hands shot up. "Okay, okay. I simply thought you might be *interested* since your *father* designed it."

"I am interested," I said guiltily, "but just not now. We had a humongous night, okay? We drank too much and stayed up all night."

"You don't think it was emotionally draining for your father and me?" Whitman snapped off the radio. "To see you barefoot with your toenails painted black?"

I couldn't tell if he was really upset or just pretending to be. "I told you it would be a surprise."

"It was a surprise, all right. I felt like I was in *Rosemary's Baby*. I thought if I turned around I'd see Ruth what's-her-name staring at me."

"What are you talking about?" my dad asked him.

"You know, Ruth what's-her-name. In the movie."

"Ruth Roman?" Dad One hazarded.

Whitman let out a snort. "Ruth Roman was back in the forties. B-movies."

"She was in the fifties," Daddy said. "Biblical epics."

"You're thinking of Debra Paget. And *Rosemary's Baby* was made in the early seventies."

"Nineteen sixty-eight," I corrected him. I read video boxes. I knew.

Whitman turned around and looked at me, irked that he was wrong. "Before you were born anyway. When were you born again?"

"Nineteen seventy-eight."

"That's right, because you were five when I first met you and that was eighty-three."

"The year before you moved to New York," I reminded him. "You were still with Carl. You hadn't left him yet for Daddy."

Whitman scratched his chin and looked out the window.

"And then Daddy moved to New York to be with you. In eighty-six. When I was eight." Just saying it brought up an old angry hurt. At one point in my life I picked at that hurt all the time, scratched it like a scab on a wound I never wanted to heal. My dad left me in 1986 to go live with Whitman in New York. Because he loved Whitman more than he loved me. And certainly more than he loved my mom. I hated Whitman back then. He was an enemy. And some part of me has been wary of him ever since.

Wary and a little afraid. He was like a big ocean liner and I was a little raft made out of boards and string, and he could so easily swamp me if he wanted to. As a girl I cast him as a conniving, black-hearted bitch and was certain that he wanted to wrest total control of Daddy, or turn Daddy against me, or do any number of the horrible things that grownups do. I always got the feeling that as far as Daddy was concerned, Whitman was the gourmet dinner and I was the leftovers. I could not compete with Whitman at any level. Before I understood it as a woman, I understood as a daughter that no female can ever win the heart of a man in love with another man.

Whitman turned back around. "What were we talking about?"

"I wasn't talking about anything," I said. "I was trying to get some sleep. You were talking about Ruth someone."

"Yes, you know, Ruth thingamajig." He turned to Daddy. "The one who was married to Garson Kanin. They wrote screenplays together. Then she started acting dotty old lady roles."

"Well, what about her?" I asked. As usual he'd managed to snag my attention even though I didn't have a clue what he was talking about.

"Gordon!" he said, snapping his fingers in triumph. "Ruth Gordon! How did I ever get onto her? Oh yes, your wedding. It reminded me of *Rosemary's Baby*. It seemed somewhat—occultish."

"Occultish?" Tremaynne said.

"You weren't invoking the devil or anything during that ceremony, were you?" Whitman asked.

Tremaynne and I looked at one another and burst out laughing.

"Whitman," I said, "it was our *wedding*. It was the way we wanted it to be. Me and Tremaynne—"

"Tremaynne and I," he corrected.

"We planned it all out together."

"Okay, honey, I know I'm unbelievably square and hopelessly yupper-middle-class, but would you kindly tell me what the aesthetic was?"

I *hate* it when I don't know what he means. "The what?"

"Well, the bride wore a black negligee. The groom wore hiking clothes. You had bare feet and black toenails. There were black candles and two blood-red roses on the altar. And that so-called Reverend What's-his-name of the Church of Whatever-it-was—"

"Reverend Lucifer of the Church of Now," I said.

"Yes, now, did I miss something here or isn't Lucifer one of the names of the devil?"

"You certainly have a bug up your ass all of a sudden," my dad said to Whitman. Quietly. Like maybe trying to get him to shut up.

"Look, I don't mean to sound antagonistic." Whitman offered us his pack of Trident sugarless gum. "I'm just trying to understand." His eyes flicked over to me, then back to Tremaynne. "This wasn't like any wedding I've ever attended."

I happened to look up and caught Daddy staring at me in the rear-view mirror. He'd been waiting to catch my attention. He smiled and his smile took me to that secret world we share, just Daddy and me, apart from Whitman, apart from Mom, apart from everyone else.

"It wasn't supposed to be like any wedding you've ever attended," I said proudly. "We made it all up ourselves."

"Mm," Whitman said, nodding.

Tremaynne suddenly sat forward. "Do you ever think about important things, like how the world's forests are being destroyed?" he asked Whitman.

The question seemed to take Whitman off-guard.

"Not just the forests," Tremaynne went on. "The whole earth. Water, air, land. All the animals. Everything." His body was tense. "You ever think about that?"

"Yes," Whitman said, "actually I do think about that."

"In your travel stuff," Tremaynne said, "when you write about fancy resorts, do you ever talk about the damage they do to the environment?"

"People don't go to resorts to look at environmental damage," Whitman said.

"So anything a developer does is okay as long as it brings in rich people?"

I couldn't tell where Tremaynne was coming from with all this. His voice always took on an angry edge when he talked about environmental issues. I liked his passion. I liked it that he was challenging Whitman, putting him on the defensive, making him squirm.

"I think you're misinterpreting my politics," Whitman said. "My sympathies are entirely Green."

Tremaynne smiled, only it wasn't a friendly smile. "So how many trees did you cut down to build your house?"

Whitman raised his eyebrows and turned to Daddy.

"If you look at the structural support and framing system of our house," Daddy said over his shoulder, "you'll see it's mostly fabricated steel. Wood was used mostly for the interior finishes."

"I meant," Tremaynne said, "how many trees did you cut down to clear the lot, before the house was built?"

"Two," Daddy said.

"Do you know how many organisms depended on those two trees?" There was an aggressive thrust in his voice that made my heart beat a little faster. It was the first time anyone I'd married or been involved with had engaged with the dads as an equal.

"Tremaynne," Daddy said, "I'm an architect. Wood is a building material to me. It's a renewable resource."

"Those corporate forests are sick," Tremaynne said. "They plant only one fast-growing species. Mono-culture. There's no diversity, so one bug or virus can wipe it all out."

"People have been using wood for building for thousands of years." Daddy kept his voice calm.

"You know how much wood people waste to build their stupid trophy homes and luxury resorts?" Tremaynne sounded almost belligerent. "There's alternative forms of building materials. Why don't you use those?"

"I'm not interested in buildings made out of hay bales or old tires," Daddy said. "Sorry."

"Everyone's going to be sorry when we're all dead." Tremaynne folded his arms and sat back.

There was an uneasy silence until Whitman said, "Would anyone mind if I put on an opera?"

Don't ever ask me a question about geography.

When I was eight, and flying out to New York for the first time by myself, I dared myself to look out the plane window. I'd never realized how huge America really was. It was incomprehensible and really scary.

Like now. Where were we? Tremaynne showed me on a map. But none of it meant much because I'd never explored the Pacific Northwest. I'd lived there all my life, but I didn't have a clue where we were or where we were going. All I knew was that we'd crossed the Cascade Mountains via the Columbia Gorge and there was a luxurious spa and a free honeymoon suite waiting for us at the end of a nine-hour car ride. It was the grand opening of Pine Mountain Lodge, a resort my dad designed and that Whitman was writing up for *Travel*. Their millionaire Dutch friend Fokke Van der Zout was one of the developers. Whitman said the opening was going to be a big to-do, and there might even be celebrities there.

"Like who?" I asked.

"I don't know. Maybe Jessye Norman or Jane Bugler. Fokke and Marielle are friends with all sorts of opera singers."

"Opera singers?" I was disappointed. "They aren't celebrities."

"To those of us interested in art and culture," Whitman said prissily, "opera singers are celebrities."

"Jennifer Lopez is a celebrity," I grumbled. "Brad Pitt."

"Ralph Nader," Tremaynne added.

Pine Mountain Lodge was in Idaho somewhere. With his finger-tip, Tremaynne traced an endless series of highways and winding roads to a green section on his map. Tree symbols were dotted all over it. He pointed to the words: River of No Return Wilderness Area.

I freaked. I sat up and grabbed Whitman by the shoulder. "You're taking us to someplace called the River of No Fucking Return?"

"It's beautiful," Whitman said. "Largest wilderness area in the Northwest. Old-growth trees everywhere."

"Land that's supposed to be protected from development," Tremaynne said. "Only now the Forest Service has this cozy new arrangement with private developers that no one's supposed to know about."

"They didn't build *in* the wilderness area," Whitman informed him. "It's on the outskirts. Venus's father created a place that's completely sensitive to the environment."

"Sure," Tremaynne smirked.

I saw the dads exchange a quick glance. Tremaynne was obviously making them uncomfortable.

Watching Tremaynne challenge the dads excited some primitive part of me. He could challenge them in a way that I never could, asserting himself as their equal. My other two husbands had never been able to do that.

Challenge and combat is this guy thing. It's how the alpha male emerges and claims the alpha female. I saw this program once on the Discovery Channel on how it all works.

The Tremaynne in the SUV with the dads was a very different

creature from the Tremaynne who'd sat docilely with the dads over dinner in that vegan restaurant. In the car with the dads, he was more like a pit bull.

Something was going on inside me. I felt like I was waking up. My senses were quickening. It was like drinking two double espressos double quick. But below the excitement there was this jangle of panic, as though I'd caught a sudden glimpse of a shadow I didn't want to see. I wasn't sure where the fear was coming from. I felt it the minute I saw those words: River of No Return Wilderness Area.

As a honeymoon destination, the name sucked major league. It couldn't have sounded more doomed unless it was called the You'll Never Get Back Alive Wilderness Area.

Stop worrying, I told myself. *It can't be that dangerous. You're with three strong men. They'll take care of you. You never have to leave your luxurious honeymoon suite. You can hole up with your handsome new husband and fuck like bunnies for three days straight. With time out for a facial, a hot-mud wrap, and a massage. And it won't cost you a penny.*

I drew my legs up, pulled a blanket around my shoulders, and tried to think calming thoughts. How would we make love the first time? A beautiful suite would be so different from my dinky, messy apartment. I pictured us in a huge room with log walls and a stone fireplace. I might even wear the scratchy Patty Cakes shorty negligee that Bruce gave me. I'd been dieting all week, just in case.

A real honeymoon! I tried to imagine how it must have felt for my mom, when Daddy took her off to San Francisco for their honeymoon. It must have been weird. She told me that Daddy couldn't get a hard-on. "So out of guilt," she said, "he ate me out and I had an orgasm that way."

A couple hours later we were, like, totally zonked and totally wired. That buzzy feeling of being exhausted and wide awake at the same time. With nothing to do. I looked up and saw the dads holding hands. They looked so sweet. Whitman's hand rested on Daddy's thigh.

It gave me this crazy idea.

We were covered by a soft Pendleton blanket, so the dads couldn't see what I was up to. I moved my hand down to Tremaynne's thigh. Gave it a slight squeeze.

Tremaynne looked at me through half-closed eyes. I kissed him, darting my tongue into his mouth to turn up the heat a little. Then I began to feel him up. First his thighs, hard as the rocks he loved to climb. Then up, slowly, until I'd cupped his crotch. I felt around until I had his prick between my fingers. He spread his legs and slid his hips forward.

The only sound was the tires humming on the asphalt.

I rubbed and squeezed and felt his cock blossom and grow hard. I stroked and teased it. It was like playing with the stubby barrel of a revolver. Then I left it, swollen against the buttons of his jeans, and traveled higher, to his chest. I inched a finger into his soft flannel shirt until I reached a nipple. His were almost as sensitive as mine.

My accomplice shot me a secretive glance, then turned to look out the window as I started a light, circular movement with the tip of my finger. The nipple stood up at attention. Tremaynne closed his eyes and lolled his head back as I worked my magic.

"You're certainly quiet back there." Whitman turned around. I snapped my eyes shut. "Oh. They're sleeping," he whispered to Daddy.

I opened my eyes again. I could see Whitman's hand moving higher up Daddy's leg. Daddy gave him a quick, bemused glance and glanced into the rearview mirror. I closed my eyes just in time.

When I opened them again, I could see what Whitman was doing.

The dads were totally unaware that I was spying on them as I jerked off my husband in the backseat.

The landscape changed. It wasn't wet, like on the west side of the mountains. It was dry. High desert, Whitman called it. "Part of the Great Basin," he said.

Whatever that was. In my mind's eye I saw a huge sink.

Tremaynne was totally engrossed in a set of maps he'd pulled out of his backpack. The maps were covered with intricate dots and squiggles and symbols marked in different colored inks. I didn't realize until then just how interested he was in where we were going.

My handsome new husband wasn't being very communicative, so I tuned into the Dads Channel in the front seat. Whitman and Daddy seemed to be having a good time. They ignored us completely. They gossiped about friends, talked about their work, discussed financial issues, wondered when the economy would get back on track, made fun of politicians, laughed and carried on like newlyweds.

Whitman told Daddy there was a secret hot springs somewhere in the vicinity of Pine Mountain Lodge. One of his "sources" had told him about the springs but begged him not to reveal their whereabouts in his travel story. Whitman was determined to find them. "These springs were sacred to the Indians, evidently," he said. "The Indians called them *si'pi.*"

"What does that mean?" Daddy asked.

"Big Fart. Big Stink. Something like that. Sulphur, I guess."

I surreptitiously studied my new husband as he studied his maps. Would we ever have the kind of relationship the dads had? Driving someplace fun with twenty years of shared experiences behind us? Getting excited about a secret hot springs?

My thoughts drifted back to my familiar world. Phantastic Phantasy, where I'd be if I wasn't on my honeymoon. In the bright desert light, with not a building in sight, that furtive half-lit world of shooting sperm and pineapple-vomit-smelling disinfectant seemed a million miles away.

I couldn't stay in the adult entertainment industry forever. I had to for a while, because I lived from paycheck to paycheck. But maybe, eventually, now that I was remarried and my bankruptcy was behind me, I could think about doing something more challenging. I could go back to school. Get a degree in something.

I didn't know what Tremaynne would contribute to our new life together. We'd never talked about finances. His bankruptcy made him very cynical about banks, corporations, and credit-card companies. He had a whole theory about it. "They set up a trap and push you into it," he maintained.

He'd started charging when he was going to school in Berkeley. Now he was totally poor. And though I sometimes wondered why he didn't go out to get a job, like everyone else in the world had to do, I also admired him for doing the kind of environmental work that didn't earn him a dime.

"Some jobs you can't do for money," he insisted. "You have to do them because if you don't, everything on Earth will be destroyed."

I didn't feel that same kind of urgency myself. But I was glad someone else did.

Whitman was the navigator. He directed Daddy to turn right and left. We began to climb higher, through a dense pine forest.

"Ponderosas," Whitman said. "Wow! Look at that view!"

I looked. Tremaynne looked up from his maps. All I saw was, like, nothing. No houses. Just a hundred or maybe a thousand miles of hills and pine trees with snowcapped mountains way in the distance. I'd never seen anything like it.

I half-expected to hear the theme music from *Bonanza* and see the three Cartwright boys gallop past with their dad.

This forest was different from the lush wet forests west of the Cascades. Or so Whitman said. He and Dad were talking geology, history, the evolution of plant species.

"These ponderosas are amazing," Whitman said. "They've learned how to benefit from disaster."

I asked how. Whitman explained that we were in a very high and dry area that got hit by lightning a lot. The ponderosas shed their needles, so lightning fires periodically swept through the dry forest floor, burning everything to a crisp. The trees, he said, had figured out an ingenious method of survival. "They use the fire. The fire is necessary to eject the seeds from their pine cones."

"Adaptive evolution," Tremaynne said.

Whitman turned around in surprise. "That's right. Adapt yourself to your environment."

"Adaptive survival," Tremaynne said. "If fire or something is your enemy, put the enemy to work for you."

"Are you saying that the trees can, like, actually think?" I asked.

"They can think, communicate, and remember," Tremaynne said, turning back to his maps as if I'd offended him. "They eat, shit, breathe, and grow, just like us."

We left the main road and drove across a flat arid plain. Then suddenly Daddy made a sharp turn and we began to switchback down the side of a steep bare canyon.

"Ladies and gentlemen," Whitman said in his tourist-guide voice, "welcome to Hell's Canyon, the deepest gorge in North America. The cliffs of this precipitous canyon drop one mile to the Snake River below."

Once I saw what was happening, where we were going, I couldn't breathe right. The road was gravel. Narrow. There weren't any side railings. A mile below us a river sparkled like a silver thread in the sunlight.

The grade was so steep that the car began to skid and slide when Daddy put on the brakes.

"Stop!" Whitman cried. "John, stop for Christ's sake!"

"I'm trying to," Daddy said, tapping the brakes as we skidded faster and faster. "It's the gravel."

I was scared shitless. I needed something to grip. I lurched over to grab hold of my husband. His mouth was open.

"If we go over the side," Whitman shouted, "everybody jump out!"

"We're not going over the side," Daddy said. He brought the SUV to a stop about two inches from a precipice, at the outside edge of a hairpin curve.

We all sat there, real quiet. Daddy was clenching the steering wheel so hard his knuckles were white.

"You need to put it into four-wheel drive," Whitman said.

"I can't, until we get around this curve," Daddy said. "It needs to go forward about a yard before it engages." His voice was measured. He licked his lips and stared into the distance.

"Why don't you two get out of the car," Whitman said to Tremaynne and me. "Just in case."

"In case of what?" Daddy said through clenched teeth.

"There's no reason for us all to die," Whitman said. "If you go over the edge, I want to go with you. But they don't have to."

Daddy, clutching the steering wheel, looked stiffly in his direction. "It's not that bad, Whit. I can back up from here and make the turn."

"You might slide on the gravel," Whitman said. "Those treads are shot. It's my fault. I should have put on new tires."

"Whit, I can do it," Daddy insisted.

"Get out of the car," Whitman said to Tremaynne and me.

"Should we, Daddy?"

Whitman snapped, "I am your daddy in this case. Get out!"

Dad One caught my eye in the rearview and gave a tense nod.

"Here's my cell phone in case anything happens," Whitman said. "All the important phone numbers are programmed in. Call everyone and tell them I was happy right up to the last moment."

"Whitman, for Christ's sake!" Daddy barked. The veins were standing out in his neck.

"You inherit the house," Whitman said to me. "The lawyer's name is Jack Sullivan. Sullivan, Delaney, and Yost. Now go."

I felt like we had to move slowly, carefully, or something would be thrown off balance and the car would tip over the edge. I carefully cracked open the door. The second I did, a hot, violent gust of wind blew in and the door flew open. Tremaynne and I slid out. Stood on solid ground. Beneath the loose gravel, the packed-dirt surface of the road was slippery as a greased waterslide.

Whitman called out, "Take the picnic basket just in case. There's foie gras and gherkins—"

"Whit, shut up!" Daddy bawled. "Venus, close the door. You two get out of the way. Way out of the way."

"Daddy, be careful!" I had a sudden horrible vision of the car toppling over and rolling down the canyon wall into the river. I couldn't look, but I had to. I could see the dads in the front seat, their faces anxious.

"Maybe you'd better get out," Daddy said.

Whitman shook his head.

It was completely still, so quiet I could hear my heart thudding. I'd never seen so much clear blue open sky in my life. The light poured down in such a way that you could see everything clearly for miles around. There weren't any trees in this canyon. There was no hiding.

Another hot blast of wind came whistling down the gorge as Tremaynne and I trudged up the steep, slippery road.

"They'll be okay." I tried to sound confident. I turned back to look at the car idling two inches from the edge of eternity. "My dad's a really good driver."

"Give me that cell phone," Tremaynne said.

"Why? It's—"

"I just need to make one quick call," he said.

I didn't want to piss him off, so I handed over Whitman's phone.

"You wait here," Tremaynne said. "I'm going to climb up that rock and see if anyone's coming. Just in case."

I wanted him there, at my side, but I didn't want to seem needy. And who the hell did he need to call out here in the middle of nowhere on his honeymoon?

I stood there, hair blowing in the hot dry wind, looking out across Hell's Canyon. The world seemed to be slipping slowly out of control. I was losing all sense of what was familiar. I hate that feeling. It scares me. I wanted a cigarette bad but was afraid to light up. With my luck, the wind would blow a spark to the grass and set all of Hell's Canyon ablaze.

For the next few minutes my attention was evenly divided between watching the dads and watching Tremaynne. My husband, the rock climber, clambered to the top of a huge boulder and stood there like a statue, silhouetted against the sky, the cell phone held to his ear. He was talking but I couldn't hear a thing except the wind hissing past my ears.

Down below me, the SUV lurched backward and stopped. Daddy turned the wheels completely to the left. He evidently thought better of it and turned them straight again. Then he gently began to back up. The SUV made it about a foot before the rear wheels started to spin.

I wanted to pray but didn't know how. When people are raised with religion, they know who to pray to. They're plugged into some God up there, and they can beg him for his help. I didn't grow up with any of that. Carolee was more interested in tarot cards, psychics and astrology. And you can't pray to a sign of the zodiac.

I shielded my eyes and glanced up at Tremaynne. He was gone. The panic tapped me on the shoulder. Then I heard a roar and looked down to see the SUV shooting backward, spitting out gravel and dust. Daddy got it far enough back so that he could make a tight right turn around the hairpin.

A second later the SUV stopped and both dads got out. Whitman waved his arms and shouted something, but the huge windy silence of the canyon sucked his words away. He ran around the SUV and hugged Daddy.

There was a crunch of gravel. Tremaynne stood at my side. He didn't say a word. He offered nothing. We silently headed back toward the dads.

Whatever you do, I said to myself, *don't ask him who he was talking to in the middle of nowhere on his honeymoon.*

Chapter
8

Tremaynne refused to eat foie gras.

"You know how they make it?" he asked me. I shook my head. I only had foie gras when I was with the dads. I loved it, and I wanted some real bad.

Tremaynne gripped my throat and forced my head back, demonstrating the process "They take this funnel," he said, "and jam it down the goose's throat and force-feed it all this corn. Am I right?" he asked Whitman, who'd suggested we stop for a picnic.

"You could just eat the gherkins and the French bread," Whitman suggested. He glanced at Daddy—that secret glance couples use to say things without saying anything.

"They force-feed it," Tremaynne went on, going through the motions of viciously grinding corn down my throat, "and don't let it move. When its liver turns all swollen and ready to burst, they kill the goose and use the diseased liver for that shit *you* want to eat." He released my neck. "Go ahead. But not me."

I coughed. His neck grip wasn't exactly gentle. I felt the sharp tang of passion. For a moment my husband turned into a handsome but brutal stranger. The stranger had me in his power. He was going to force me to strip, slowly, and perform lewd sex acts. What would I do?

"Maybe there's a restaurant somewhere," Daddy said. He was getting a little punchy, the way he does when he needs protein. "Maybe they serve salads."

"This does not look like salad country," Whitman observed.

We'd come very slowly, in four-wheel drive, down to the bottom of Hell's Canyon, another charming-sounding honeymoon destination. There were a few box-like houses scattered along the river but no sign of a restaurant.

"Let's ask that man." Whitman pointed to a skinny old guy standing next to a dusty pickup truck. He had a wide red nose, close-set eyes, and was wearing an orange vest and feed cap. Daddy pulled over and Whitman rolled down his window. "Excuse me, sir," he called. "Do you know if there's a restaurant around here? Someplace that serves salads?"

The man looked at him as if he were crazy. "Restaurant?" he said finally.

"You know," Whitman said, "plates, silverware, food?"

"Nothin' like that around here," the man said, tilting his hat back and frowning. "Gotta go to Snakebite."

Of course we do, I thought.

"And where's that?" Whitman asked.

"Keep goin' and you'll come to it," the man said. He turned away, reached into the back of his truck, and pulled out a rifle.

We all stared at the gun.

The man grinned, showing a mouthful of stumpy brown teeth. "Bear season," he said.

"Oh," Whitman said. "I didn't know there were any bears left around here."

"Yup. And I'm gonna shoot me one of them motherfuckers right between the eyes," the man said. He raised the gun and looked through its viewfinder. "And if I don't get me a bear, maybe I'll get me one of them tree-huggers." He put his gun down and bent forward to squint into the back seat.

"Tree-huggers?" Whitman laughed a little too loudly. "Are those like hip-huggers?"

"Like Earth Freedom," the man said. He stepped closer, blatantly peering into the back seat.

Tremaynne averted his face. His sudden passivity seemed odd because he was usually challenging people. But I was afraid to look into the old man's eyes, too. They were really hostile. I crossed my arms over my chest, depriving him of ogling rights.

"I'll bet you've heard of Earth Freedom," the man said. His voice was vaguely threatening. "They're huggin' trees all over the place up here. Huggin' 'em so fuckin' hard that nobody can even cut down a tree no more."

"Well," Whitman said politely, "if we see any, we'll *certainly* let them know how you feel. Bye now!" He rolled up his window and whispered to Daddy, "Get the hell out of here."

"Yeah," I agreed, "get the hell out of Hell's Canyon."

Daddy started up the road on the other side of the canyon.

Whitman whistled and blew out a big loud breath. "Did you see that gun? That was a real gun." He turned to Tremaynne. "He seemed to recognize you."

I laughed. "Whitman, he was looking at my tits."

Whitman continued to stare at Tremaynne. "What was the name of that group you were with?"

It was a simple question, but whenever Whitman asked a simple question, it meant he was digging for something more. I knew how his sudden interrogations worked. His nonchalant tone put me on high alert.

Tremaynne kept looking out the window. "What group?"

"Those environmental activists," Whitman said. "The ones down in the Siskiyous."

Tremaynne licked his lips. "Arbor Vitae."

"Oh yeah." Whitman turned back around. "They're nonviolent, right?"

"Right," Tremaynne said.

"Look." Daddy pointed at a sign. "We're in Idaho."

* * *

When he was working on Pine Mountain Lodge, Daddy always flew to Boise, rented a car, and drove from there. He'd never been in Snakebite, and Whitman couldn't find any mention of it in his cache of reference guides. He said the town must have gotten its name from its proximity to the Snake River.

"More likely because it's full of snakes." I hate snakes. I was on my guard.

"Don't step on any rattlers," Daddy warned. He told us how one of the carpenters working on Pine Mountain Lodge had come out to hike in Hell's Canyon and was bitten by a rattlesnake. "If it hadn't been for his cell phone," Daddy said, "he'd be dead. They had to airlift him out in a helicopter. He couldn't walk because his leg swelled up as big as an elephant's."

"Don't scare her," Whitman said. He reached back and patted my knee. "Don't worry, honey, I brought our snake kit. If you get bitten, I know where to cut and how to suction out the venom."

My faux pa always teased me like that. He knew perfectly well that snakes made me faint, spiders made me scream, roaches made me weep, and mice took my breath away.

"Maybe there's a McDonald's," I said hopefully, "with a drive-through so we don't have to get out of the car."

"I'm not eating in a McDonald's," Tremaynne huffed.

"McDonald's is inappropriate for a honeymoon meal," Whitman agreed. "But I have to say, a quarter-pounder with cheese would taste pretty good right now."

"Double quarter-pounder," I sighed. "No onions."

"I'd get the pâté de foie gras burger," Daddy said. "With fries."

We were just joking around, but Tremaynne became all indignant. "Do you know how much nondisposable waste those places generate?" He glared at me. "Do you know what they do to make those seven trillion hamburgers a year?"

I saw Whitman take a deep breath, like he was trying to control himself.

"They're burning up the rain forest because of fast-food restaurants. So they can raise these huge herds of cows that don't eat any natural food and get shot full of growth hormones."

We pulled into Snakebite.

"I don't think we have to worry about a McDonald's," Daddy said.

"Take a picture." Whitman handed me his small digital camera and led Daddy over to a sign that said *Snakebite. Pop. 34.*

"Get the sign in. Use the zoom. Just our faces and the sign." He pulled Daddy into an embrace and was kissing him on the cheek when the old guy's black pickup slowly jolted up the rutted gravel road. The truck stopped just as I snapped the photo.

The old man stared at us through narrowed eyes. Whitman gave him a friendly wave, but the man didn't acknowledge it.

"Canyon of the damned," Whitman stage-whispered. "Okay," he said with a show of bravado, "now I'll take one of you two."

I took Tremaynne by the arm, but he pulled away. "I don't want to," he said. Which was weird, because he was the sort of photogenic person who always gravitated toward cameras.

"Okay, then I'll take one of Venus and her alpha dad." Whitman motioned for Daddy and me to stand together.

But we were all immobilized by the man. He just sat there in his truck staring at us like we were bears in his viewfinder. Finally Whitman aimed his camera at the old man. "Say Brie, darling!" He snapped the photo.

Springs creaking, the truck slowly lurched off down the road.

Snakebite was one of those places where it's impossible to imagine anyone really living. It was set in a gully with a creek rushing through as if it wanted to get away as fast as possible. One gravel-covered street with about five ramshackley wooden houses and a couple of trailers made up the entire town. The rusty skeletons of dead cars, weeds poking through their vanished windows, were scattered along the side of the road. Tires and discarded appliances had been pitched down into the creek. Everything looked dusty and forlorn.

"Don't judge a book by its cover," Whitman said cheerfully. "You never know where you'll stumble across a three-star Michelin restaurant."

We trudged over to a brown wooden building with Snakebite Café painted above the door. *Spoted Owl Served Here* was written on a piece of cardboard taped in the front window.

"Obviously a logging town," Whitman said.

"Former logging town," Daddy said.

"Whatever you do," Whitman whispered, "don't order *spoted owl*."

I'd never felt such a hostile atmosphere in my life. It really gave me the creeps. I wanted to leave, but it was like we were being sucked into this bad dream and couldn't get out of it.

First of all, there was a low funny smell. I don't know what it was. Something stale and icky-chemical-sweet at the same time. Like old grease and roach powder.

Deer and elk heads stared blindly from the walls. A giant black bear, stuffed to look like it was about to attack, reared up on its hind legs next to the cash register, fangs gleaming, claws ready to rip and shred. There were other stuffed animals, too. Small hairy things, arranged to look as though they were scampering along the shelves.

A woman with dark bags under her eyes, several chins, and thin yellow hair stood behind the counter drinking coffee and puffing on a cigarette.

"Can we sit anywhere?" Whitman asked.

Her ice-blue eyes moved slowly from me to Tremaynne to Daddy to Whitman. "Where you from?" she asked.

"Portland," Daddy said.

"Where you headin'?"

"Pine Mountain Lodge."

She sniffed. "Won't find that kind of food here."

"Well," Whitman said, scanning a menu, "we've been driving

since seven this morning, and we're all pretty hungry so we thought we might get a salad or something."

"No salads," she said.

"Okay." Whitman slid into a chair and the rest of us followed his lead. "How about—"

"Ain't got it," the woman said, smoke streaming out her nostrils.

Whitman cleared his throat. "How do you know, when we haven't ordered anything yet?"

"I just know," was her cryptic reply.

Daddy groaned in disgust and made a motion to leave, but Whitman put a restraining hand on his wrist. One thing about Whitman, he never backs down from a potential fight.

"Is there anything on the menu that you recommend?" he asked pleasantly.

"No." the woman crossed her arms. It was a showdown. "We don't serve nothin' you want."

I hadn't had a smoke all day and the first drag made me light-headed. I was so nervous I kept my eyes on my cigarette and away from Mrs. Multichin.

"I'll have the spoted owl," Tremaynne said.

I kicked him under the table.

The woman glared. "The what?"

"That sign in your window." He pointed to it. "It says you served spoted owl."

"Spotted," she spat.

"Oh," Tremaynne said. "It's spelled s-p-o-t-e-d. Well, that's what I'll have."

The woman half-closed her eyes, took a deep drag of her cigarette, and let out a wet hacking cough. "Smart ass," she muttered.

Whitman whirled around. "Do you refuse to serve everyone who comes in here?"

"No," she said, "just rich smartasses that like to cause trouble."

Now it was Daddy who restrained Whitman. It was just a touch on his arm. "Whit, let's go."

Daddy Two let out a loud Buddha breath. "Have we done something to offend you?" he asked the woman.

"Rooms at that Pine Mountain Lodge cost four hundred bucks a night," she hissed.

Whitman stood and slowly walked toward her. He held his hands up, as if she had a gun pointed at him. He smiled. "So is that the problem? You don't like Pine Mountain Lodge?"

The woman moved closer to the stuffed bear. "It's your kind spoils it for the rest of us." She angrily stubbed out her cigarette and shook out another. Whitman grabbed her Zippo from the counter and offered to light her cigarette, but the woman backed away.

He put the lighter down again. "Sorry. Old habit. I was raised to be polite."

She took the lighter and silently stared at him.

"Okay," Whitman said. "It's obvious you don't want our business, so we'll leave."

Daddy, Tremaynne, and I leaped up and got out of there as fast as we could. Whitman stayed a moment longer, examining the bear, then he too started out.

"We gotta live here all the time," the woman called to his back. "We can't afford no Pine Mountain Lodge."

"Especially if you keep turning customers away," Whitman called over his shoulder. He stepped outside and looked at us. "Well. Pâté anyone?"

"Let's find a spot outside of town," Daddy suggested. "Tremaynne, you'll just have to eat bread and cheese."

"I'm not your little boy, okay?" my husband said grumpily. "I don't have to eat anything I don't want to."

Whitman's voice was sharp. "Then don't. But let us enjoy our goddamned diseased goose liver, okay?"

I'd been tracking the advance of another pickup rattling into town. You couldn't miss it; it was the only moving object in the landscape and it was barking.

The truck pulled up next to the café. Two men wearing camouflage jackets and feed caps peered at us through the dusty wind-shield. With the glare and the dust, I couldn't see much. One of them had a black beard; the other one had pale, shoulder-length hair.

The back of the truck had been fitted with a large cage. There were three furiously barking dogs in it. Big dogs, mixed breed, vi-cious looking. Their barks were slightly muffled by a brown hairy blanket draped over the top of the cage.

Only it wasn't a blanket.

"Jesus Christ!" Tremaynne cried.

I thought I was going to be sick to my stomach. Once I saw it, I couldn't not see it. I didn't want to look but I had to.

The bear's belly had been slit open. It was gutted. Strings of slimy blue and red entrails hung down into the cage, dripping onto the enraged dogs. A smell like blood and shit reached my nostrils. Next to the cage I saw two plastic pails full of raw oozing guts. Then, with a jolt, I saw the bear's face, its small, startled eyes, its dangling pink tongue.

I raced around the side of the Snakebite Café and threw up my latte and the barbecue-flavored potato chips I'd eaten hours earlier. It was horrible. There were flies everywhere. I had to wave them away while I puked. They buzzed down to dine on my vomit.

I heard a loud voice. Tremaynne's. Accusing. "You killed a bear! Why did you have to kill it?"

Another voice. Unfamiliar. Angry. "That ain't none of your god-damn business."

"There's hardly any bear population left!" Tremaynne shouted.

"There's tons of bear around here. They're like rats."

Tremaynne's voice sounded like a sob. He must have really lost it. "Do we have to kill everything?"

There was a moment of silence. Then I heard laughter. It sounded like the hunters hadn't heard anything so funny in their en-tire lives.

* * *

"The air." Whitman sucked in a deep breath. "Delicious."

I sniffed, cautiously. It did have a pleasant tang, sort of like Western Wind room deodorizer.

I scrunched my butt down good and hard on the earth, so the vertigo wouldn't get me. We were sitting at the top of Hell's Canyon, looking out over miles of nothing.

"It's mostly sandstone," Daddy said, tearing off a hunk of French bread and carefully positioning a slab of foie gras on top. He closed his eyes and took a rapturous bite.

Tremaynne was watching me to see if I'd eat the pâté, so I didn't. And I was keeping a close watch on him, my prisoner of love. I was afraid that he was pushing me away. Was it because of the dads? Because he didn't like them?

The dads didn't particularly like Tremaynne, either. I could tell. But at least they were making an effort.

Something was troubling my husband. I didn't know what it was, but I was afraid it might have something to do with getting married. Second thoughts. Cold feet. I knew from experience that the first time was the weirdest. Maybe he was thinking: She's the wrong one. Buyer's regret.

Or else . . . but I didn't want to go where my thoughts kept leading me. Ever since Whitman's simple question, ever since he'd asked Tremaynne about his involvement with Arbor Vitae, I'd been wondering about it myself. More than once he'd expressed a kind of exasperated displeasure with the group. Earth Freedom, as I'd learned by accidentally opening and reading an e-mail addressed to Tremaynne on my AOL account, was a splinter group of Arbor Vitae. They were far more extreme. Tremaynne must have known at least some of them.

But he'd never mentioned Earth Freedom. I reassured myself with that.

I sat there looking at the three men in my life. There was so much space around us. Vast, interminable space. I hated the way all that empty space made me feel. So tiny, so insignificant. So vulnerable. So much could go wrong when you had all that space around you. The world stopped being solid and familiar, and slipped into something vaguely menacing.

I posed a question to myself: If something went wrong right now, if there was a disaster or a calamity, who would I want to be with? My dads or Tremaynne? Who would give the most help, comfort and guidance?

"Listen," Whitman said. "Silence. Absolute silence. Do you know how rare that is?"

Daddy sighed and bit into a tiny sweet green pickle.

Silence was not what I was after. Silence is boring and scary. Maybe dangerous. I wanted noise, bustle, chatter. I wanted to walk with my new husband through a fun glam scene with background music and beautiful clothes. I wanted him alone, away from the dads, in our honeymoon suite. If I could just get him back into my arms, he'd be mine again. I was sure of it.

"It must have been quiet when you were up in that tree," Whitman said.

My moody, difficult husband was gnawing on a piece of bread. "It's never quiet in a tree," he mumbled.

"That experience must have changed your life."

Tremaynne didn't answer. He wouldn't sit with us on the blanket Whitman had spread out. He wouldn't touch the pâté or the cheese. When Whitman offered him a glass of champagne, he turned it down.

"Well, here's to you, then, daughter dear," Whitman said, clicking my glass. Of course he'd brought crystal champagne flutes. "I hope you'll be as happy as your dad and I have been."

"I hope so, too." I looked up at my husband. His back was turned. He was staring off into the distance.

Whitman quickly spread some pâté de foie gras on a piece of bread and popped it into my mouth. And I ate it. It was our secret.

Chapter
9

He made a second phone call outside of Boise.

We stopped for gas at a huge eight-lane station beside the highway. In Oregon someone pumps the gas for you. Everywhere else in the nation, you have to do it yourself. (Whitman always said that's why he lived in Oregon.) While Daddy worked the pump, Whitman washed the dust and squashed bugs off the windshield. He was meticulous; "streaks" gave him a headache.

"Pee if you have to," Daddy said, stretching his back, "because we're not stopping for the next hundred miles."

Tremaynne jumped out and hurried over to the busy minimart. I followed. There was only one restroom.

When he went in, I seized my chance.

I nabbed a scarred wiener from the rotating grill, stuffed it into a stale bun, slathered relish, mustard and catsup on it, and snarfed it down in three huge bites. While I was eating the hot dog, I darted over to the candy shelf and grabbed a box of red hots and a giant Reese's peanut-butter cups. I'd paid for it all, swallowed my last bite of hot dog, and hidden the candy in my purse by the time Tremaynne came out of the restroom. I must have set some kind of record. A bulimic couldn't have gorged any faster.

"My turn," I said, smiling sweetly. He nodded absently and wandered over toward a rack of maps.

I wanted so bad to know what was going on in his mind. Something had happened to him. Something was out of kilter. It was bigger than a mood. He hadn't been the same since seeing that butchered bear in Snakebite.

Something told me to leave him alone with whatever he was wrestling with. Men don't like it when you pry into their emotions. I let him be, but I felt lost and out of sync with him—not exactly the kind of feeling a woman wants on her honeymoon.

It's always weird looking at yourself in minimart restroom mirrors. This one wasn't glass but a kind of thin metal sheet bolted to the wall. It was like looking into aluminum wrap. The surface had been scratched and gouged by every kind of sharp object imaginable. It reminded me of the windows in New York subway cars, their surfaces mauled by frantic, destructive male energy.

With a mirror like that, applying fresh black lipstick was not easy.

It was just as well that I couldn't clearly see my reflection. I was starting to look and feel car-tired. My hair was a windblown mess. My skin was coated with dust. My face felt dried out. My breath smelled of meat and stale vomit. Worst of all, my wedding high was pulsing away as fast as blood from a slashed artery.

All I wanted now was to get to that luxurious honeymoon suite, brush my teeth, wash my hair, and take a long seductive bubble bath with my new husband. I wanted privacy, just the two of us. Away from the dads, we could play bedroom games all night long.

Once I'd coaxed four orgasms out of Tremaynne. Maybe tonight I could claim five.

I poured a stream of fiery, heart-shaped red hots into my mouth.

I needed courage to confront the toilet. I hate toilets in gas stations and truck stops. This one was metal, without even a seat. The floor around it was sopping wet. A toilet like that brings out the desperation in a girl. There was no toilet paper. It smelled. Moving closer I could see a big Tootsie Roll of a turd floating in the bowl. Tremaynne's? It didn't smell like his shit.

No way I was going to wade in to that vile stall, or touch anything with my bare hands.

The urinal looked a little cleaner. It was one of those low ones designed for kids and the handicapped. I gingerly pulled my pants down, squatted, and peed into it. There was only cold water to wash my hands. No soap. No paper towels, no cloth towel on a roller, no air-dry machine. An altogether icky place.

When I came out, I saw Tremaynne standing in the corner, half hidden by the display of road maps. His back was to me. It took me a moment to register that it was a phone alcove, and he was on the phone.

He hung up, turned around, and saw me.

His dark eyes flickered but gave nothing away.

Maybe it was the red hots taking effect. Or maybe I was so insanely jealous I couldn't admit it to myself. My face was suddenly burning.

I tried to control my voice. "Who were you talking to?"

He flipped the hair out of his eyes. "Nobody. A friend." He put a hand on my back and tried to steer me away.

"What friend?"

"Just a friend."

"Who?"

"For Christ's sake," Tremaynne snapped, "do I have to get your permission every time I make a fucking phone call?"

And that was, like, *exactly* my fear, that it was a fucking phone call. That my day-old husband was calling someone he used to fuck and probably wanted to fuck again. "Why can't you tell me who it was?" I pleaded.

"Because it's none of your business," he snapped.

A sharp sudden half-crazy fear took hold of me. "Is it someone from that group?" I blurted out. "Earth Freedom?" The moment I said it, heard my fear materialize into words, I realized I'd made a major mistake.

He jerked his hand from my back and brushed past me. His face was tight, angry. I wanted to cry and run after him, but just then the dads came in to pay for the gas.

"What's the matter?" Daddy asked.

"Nothing."

Whitman looked at Tremaynne's retreating figure and then at me. "Did you have another fight?"

"We didn't have a fight."

"Yes, you did," Whitman insisted. "I know body language when I see it."

I turned away.

"Was it about food?" Whitman wanted to know. "I hate to tell you this, kid, but you married a real food fascist."

Daddy moved closer. He put a finger under my chin and lifted my head so I had to look at him. "Are you all right?"

I nodded morosely.

"This is your honeymoon," Daddy said. As if I needed reminding. "You're supposed to be having a good time."

"It'll be okay once we get there."

I said the words, but I was beginning to wonder.

We didn't say a word for the next hundred miles. Whitman drove with his left hand and held Daddy's hand with his right. I resented their calm happiness.

My new husband wouldn't touch me. He sat scrunched over to one side, staring out the window like a sullen boy.

I was miserable. Why wouldn't he tell me who he was talking to in the gas station or out in Hell's Canyon? It must have been a woman. Yes, I was sure of it. He wasn't thinking about me, his wife, he was thinking about *her*.

My mind flipped through various seduction scenarios. He'd liked that secret hand job in the car. What could I do next to restore his interest? I had to get him back. It was our honeymoon. We were supposed to be cementing our future. Like Daddy said, this was supposed to be fun.

Whitman turned off on a side road, a two-laner, and we plunged
into a thick pine forest. The road curved up to a high, rocky plateau
and then down past some small, still lakes that sucked up the hot
blaze of the afternoon sky.

Whitman turned down a gravel road. We bounced across an open
field and stopped beside a deserted lake.

"Are we there?" I didn't see any sign of a resort.

"Almost. I thought we could have a quick swim here."

"Isn't there a heated pool at the resort?"

"Yes, but you have to wear a suit. My source said this was the best
lake for FKK."

"What's that?"

"*Freie Körper Kultur.* Free Body Culture. German for skinny-dip-
ping."

The dads were already out of the SUV. Whitman pulled out a
stack of striped towels. The same towels we used to take to Jones
Beach in New York. I flashed on that strip of white
burning-hot sand with wall-to-wall bodies, all of them greased and
baking in the sun like sausages on a griddle. I was twelve when the
dads first took me there. I remembered the hungry glances of the
dark-eyed, dark-haired New York men, the way they eye-stripped
me wherever I went, and made little noises that only I was meant to
hear.

"Coming?" Daddy asked.

"I don't want to swim in a lake," I groaned. "There might be fish
in it." Or weeds, or slime, or something that brushed against my legs
underwater.

Tremaynne shot me a disgusted glance—like, *what a wuss*—and
got out. He silently trudged after the dads.

"I don't want to unpack my suit," I called out forlornly.

"Don't need one," Daddy called back.

Yeah, right. Like I was really going to strip in front of the dads
and Tremaynne, out in the open. I was no longer the girl who
danced, tits flying, at Terry's Topless. I was no longer a lingerie
model. I'd put on weight. I'd become self-conscious about my body.

Tremaynne, who never touched refined sugar or junk food, probably thought I was turning into a fat slob.

They were moving farther and farther away, crossing the field and heading towards the stand of enormous pine trees that surrounded the lake.

"Is the water, like, cold?" I called.

They didn't hear me. The three of them disappeared down a slope.

I sat there for a couple of minutes, nervously nibbling on my peanut-butter cups. The silence hummed in my ears. Then in the distance I heard a faint cry of delight. It couldn't be Tremaynne? He couldn't be having a good time with the dads, without me.

I kept a sharp eye out for snakes as I hurried toward the pine trees and the sounds of whooping and splashing. A hot, sun-baked heaviness rose from the earth. The air was breathlessly dry and smelled like the incense Carolee used to burn at Christmas.

The pine trees reared up in a stiff barricade. I'd never seen trees so big. The ground beneath them was thick with fallen cones and needles.

"*Yee-ha!*" I heard Whitman yell. And the sound of splashing water.

Their clothes were arranged on big flat rocks near the shoreline. And there they were, all three of them, naked, happily playing in the water. They looked as wet and cool as otters. Whitman's chest was covered with thick black hair that was turning gray. Daddy's body was white and completely smooth; he always shaved off the few hairs that sprouted around his nipples. The dads were both in amazingly good shape, although Whitman was thickening in the middle and Daddy's buns were starting to sag.

Tremaynne was shorter and didn't work out at a gym like the dads did. But Lordy Lordy, did he look fine. Watching his slim, dark, slippery shape against the sun-dazzled water, I felt my knees go weak with desire.

Tremaynne was an outdoorsman. All that hiking and climbing had given him muscular thighs, a narrow waist, and what the dads called a bubble butt. The hair on his chest was black and soft as sable. It spread in a *V* from his groin to his shoulders, hiding his small dark nipples like berries in a thicket. I longed to stroke it, lay my head against it.

Dry or wet, my husband always looked good to me. He was short but beautifully proportioned. Women eyed him every time we went out together. He could be criminally charming when he wanted to be.

I figured it must be my fault that he was in such a foul mood. But what had I done? Was it a crime to ask who he was talking to out in the middle of nowhere?

"It's so cold it burns!" Daddy gasped.

"All in your mind." Whitman's teeth were chattering. "Stay down a little longer."

The dads' dicks, which I'd seen on a couple of memorable occasions, had contracted in the cold lake water.

Or had they?

I couldn't be sure. They were jumping up and down in water that came up to their belly buttons.

I looked at Tremaynne's cock.

It was definitely not contracted.

"I'm going to run back and get my suit!" I called. "Wait for me!"

As I was scrambling back up the slope, I heard Daddy challenge Whitman and Tremaynne to a race. "Out to that big rock and back again. Go!"

That's what he used to do with me, when I was seven. On hot summer nights he'd pick me up after work and we'd go to the neighborhood pool. I was a good swimmer back then. Racing Daddy toward the deep end of the pool always filled me with furious excitement.

The three of them dove forward like dolphins and headed out into deeper water.

Something in me was flashing Danger! Danger! But I couldn't identify what the danger was, or who was imperiled. My one and only goal was to get into that horrible freezing water, close to my husband, as fast as possible.

My bell-bottoms and open-toed sandals were totally inappropriate for scrambling up the rocky rim of the lake. The rocks gave way beneath my feet. There was nothing to grab on to. I slid back down. Finally, panting, I picked my way to the top. The forest stretched for what looked like a quarter mile, ending at the grassy meadow where the SUV was parked.

I looked back at the lake. There they were, the three of them, cutting through the water with all the concentrated force of their masculine strength. Daddy was in the lead.

Your husband doesn't want a marshmallow, a voice in my head angrily scolded me. *He wants someone who will share his activities. Starting now, girl, you'd better get in shape.*

In my fantasies I had the power and agility of an Amazon. I rode, I ran, I swam, I even flew. *Wonder Woman* used to be one of my favorite TV shows.

But in real life I was ten pounds overweight and smoked. I didn't have the lungpower to run. I started out at a jog and was about halfway through the forest when I began to gasp, then to cough. I stopped, chest heaving, lungs stinging, and tried to catch my breath. Sweat poured down my forehead. I coughed up something thick and mucousy.

I tried to continue with a power walk, but a stitch in my side put an end to that. I puffed on. All my muscles and internal organs were, like, twitching and burning. Then something rammed into the open toe of my sandal and I pitched forward, twisting my ankle. My shoe was impaled on a low, half-buried stump fringed with thornlike knobs. The force of my fall had torn the shoe.

I felt like a frightened little girl in a fairy tale. I started to cry. I was all alone and I was afraid. There was no one to help me. Tremaynne and the dads were out in the middle of the lake having fun.

I gingerly pulled my foot free of the stump, then leaned back against one of the giant pines. The sun blazed down in the nearby meadow and out over the open bowl of the lake, but in the forest it was dark and still.

I heard a snapping sound behind me and peeked around the tree. An elk was headed straight for me.

At least I thought it was an elk. It wasn't a deer. I didn't know what it was. All I knew was that it was huge, it had antlers, and it was moving toward me.

I couldn't catch my breath to scream. I flattened myself against the tree. Then, with a sudden jolt of adrenaline, I sprang forward and started to run. My goal was to get into the SUV as fast as possible.

I hazarded a glance over my shoulder. The elk had stopped. It was joined by four or five others. They were smaller and didn't have antlers. Cows. His harem, maybe?

I crouched behind a tree, gasping for breath, then peered around the trunk. I was certain the elk was glaring at me. Getting angry. He lowered his nose, pawed the forest floor, then lifted his mouth high into the air and let out a weird trumpeting bugle.

The sound totally freaked me out. It was like a voice, a communication, a prelude to action. It was saying something about me. *Get out of here!* or, *Let's kill her!* I turned to run. And then I saw the other one.

It was even larger. A great shaggy beast with black eyes and antlers that rose up like a giant coat rack. It trotted into the field between me and the SUV. There it stopped and let out a fierce, belligerent cry. And so did I. I opened my mouth and filled the forest with a piercing scream.

The elk in the field raised its head and flicked up its ears. It trotted angrily back and forth, just outside the forest. I heard a heavy snort behind me and turned. The first elk was moving in my direction.

An ambush.

This time I screamed "Daddy!"

I couldn't stay where I was, clasping in terror the scaly trunk of a pine tree. The forest elk was coming closer. It could ram and squash me against the tree, or it could bite off my arm or kick and trample me. It was a wild animal. I didn't know what the fuck it could do. It was huffing and snorting.

At the edge of the forest I paused for one second to take my bearings. I could see the SUV about fifty yards ahead of me. The field elk stood stone still about a hundred yards to my right. Its body looked tense, like a runner's before the gun.

I made a dash for it, streaking toward the SUV. I ran as fast as I could. My foot hurt and my ankle throbbed and my mouth was dry and my lungs stung, but I kept going. Halfway there I was aware of two things: the field elk had put its head down and was charging, and, good city girl that I was, I'd locked the SUV.

I could hear the heavy thud of its hooves as it raced toward me. My eyesight became extremely sharp. I knew what I had to do, but I didn't know if I had the time to do it.

Wheezing, I reached the SUV and darted around to the driver's side. The elk butted the front passenger door with its antlers. There was a loud wham that shook the SUV. The beast backed away, nose dripping, eyes crazed. It saw me cringing on the other side, let out a furious snort, and stepped back. It seemed to be considering how best to get me. Suddenly, it leaped to one side, turned, and made straight for me.

I screamed and dove under the SUV. I saw giant hooves, hairy legs . . .

Wham! This time it crashed into the driver's door. The SUV rocked above me. I sucked in my breath, too afraid to cry, and wriggled toward the other side. With a belligerent snort, the elk backed away. Then it lowered its massive head and tried to peer under the SUV, but its antlers got in the way. It was breathing as hard as I was. Frustrated, it thrust its antlers into the earth and threw up clumps of grass and dirt. Then, with another bugling cry, it bulldozed forward and rammed the SUV again and again. *Wham! Wham! Wham!*

It was, like, totally weird. I thought; *So this is how you're going to die, killed by an elk on your honeymoon.* I moaned one last time, squeezed my eyes shut, and prayed it wouldn't hurt too much.

A moment later I heard Daddy and Whitman calling my name. Whitman cried, "Holy Christ!"

I heard the sound of hooves thudding away. I could feel their vibration in the earth. And the vibrations of feet pounding across the field. I didn't dare to open my eyes so I wasn't sure what was happening.

"Venus!"

"Honey!"

"Sweetheart!"

Daddy was on his belly, trying to pull me out. Whitman was on the other side pleading with everyone to stay calm.

Dazedly I inched myself out from beneath the SUV. Looked up to see their concerned comforting faces. Oh, the sky was so blue.

Then I felt myself roughly scooped up in a pair of arms and held tight.

He didn't say a word. Neither did I.

I looked into my husband's eyes. There were tears in mine. Bette Davis couldn't have done it any better.

No bones were broken. The SUV was scratched and dented but the door still worked okay. When everyone's excitement died down and we were on our way again, I rested my head on Tremaynne's shoulder and held him around the waist. He wasn't wearing a shirt. His skin was hot and smelled like fresh fishy lake water. He wrapped his arms around me.

"Drink some Evian," Whitman urged. "Breathe deeply. We'll be there in half an hour."

I felt fine. Shaken but extremely alive. In my husband's arms. I was surprised at how good I felt. But I was the star now, so I had to play it up a little.

* * *

Pine Mountain Lodge was even classier than I'd imagined. There was a huge gate with an intimidating security guard. Former Army. A buzz-cut and a tendency to salute or shout. Since I left the army I can spot them a mile off.

"Whitman Whittlesley the Fourth," Dad Two grandly announced.

The security guard wasn't impressed. "The fourth what?" he asked.

"*Travel* magazine," Whitman said.

"Which?" The guard eyed the battered SUV doors suspiciously.

"*Travel*. Highest circulation in the United States."

The guard scanned his clipboard. "How do you spell your name?"

Whitman spelled it. "Look, we're in kind of a hurry. One of my assistants was charged by an elk. She needs to lie down, maybe have a massage."

The guard peered into the window. "The two in back your assistants?"

"Yes. Tremaynne Woods and Venus Gilroy."

"Venus Woods," I corrected him. I looked at Tremaynne, expecting him to beam with pleasure because I was going to take his name. But he looked anything but thrilled. He'd slipped on his dark glasses and pulled a hat down to his eyes. He stared straight ahead, his breath shallow.

"And this," Whitman said, indicating Daddy, "is John Gilroy, the architect of Pine Mountain Lodge."

"Okay." The guard stepped into a gatehouse and pressed a button. The high iron gates slowly began to fan open. "We're just being super-cautious, Mr. Fourth. I'm sure you understand why."

Daddy leaned forward and said, "Earth Freedom?"

The guard nodded. "Yes, sir. They've been spotted in the vicinity."

"What, exactly, is it that they do?" Whitman asked.

"Set fires," the guard said. "Destroy property." He put up a hand

and stopped us just as we were inching forward. "By the way, where was that elk you seen? Tomorrow's my day off."

It was about a mile from the gates to the lodge. The freshly paved road wound smoothly through a grove of gigantic trees, skirted the side of a meadow brilliantly colored with wildflowers, and followed alongside the cleanest-looking river I'd ever seen. The water, clear as vodka, rippled in a wide, gurgling sheet across a bed of smooth greenish-brown stones.

"We kept all the natural features of the landscape," Daddy said.

"Even for the golf course?" Tremaynne stuck his head out the window, gaping at everything.

"The golf course required some terrain adjustment," Daddy admitted.

Whitman stopped when we came in view of the lodge. "Wow! John, it's beautiful. The setting is perfect."

Daddy beamed. "Like it?"

"Gorgeous. I want a photo of you here, in front."

Daddy didn't need any prompting. He stood, proud and happy, as Whitman arranged the photo. A syrup of yellow-gold sunlight poured through the trees and struck the stone and wood of the lodge.

"Northwest Vernacular," Daddy said in response to a question from Whitman.

I cuddled closer to Tremaynne. "They're so cute," I whispered.

"I don't want you to use my last name," he said quietly.

I drew back, confused. "What?"

"It's my name. Not yours, mine. I changed it for myself, not for anyone else."

"You mean your real name isn't Tremaynne Woods?"

He let out a dismissive snort. "It is now."

"What was it before?"

"Phillip Klunk."

"Why did you change it?"

He turned to me, his dark eyes narrowed. "Do I look like a Phillip Klunk to you?"

There wasn't time to answer because the dads got back in. Whitman rubbed his hands together. "This is really going to be fun."

Chapter

10

When we pulled up in front, a smiling uniformed attendant came out and greeted us with: "Welcome to Pine Mountain Lodge!"

Three college-age guys and one cute woman, all of them wearing black khakis and white cotton-knit shirts with the collars turned up, were stationed by the lobby entrance. They swooped down in formation and opened the doors of the dirty, dented SUV as if it were a limousine. The young woman gave me a discreet but unmistakable once-over as she helped me out. Our eyes met. Mine moved nervously away.

I'd never been in such a swanky place. It was completely off limits to someone with my credit rating. The pine trees seemed to whisper, "Big Money." A couple of black Mercedes with tinted windows were parked nearby. The people milling around the lobby and grounds had obviously spent a fortune to look casual. One woman was wearing a pink golf shirt and three strands of pearls.

As I struggled to pull out my junky old suitcase that didn't close properly and had to be wrapped with a bungee cord, Daddy Two quietly said, "Just leave it, sweetheart."

I didn't understand. "Why?"

"I'll take care of that, ma'am." The young woman, skin tanned, hair bleached by the sun, eyes sparkling green, hauled out my suitcase and piled it on a trolley with the dads' fancy leather bags. When she tried to take Tremaynne's backpack, he grabbed it from her hands and slipped it on.

Our greeter gestured toward the lobby. "If you'll please follow me into reception?"

"Mr. Whittlesley," the red-haired desk clerk said, "we're so pleased you could join us for the opening. And Mr. Gilroy, good to see you again, sir."

"Hi, Mike. Everything working all right?" Daddy asked.

The desk clerk nodded. "A couple of short-term power outages, but we've got it covered with the backup generator."

Now a tall, tan, ruggedly handsome man of about forty, wearing a dark suit, came forward. "John." He and Daddy shook hands. "So glad you could make it back for the opening. We're already getting raves. Harrison loves it."

From the way he said it, I figured he meant Harrison Ford. I kept my eyes peeled for celebrities.

"This is my partner, Whitman Whittlesley," Daddy said.

"Oh yes, from *Travel* magazine." The man shook Whitman's hand. "Geof Killingsworth, general manager. We've got a really full program planned for you." His brilliant blue eyes flicked over to Tremaynne and me. "These are your assistants?"

"Yes." Whitman beckoned us over. "Venus Woods—"

"Gilroy," I muttered.

"John's daughter, and her husband, Tremaynne."

Geof Killingsworth smiled and clasped my hand. Tremaynne wouldn't come near. He kept his back to us as he intently studied a scale model of the lodge, shipped from Daddy's office, that sat in a Plexiglas display case on one side of the lobby. His rudeness embarrassed me. He'd been so sweet after the elk attack. Now he seemed to be turning hostile again. I had a sudden sinking feeling that I was seeing him as he really was, that I'd made up a more pleasant personality for him than he really had. Why couldn't I ever fall in love with someone who fit into the dads' preferred world of money and social grace?

"Venus and Tremaynne will be helping me out with my research," Whitman lied.

"A real family business," Geof Killingsworth said affably. "We like families at Pine Mountain Lodge. I hope you'll mention that in your article."

Tremaynne's voice carried across the vast lobby. "What kind of family could ever afford to stay here?"

We all looked at him. I sensed trouble.

"You'd have to be, like, a millionaire," Tremaynne said.

Geof Killingsworth didn't know what to say. He smiled and rubbed his hands together. "Well, why don't you all get settled and we'll see you for cocktails in the Great Hall in about an hour. Prince Brunelli and all the other investors will be there with their special guests. There's lots of star power here, so we'll be taking lots of photos." He turned to Daddy. "John, I wonder if you'd mind having a quick look at the backup generator building."

"E.S.S. four? Is there a problem?"

"I'd like your opinion." Before starting off, Daddy at his side, Geof Killingsworth gave a quick, admiring glance to his new domain: the beautiful sweep of flagstone floors, the giant stone columns holding up the wooden ceiling, the two-story glass entry wall.

"I'll see you in the room," Whitman called after them. He and Daddy acted differently in public. More like straight men.

When Daddy and Geof Killingsworth were gone, Whitman slowly walked over to Tremaynne. He stood there for a moment, regarding him. "Are you going to ruin this?"

"Ruin what?" Tremaynne asked, feigning innocence.

"Venus's honeymoon. Your honeymoon. Our honeymoon."

"I just asked a simple question," Tremaynne said. "Isn't that what a writer's supposed to do, ask questions?"

"This place is not for everyone," Whitman said. "It's not supposed to be."

"No," Tremaynne said, "it's for rich people. Like you."

"For three days," Whitman said, "it's for you and Venus, too. You can enjoy it or you can hate it, Tremaynne. It's up to you. But if you hate it, I don't want to hear about it. And neither does anyone else."

I moved to Tremaynne's side and took his arm. "He was just asking a question, Whitman."

Whitman sighed. "I'm a writer, Venus. I know a subtext when I hear one."

Yet another uniformed staff person joined us. "Mr. Whittlesley? We've put your party in adjoining suites. If you'll follow me?"

I didn't dare smoke in the room, but I was excited and wanted a cigarette real bad.

Our suite was fantastic.

The outdoors was right there. There was a floor-to-ceiling glass wall that angled up so that part of the ceiling was glass, too. Everything was made of wood. Beyond the glass wall, there was a deck with a flagstone floor and a stone hot tub. Giant pine trees rose up just beyond the patio. The river sparkled through the trees.

"Wow." I kicked off my sandals and stretched out on the enormous bed in what I hoped was a provocative pose. "It's like being in a movie."

Tremaynne shook his head and frowned as he examined everything. He ran his fingers along surfaces like a blind person reading Braille.

"Don't you think it's beautiful?" I asked him.

"Beautiful? What does that mean?" he said.

"The materials. The way it looks. Everything." And it was my daddy who did it. It came from his brain. It represented the way he thought. It made me feel proud, special somehow.

Tremaynne cocked his head and shot me a squinty, disapproving glance. "Can you really feel comfortable in a place like this?"

"Sure." Anything was an improvement on my tiny, messy apartment in Portland. "It kind of reminds me of their house."

Tremaynne opened the minibar and scanned the contents. "Whose?"

"The dads'." I paused, wondering if this was the right time to bring it up. "Who won the swimming match?"

"I did."

"It was nice of you to go swimming with them. Nude."

He pulled the bottle of wine from its bucket and examined the label.

"You seemed to be having a good time."

He plunged the bottle back into the ice and started picking through the giant fruit basket.

"Do you find them attractive?"

He smiled but wouldn't look at me.

"Sexually, I mean?"

"Got any aspirin?" He opened my purse and started pawing through it.

I darted up to snatch it from his hands. But instead of handing it over, he turned away and began rifling through the contents. "Plenty of candy, I see. Cigarettes. All the consumer shit you can't live without."

"Tremaynne, if you're mad at me, let's talk about it."

"I'm sick. I've got like the worst headache in the world." He drew out a plastic case. "What's this?"

"My birth control."

He tossed the case at me and said, "Please don't stop eating *those.*"

I was burning up. Part of me wanted to fight this out. But I was too scared. I didn't want to find out what was bothering him, because I was afraid it was me. And it was too soon after the wedding to start fighting. I wanted to live in ignorant bliss awhile longer.

"Was it the bear?" I asked.

He looked at me like I was crazy. "What are you talking about?"

"You changed. After you saw that bear."

"Yeah. That really freaked me out." He slowly walked over to the glass wall and stood there, looking out. "I just can't stand it that people kill animals."

"It was horrible."

"I saw a lot worse than that when I worked at the animal research labs."

I covered my ears. But he told me again.

How, in these labs, they sever the nerves in cats' ears in order to study the effects of hearing on balance. They inject monkeys with cancer cells, expose their brains, blind them, chop off limbs, raise babies in isolation from their mothers, and subject males to electro-ejaculation so the facility can clone more monkeys for more research. The research labs did all kinds of things I tried not to think about.

Just like I didn't want to think about those phone calls he'd made.

All I wanted was to lie with my lover in wedded bliss.

"Tremaynne," I pleaded, "we're on our honeymoon. This isn't an animal research lab. It's our honeymoon suite."

"Oh, I get it." He threw my purse aside, grabbed my wrists, and pushed me down on the bed. "You want a little penis-imo."

"I just want to know that you love me."

He pulled back and looked into my eyes.

"If I've done something to piss you off, just tell me."

"No," he whispered, stroking his cheek. "It's not you. It's not you, Venus."

I could feel him coming back to me. "Then what?"

There was no answer. There was just this sudden surge of mutual lust. He ground his hips into mine. I ground back. He let out a sharp, sudden groan of desire and dove for my mouth. His tongue was everywhere. I raised my legs and grabbed his ass tight. He tore open my blouse and pulled my breasts free, hungrily sucking and licking my nipples.

He unzipped my bell-bottoms and yanked them off. I was wearing some new French thong underpants that my mom bought me for the honeymoon. Tremaynne slipped his hands under the elastic sidebands, caressing my hips and belly, and peeled the thong away. He lifted and spread my legs, eyed my pussy, and dove in.

I was torn between sex and sanitation. I wanted to go wash myself, but his tongue was already probing and licking. My clitoris hardened. My nipples grew stiffer. My back arched. I moaned in ecstasy.

But then he stopped. Drew back his head. Looked at me.

"There's just one thing I want to know," he said.

"What?" I panted.

"Why didn't you tell me you have genital herpes?"

I stared at him through my raised legs, desperately hoping it was a bad joke. "I don't."

He raised his eyebrows. "Then how did I get it?"

I clamped my legs together and rolled onto my side. "You have genital herpes?"

"It just appeared today. I saw it in that gas station. It freaked me out. I never had it before."

The accusation stung me. "I don't have herpes."

"Well," he said, "someone gave it to me."

I didn't have to go out into the hallway to get into the dads' room. Our suites were separated by a large, fully equipped conference room.

Their door was unlocked.

"John?" Whitman called from the shower. He has supersonic hearing. "Come in here and I'll scrub your back."

A minute later the water shut off. A minute after that he stuck his wet head out the bathroom door. "Oh. I thought it was your dad."

"No, it's me."

He slipped into a thick white guest bathrobe like the one I was wearing and began vigorously toweling his hair. "Like your room?"

"It's great."

"Your dad did a beautiful job. Everything's so carefully thought out. Make sure you tell him that." He strode admiringly through the room. "I'm so proud of him for pulling it off. This project was a nightmare. He almost quit, you know."

I didn't know. Daddy never told me anything about his work. Or maybe he had and I hadn't bothered to listen.

Whitman opened the door to the deck. The sound of chattering birds wafted in. A big squirrel skittered up a tree. Whitman sucked in a deep Buddha breath. "How can you not love it?" he said.

"What?"

"Life! This!"

"Yeah," I said. "Life is a banquet and most poor assholes are starving to death." I'd watched *Auntie Mame* with the dads every year since I was eight. I knew the whole thing practically by heart.

"The voice can be a mellifluous instrument, Venus. It doesn't have to be a flat, depressed monotone."

"Yes, Auntie Mame."

"And speaking of banquets, you're expected to be at the big bash tonight."

"No," I said firmly. "We're not going. I came over to tell you."

"You can't pretend to be my assistants for the duration of one cocktail party?"

"It's our honeymoon, Whitman. We want to be alone."

"Away from us, you mean."

I blurted out, "Do you have any condoms I can borrow?"

Whitman shook his head. "We don't use condoms. One of the perks of a long-term monogamous relationship."

"Okay."

"But I'm glad to know that you're protecting yourself. There are so many awful love bugs out there. It takes just one—"

It could be simple chafing, I thought. I had no clue what genital herpes looked like. Maybe it was just dry skin, or irritation from the hand job I'd given him earlier in the day.

Or maybe he'd picked it up from that bitch he'd been calling. She'd given it to him, and maybe he'd passed it on to me.

At least now I knew why Tremaynne had been acting so weird. It was the shock of discovering he had a STD. I was dealing with it myself.

"I wonder if they sell rubbers in that chic little boutique off the lobby," Whitman said.

I shook my head. "They don't."

Whitman scratched his head. "Then I'm sorry, I don't know where—" His face brightened. "Maybe we could get you some industrial-strength Saran Wrap from the kitchen."

I smiled politely. "Could we borrow the car and drive into McCall? There must be a drugstore there."

Whitman picked up his pants and dug through the pockets. "Maybe Tremaynne could go and you could come to the cocktail party with us."

"I think we'll both go into McCall."

He drew out the car keys. "I just thought since you were so keen to meet celebrities."

"Why? Who's here?"

"Who isn't?" Whitman said.

"Harrison Ford?" He was old, but major.

Whitman waved me away. "You just go into McCall and get your rubbers. Your dad and I will have to meet all the stars ourselves."

There was a click of the door release and Daddy came in. "I just saw Susan Sarandon," he said. "At least I think it was Susan Sarandon."

"Where was she?" Susan Sarandon was my favorite movie-star mother. She was my mom's favorite actress after Bette Davis.

"Everyone's on their way down to the cocktail party," Daddy said. "Whit, I don't know if I brought anything dressy enough."

"Whatever you wear, I'm sure the women will be all over you," Whitman said. "As usual."

"It's been set up as a big photo op," Daddy told me. "So the investors can shake hands with movie stars."

Whitman glanced at his watch. "Holy cow. John, go hop in the shower." He tossed me the keys. "Venus, drive safely."

"Where's she going?" Daddy asked as I raced towards the connecting door.

"Into McCall to buy some condoms," Whitman said.

"Tremaynne can do it." I was suddenly breathless with excitement. "I'm going to that party with you guys."

I had two evening dresses with me. The one I chose was a kooky-looking pink satin thing from the Sixties that I'd found at Goodwill for $4.00. The low-cut bodice was partially covered with sequins and there was a weird bow in the back that looked like a propeller. The calf-length skirt was partially slit up the sides. It was sort of Jackie Kennedy Goes to Las Vegas. I slipped into the orangey-red nylons my mom had given me, and my purple, scuffed stilettos. Around my shoulders I artfully draped the white silk and cashmere shawl the dads had brought me from one of their trips to Italy. If I folded it right no one would see the big coffee stain.

Tremaynne sat on the bed, playing with Whitman's car keys, watching me. "It's just a bunch of stupid movie stars," he said.

I stared into the magnifying cosmetic mirror and carefully applied pale pink lipstick. I had about ten dozen cases left over from my days as a Lorrie Ann Lady.

"You'd rather hang out with a bunch of stupid movie stars than me?" He sounded wounded and a little incredulous.

"Come with me," I said, keeping my tone light.

"I hate movie stars."

"Why?"

"They're not earth-conscious," Tremaynne said. "Nobody here is. They couldn't build this place if they were."

"I think it's beautiful."

"That's because your dad was the architect."

"Maybe. So what?"

"You're never going to get away from them," he said.

"Who?"

"The dads."

I looked at him.

"You're like their little puppet," he mocked. "They pull your strings and you move."

I was determined not to react.

"You're so brainwashed you can't even see how they manipulate you."

I stood there wondering if he was revealing some terrible psychological truth or if he was just jealous and trying to turn me against them.

"They're part of the corruption," Tremaynne spat.

"Excuse me? What corruption?"

"The corruption that creates places like this. Do you know what was here before?"

I shook my head.

"Nothing. Totally unspoiled land." He got up and came close, gently tracing the pattern of the rose tattoo on my breast. "Untouched wilderness habitat."

He was like a snake charmer, and I was the snake.

His hands slid under my skirt, up my thighs. With sudden fierce kisses he pressed me back against the marble sink. "Let's get out of here," he whispered. "Let's go someplace else."

"Where?"

"Out into the woods."

"In what?"

He jangled the keys to the SUV. "We'll take a blanket. Swim in the river. Sleep under the stars. Come on, Venus."

"Not this time," I said. "Next time."

He was instantly off me. His voice turned harsh. "There is no next time. There's only now, Venus. This is it."

"What are you saying?"

"It's me or the dads, babe."

My heart was racing. "You said you *wanted* to come out here. To the lodge."

"I wanted to check the place out. I did. And now I know."

"Know what?"

"It's even worse than we thought."

"Who's we?"

He turned away.

My throat clenched but I was determined not to cry. "You've treated me like shit all day," I managed to choke out. "You even accused me of having genital herpes, which I don't. But *you* do. So *you* go get the fucking rubbers, and then you'd better do something nice, so I'll want to be with you."

"Hey, Venus—"

"Life's a feast, Tremaynne, and I'm not going to starve to death."

"Venus, wait—"

I was out the door before he could stop me.

Chapter

11

Party sounds rose from below as I gloomily made my way along the second-floor hallway, stilettos clicking on the flagstones. Part of me wanted to run back to Tremaynne. Part of me wanted to punch him. Part of me wanted to rewind my life up to the point where I met him and then start all over again from there.

Would I marry him again, knowing what I knew now?

It was almost like he'd turned into a complete stranger. Alone, in my apartment, unmarried, we'd been so happy. But now that spell had been broken. We'd been hatched into a new world. And the real test of our love was just beginning.

In my heart of hearts I was praying that Tremaynne would make an effort, come after me, surprise me. It wouldn't take much. Everything in me was yearning to make up. To be with him. But in this world, not outside in the wilderness.

Some honeymoon. Maybe it was time to morph into someone else for a while.

Sometimes the best thing to do is become a little girl again. Whenever my own life seems too crappy and confusing to deal with, I just switch it off and turn into a mindless daddy's girl. I follow the dads around and watch from the sidelines, the way I used to do when I was eight and thrown into their social life in New York. All their friends were nice to me. I got a lot of attention. A kid in that Manhattan world of careers and connections was a rarity, a curiosity. I didn't have to do anything except pretend not to be the angry little girl I really was.

I hated the dads back then. I could never be the absolute sum total of their existence, the way I was with my mom back in Portland. The dads would buy me expensive new clothes, dress me up the way they wanted me to look, and then drag me along wherever they went. In Manhattan I was always terrified and excited at the same time. I never knew where I'd be next, and I had no identity except as the dads' part-time daughter.

All those Manhattan parties. The endless introductions. The nonstop networking. The insane devotion to careers and money. "What do you do?" one of their friends once asked me.

"I'm a child," I said.

Much as I resented them and their endless social drive, I wasn't blind to the fact that the dads were in love. It was *their* relationship that came first, not Daddy's and mine. And it was their love that I found so puzzling. Where did it come from? It seemed to give the two of them a kind of mysterious stability that was entirely lacking in my chaotic, rummage-sale life with Carolee back on the West Coast.

I was jealous of their love.

I still was.

The partners I found never gave me that quiet, steady glow of happiness I always associated with the dads. It was starting to worry me. Like my mom, I seemed to have absolutely no ability to judge character. I was so greedy for love that I took whatever presented itself. I was like a starving dog. Throw a bone my way and I was on it in a flash.

I clicked on down the hallway, half taking in Daddy's calm, orderly building. Stone and wood walls were interspersed with giant out-thrust windows. At the end of the hallway I came out into a bright open space over the lobby. The walls and ceiling were glass. There was a dramatic staircase, perfect for making an entrance, but I pressed the button for the elevator instead.

A light went on. The elevator door opened. A movie star was standing inside. A name so big that I couldn't even say it to myself. He smiled. I stared. I couldn't move. The door closed.

I ran over to the banister to watch him get out on the lobby level, right below where I was standing. Was it really? It was. You could sense the atmosphere changing, shifting to accommodate his fame. People tried not to stare. He smiled. Waved at someone. Everything he did looked casual, but you could see it as a picture in *People* magazine. A man wearing a black suit came forward to shake his hand. Cameras flashed.

The vast two-story room next to the lobby, called the Great Hall, was crammed with laughing, chattering people. From above, I could see all the little groups of twos and threes and fours. Gleaming bald heads, slender tanned shoulders, lots of blonde hair, gold jewelry and diamonds. People were talking, drinking and eating. Three stuffed birds with long tails—pheasants maybe?—were artfully arranged along a gleaming wood table piled with food. Another table served as a bar. The enormous stone fireplace was banked with urns of wildflowers. Some guy was playing tunes on a grand piano. He must have been famous because a lot of people were standing around watching him.

I looked for Harrison Ford and Susan Sarandon but didn't see them.

The Really Big Name carefully swam out into the crowd. His presence goosed up the level of conversation. There were shrieks of laugher. Heads swiveled in his direction.

I remembered the lurid stories about how he'd been arrested in L.A. with a young black prostitute. I was, like, totally shocked. Someone that famous, and that handsome, had to go to a prostitute for sex? His career nose-dived, but lately he'd made a comeback with three hit movies. Romantic comedies. There was talk that he was going to boost his career by doing an action flick with lots of kung-fu and car crashes.

The Great Hall where the party was being held opened out onto broad stone terraces front and back. People went in and out, back and forth. The glass roof and walls were so clean they looked invisible. It was like being outdoors. I could see the sky glowing with the last of the soft evening light. It all looked magical, unreal. If my husband had been with me, everything would have been perfect.

As I stood there watching the scene, I was suddenly overcome with a wrenching sense of loneliness. I'd felt this before, but never so acutely. It's because of this feeling that I got into drink and drugs when I was fifteen.

The feeling was that I was a complete outsider. Always had been and always would be.

Like now. Where did I belong?

I could enter that glittering world below only as the daughter of the dads. I had no other claim to be there, amidst fame and money and beauty and talent. Or I could go back to Tremaynne, the husband who hated everything this place stood for, and sneak away into the woods with him.

But I'd gotten my fill of nature that afternoon. I was afraid to go back into the forest. I could see it out there, looming in on all sides, dark, mysterious, full of bugs, snakes, and wild animals.

So there I stood, stuck between two identities, neither of them my own. If I wasn't daughter or wife, who was I? I had no career. I was a twenty-five-year-old twice-divorced bankrupt chick who worked in a porn shop. There was nothing that made me unique.

"I thought you were dead," I heard a breathless voice behind me say.

Startled, I whirled around. It was the cute young woman who'd been working as a valet when we arrived. Now she was wearing a bow tie and standing there in front of me with a tray of bottled waters.

"Didn't you die in a car accident?" she asked, sounding worried. "In Europe somewhere?"

"I don't think so."

"I read it somewhere," she insisted.

"Shouldn't believe everything you read." I had to stop myself from automatically flirting with her.

"You hardly have any accent at all," she gushed. "If I didn't know, I'd think you were American."

I smiled dumbly, not knowing what the fuck she was talking about.

Her green eyes bored into me. "You're, like, Swedish or Icelandic or something, aren't you? It's hard to tell from your name."

And just what was my name, I wondered. Mrs. Phillip Klunk? Ms. Venus Woods? Miss Venus Gilroy?

"I saw your last music video," the young woman went on. "Kristin" was printed on her name tag. She wore no makeup. Freckles were splattered across her nose like cinnamon on cream. She looked disgustingly healthy, like an older version of Pippi Longstocking. "It was so awesome."

I could see the worshipful awe in her big green eyes. It gave my sagging ego a sudden boost.

"My parents caught me watching it," Kristin confided. "They grounded me for a *month.*"

"Why?"

"The church!" she exclaimed. "That was three years ago. I was only eighteen." She gave me a bold look. "I've got my own place now."

"Which video was it?" I asked nonchalantly.

"That one where you're naked on the big white horse." She momentarily came to her senses. "Oh gosh, I'm so rude. They're going to fire me." She proffered the tray. "Would you care for an advanced hydration delivery beverage?"

"A what?"

"Water. That's what we have to call it."

"Why?"

She shrugged. "Someone who owns the company was an investor or something." She couldn't take her eyes away from the rose tattoo on my boob. It seemed to fascinate and frighten her.

I recognized a groupie when I saw one, having groupie tendencies myself. I suddenly understood how JD or any performer would get high off adoration. It felt kind of dangerous. Like I had this secret power if I ever dared to use it.

Down below, I finally caught sight of Daddy and Whitman. They were standing with Marielle and Fokke, their Dutch friends. Fokke was an investor in Pine Mountain Lodge.

Daddy saw me first. He waved. The others looked up and waved. I waved back.

Kristin hungrily watched my every move. "Are those your handlers?"

I spit out a laugh. "Sort of."

"Famous people *never* travel alone," she affirmed. "They've all got, like, an entourage. Before I started working here, I never heard that word used for people. Handlers. Only for animals."

My handlers, all four of them, were motioning for me to come down. Even from a distance Marielle looked stunning. She was wearing a shimmering pure white Chinese-looking neck-to-ankle sheath that accentuated her height. Her big yellow diamonds flashed and sparkled.

I adjusted my coffee-stained shawl. "I gotta go."

"Oh, sure," Kristin nodded. "Hey, do you think you could give me your autograph?"

"I don't have anything to write on."

Kristin set down her tray. She pulled a piece of paper and a pen from her pocket and thrust them at me.

I still didn't know who I was supposed to be. "What do you want me to write?"

She thought for a moment. "Just put: 'To my dear friend Kristin. Who's not the geek she looks like. I hope you'll look me up when you come visit me in'—where?"

"Iceland?" I suggested.

" 'Iceland. My number is—' " She looked over my shoulder. I could feel her warm breath, smell her apple-scented shampoo. "Then write down your phone number."

"I probably won't be there," I said. "I'm always on tour."

"Oh," She sounded disappointed. "Sure."

I handed her the paper.

"Thanks." She read it, smiling, then suddenly looked crestfallen. "You didn't sign it!"

I took the paper back. "How do you want me to sign it?"

"With your name, of course," she laughed. She saw me hesitating. "Just put, 'Love, Godiva.'"

It was such a relief to finally know who I was.

Daddy was famous for his dramatic staircases. They were like his signature in a building. The staircase at Pine Mountain Lodge was a long curving swoop of stainless steel and wood unattached to the wall. I decided to make my entrance that way instead of by elevator.

I knew that people were watching me. Maybe they all thought I was Godiva, whoever she was. I gave all my fans a big closed-mouth smile as I headed down to pick up my Grammy.

Just as I reached the next to the last step my ankle gave out. It didn't hurt, but it just, like, collapsed. I let out a gasp of surprise and pitched forward on my stilettos. Arms flailing, desperately trying to keep my balance, I careened across the lobby and was about to crash into a wall when a pair of strong arms suddenly caught and held me.

"Jesus Christ!" I gasped. I was so embarrassed I couldn't look into my rescuer's eyes.

A deep voice with a foreign accent asked if I was all right.

"Yeah, I think so. My ankle just sort of collapsed." I straightened up and put my full weight on it. "Seems okay now."

It was then that I looked into his dark eyes and realized who he was. I sucked in a shocked breath. He blinked, as surprised as I was.

"It's you?" He smiled. "Laurie Ann?" But then, as if some inner warning had gone off, his eyes flicked nervously back and forth, scanning the crowd. "What are you doing here?" he whispered.

"I'm on my honeymoon," I whispered back.

"But I thought you were already married."

"I was. This is a new one."

Daddy and Whitman hurried over and began fussing.

"Well, you certainly know how to make an entrance," Whitman said.

"It was her ankle," my rescuer said.

"Lean back," Whitman ordered, "let me feel."

Daddy clasped me under my armpits and tilted me back while Whitman lifted my leg and examined my ankle. I felt like we were part of a dance team.

"Thanks," Daddy smiled at my rescuer. "We'll take her from here."

"Which one is your husband?" Marcello whispered in my ear. I couldn't help it. I started to laugh as the dads led me away.

"Is that who I think it was?" Whitman asked Daddy in a secretive undertone.

Daddy nodded. "We'll go back and I'll introduce you."

Those were the hushed, tactical tones they used for business or professional maneuvering at parties in New York. But it was Marcello they were talking about, wasn't it?

He'd called me Laurie Ann! The fake name I'd used as a lingerie model.

Whitman commandeered a big soft white chair and the dads eased me into it like I was an invalid. Daddy sat on the arm of the chair and rubbed my neck. Whitman sat opposite me on the ottoman. He slid off my shoe and lifted my foot to rest on his thigh.

"What are you doing, Whitman?"

"Massaging your ankle." He pressed in with his fingertips.

"Here?"

"Why not?"

"Everyone's, like, looking."

"Shyness from a former, like, topless dancer?" Whitman teased. "So let them look."

The looks I got, or we got, were not like the adoring looks given to Mr. Famous English Actor. The thin tan blonde women wearing simple black cocktail dresses accessorized with gold, pearls, and diamonds eyed me like a disgusting bug they wanted to squash. Their husbands, on the other hand, were like gluttons eyeing the first course. I'd been familiar with looks like that since I was twelve.

"Let me get you a plate of food," Marielle suggested. "The chef is brilliant."

"Whudda they got?"

"What do they *have*," Whitman corrected.

"Delicious little trout tartlets," Marielle said.

I was more in the mood for sour cream and onion potato chips with really hot salsa. I didn't have a clue what a trout tartlet was.

"A little pastry shell," Marielle explained, "with smoked trout and a tiny dollop of eggless lemon mayonnaise. There's also fresh alder-grilled Copper River salmon. Sautéed wild mushrooms. Pheasant roulades. Halibut cheeks. A divine orzo salad with lots of flowers and seeds." She gave me an affectionate smile. "You can eat everything and not get fat."

"Well," Whitman said, "underneath all the glamour it's just a simple fat farm, after all."

"I guess I wouldn't mind some tartlets and roulades," I said.

"Yes, eat now," Whitman said, "before the food fascist appears."

Right there in front of me, he told Marielle and Fokke about my husband's aversion to foie gras and meats of all kinds. "Living in that tree must have turned him into an epiphyte."

They laughed. I didn't. Number one, I didn't know what an epiphyte was, and number two, I thought it was pretty rude of my faux pa to make fun of my husband's eating preferences. Was I supposed to side with them against Tremaynne? Laugh at him?

A wife was supposed to defend her husband.

"Where is he now?" Fokke asked me. "Up in a tree? With the squee-rells?"

"I hope not," Whitman said, smiling at me.

"All the trees left on this property are protected," Daddy said.

"We didn't cut down any more than we had to," Fokke nodded.

"For your damn golf course." Marielle glided off. I thought she was the most beautiful middle-aged woman I'd ever seen. She had a kind of imperturbable serenity. Fokke, her millionaire husband, was just the opposite. He could never sit still and when he spoke it always sounded like he was gargling gravel.

Fokke asked me what I'd like to drink, then suggested a glass of

1997 something or other from a vineyard in Burgundy. "Good year," he gargled, "you'll like it."

Whitman, meanwhile, continued to massage my ankle. Daddy absently caressed the back of my neck as he sipped his wine and gazed around the room he'd created.

"You look happy, Daddy."

He smiled. "Every once in a while I get to do a building I really love," he said. "Something I'm proud of. It's always a battle, but sometimes you win."

I could see how my mom would fall in love with him. Daddy was always so calm and purposeful. He was an artist, but his art was about creating order. That's really appealing when you're a woman living a scattershot life, making it up as you go along.

Whitman's hands felt good on my ankle. I wondered what it would be like to be Daddy, and have Whitman make love to me. I leaned back and tried to relax, but couldn't. I wanted to be with Tremaynne. I wanted Tremaynne's hands all over me. I wanted to be sucking his hot wet tongue into my mouth.

We made chitchat, going over the elk attack for the umpteenth time. I told them about my close encounter with the famous movie star.

"That pederast? Who cares about him?" Whitman said dismissively. "Jane Bugler's here. One of the most famous opera singers in the world. The greatest Norma of her generation."

"She's going to sing later on," Daddy said.

As if I cared.

My eyes wandered, scouting for real celebrities. I caught a glimpse of Marcello across the room. He was standing with an elderly woman wearing a dowdy flower-print dress. His eyes wandered, looking for someone else. They landed on me. He smiled, but I looked away, not wanting to plug in. I didn't want to acknowledge our guilty secret.

Fokke returned with my wine. "Where is your husband?" he asked.

I saw Daddy and Whitman exchange glances.

"He went into McCall," I said.

"So you really love dis guy who sits up in de trees?" Fokke wanted to know. "What does he do dat for anyway?"

"He's a professional activist," I said.

"How can you be active sitting in a tree?" Fokke asked.

"When you sit in a tree," Whitman explained, "they can't cut it down."

"Dat's ri-dic-a-lus," Fokke insisted. "What would we do without timber? The building industry would collapse. Your fodder would have no verk. Where do you think the wood came from to build this place?"

"Tremaynne works for animal rights, too," I said stubbornly.

"Ya," Fokke said nervously, "don't tell that to Marielle. She's crazy for all these animals, too."

"You know what they do to those poor little monkeys in research facilities?" I said.

Fokke shook his head.

"Instead of letting them have sex, they electro-ejaculate them. For their sperm. They clamp this electric—"

Marielle returned with a plate of food. "I just saw your husband," she announced.

I jumped up from the chair. "Where?"

"Outside," Marielle said. "Down by the stables. I'm sure it was him."

"What stables?"

"Outside. Down there." She pointed beyond the food table. "He was talking to someone. Down by the horses."

I ran outside, shoeless. Three broad flagstone terraces led down to an Olympic-size pool. Beyond that there was a strip of thick green grass, and then a winding path through giant pine trees to a corral, pasture and stables. Guests at Pine Mountain Lodge didn't have to stay in the lodge itself. They could rent luxurious cabins way out in the woods and ride back and forth on horseback. There was a long line of saddled horses tethered to a railing, waiting like cabs outside a New York nightclub.

"Tremaynne!" I shouted, skirting around the corral. The ground was hard and rocky. The soles of my nylons got shredded. "Tremaynne!"

The college-age kid working in the stable said he hadn't seen anyone who looked like the man I was describing.

"He was here just a minute ago," I said. "Outside. Talking to someone."

"I been in here," he shrugged. "Feedin' the horses."

I looked everywhere I could without going any deeper into the forest. The sun had gone down and the night turned suddenly cool. The air smelled sweet, like fresh water and crushed herbs. Nearby, the river flowed with a restless voice through the trees. Two horses, one gray and one white, grazed in the lush pasture beyond the corral. And way beyond that there was a landing strip with three single-engine planes parked outside a hangar.

Marielle must have mistaken someone else for Tremaynne. He'd probably taken the SUV and gone to McCall, as the original plan called for. All I had to do was go check with the valets.

But then I did see someone. Across the river. Near a clump of bushes in the woods. It was just a glimpse, but I thought I saw a flash of Tremaynne's orange backpack.

I called his name and headed for the bank of the river. No way I was going to cross. It was deep and fast and ice-cold.

I knew how much Tremaynne loved the wilderness, but I couldn't believe he'd just leave me on our honeymoon and go out into the woods to camp by himself.

I decided to postpone freaking out until I found out if the SUV was gone or not.

It got darker and darker as I hurried back toward the lodge. A bird with a sharp, raucous voice seemed to be laughing at me. Tiny bright lights flicked on along the path. My feet were sore from stepping on rocks. Above me, at the top of the three terraces, Daddy's beautiful building was silhouetted against an indigo sky salted with stars. From inside the lodge came a high soprano voice singing an opera aria, maybe in Italian, I couldn't tell.

It was like a concert. No one was talking.

"Now where are you going?" Whitman whispered when I snuck in between songs to retrieve my shoes and bag.

"Out for a smoke." I crammed a trout tartlet into my mouth and washed it down with a gulp of burgundy.

"It's Jane Bugler," Whitman whispered, nodding toward an enormously fat woman in a long orange crushed-velvet dress that made her look like a pumpkin. "Fokke flew her over from La Scala just for this."

"Pretty voice but her dress sucks major league." I decided to take the wine with me.

"Did you find Tremaynne?" Daddy asked.

I nodded and gave him the kind of lying smile I've always been so good at. "See you guys later."

I slipped back outside and decided I'd have a smoke before going to check on the SUV. A glass of wine does not make sense without a cigarette.

I lit up and stood outside the giant glass wall, listening to the music and looking in at all the reverent faces. I'd been hearing about this Jane Bugler for years. She and Marielle had been students together at some famous music conservatory in Paris. At one time Marielle was training to be an opera singer, too. But then she met Fokke, and instead of an opera career she got yellow diamonds.

Someone coughed softly behind me. I turned around. Marcello was standing in the shadows, cigarette in hand, staring at me.

I was used to seeing him in a dark suit. I'd never seen him dressed casually. Tonight he was wearing a white short-sleeved shirt tightly tucked into loose gabardine slacks. There was no flab around his waist. His thick hair glowed silvery-white against his bronzed face. It was dark, but not so dark that I couldn't see a giant Rolex watch on his tanned, hairy wrist.

He sidled up to me and whispered, *"Buona sera."*

"Bona sera." I kept my distance. I didn't want him to think just because I'd posed for him in lingerie, and seen him jerking off into a hanky, that he could be intimate with me. I was, after all, on my honeymoon.

"You enjoy the music?" he asked, his voice pitched low, just for me.

"Not really." I took a really deep drag, chased it with a gulp of wine, and let the smoke pour out of my nose.

"What are you doing with those men?" he asked.

I knew who he meant. "They're my dads."

"Your sugar daddies?" There was a knowing edge in his voice.

"No. My fathers. My *dads.*"

"They are homosexual?"

I laughed at his impertinence.

"Laurie Ann." He moved ever so slightly closer. "I still think of you," he said with a sudden gust of passion. "I still desire you."

It was so totally unlike anything a man had ever said to me that I burst out laughing. Only I kept my lips shut, so instead of letting out a ladylike peal, I sounded like a snorting horse.

I could tell Jane Bugler was getting close to the end of her song. Her voice swooped up and down, gathering intensity. It had to be something about love. It always was, in opera. *"Amore!"* she sang. *"Ti amo!"*

"You don't believe me?" Marcello's voice was husky in my ear. A stream of his warm cigarette smoke brushed my cheek. I could tell he was excited. I could feel it emanating from his body.

"It doesn't make any difference," I said.

"Of all the women here," he breathed, "you are the only one who excites me. You are the only one who could make me love you."

"Thanks, but I don't love you."

He turned away. "You think I am too old."

Now I'd hurt his feelings. "No, it's not that."

"Then what?"

"I'm *married.* Get it? This is my *honeymoon.*"

"You were married before," he said. "You posed for me when you were married the last time."

"I needed the money," I said.

He was silent for a moment. "Your husband must be very rich."

I didn't say anything.

He let out a frustrated sigh. "If only I could touch your breasts."

I stepped away, insulted, and crossed my arms.

"If I could just look at them."

I tossed my cigarette into my wineglass. "Forget it."

"I'll pay you one thousand dollars."

The shock of it made me wheel around. I straightened my back. Marcello must have thought I was going to take him up on his offer because he was staring at my sequined boobies with fire in his dark eyes.

Jane Bugler's voice was getting louder and more dramatic, throbbing with emotion. *"Perché?"* she bellowed. *"Perché, perché, signor?"*

As she sang I felt something drop onto my shoulder and skitter softly down my bosom. I looked down and saw it . . . a huge spider, just standing there on all eight legs right between my tits. I let out a gasp and threw up my hands. Red wine flew out of my glass and into Marcello's face.

Jane Bugler's last *"Perché"* was a really high note. But my scream was much higher and much louder.

I didn't hang around for long.

I sort of heaved my tits forward, brushing frantically with my shawl, hoping the spider would fall or jump off.

Marcello, his face dripping, his immaculate shirt soaked with burgundy, watched me in a shocked daze. I must have looked insane. The room inside became totally quiet.

"It's Godiva!" I heard Kristen's excited voice coming from somewhere inside the Great Hall. "She's a famous Icelandic rock star."

I dropped the shawl and took off. I didn't know where I was going. I just wanted to get out of there before anyone could attach my face to the shriek that drowned out Jane Bugler's last and highest note.

I fled. Man, did I run. I ran the way I used to run when that gang of black girls in middle school chased me, furious if I didn't give them my lunch money. I ran the way Cinderella had to run when the clock struck midnight and her Mercedes was about to turn back into a beat-up Toyota Corolla with duct tape holding up the windows.

I flew down the flagstone terraces and around the back of the lodge. There were service doors down at the bottom level. I could see a big kitchen, hear the clatter of dishes, see food-service workers carrying plates and platters. That's where I really belonged—downstairs with the help.

I dashed on, my sides aching. Turning the corner I came to the ramp leading down into an underground garage. I darted in and searched for a dark corner where I could hide and catch my breath and collect my thoughts.

I huddled down in a recess back in the furthest corner of the garage, luxury cars and SUVs all around me. I looked for the dads' dusty, battered Rodeo but didn't see it.

Hands shaking, winded, I fumbled in my bag for a cigarette. Stray thoughts flashed and collided with memories. Getting back home and locking myself inside before the gang of black girls got me. Lingerie modeling. My wedding the day before. Whitman's disapproval. Tremaynne's hostility. Being refused service in Snakebite. The dead bear. The charging elk. Genital herpes. The terrifying long-legged spider . . .

I looked down to make sure it was gone. Pried open the front of the sequined bodice and looked inside. My breasts were very hot. And they'd suddenly taken on a weird new importance. Marcello had offered me a thousand bucks just to look at them.

But Tremaynne was my first concern. I needed to verify that he had, in fact, gone into McCall and wasn't hanging around the lodge waiting or looking for me. I decided it couldn't have been him I saw across the river. That would be, like, abandonment.

When I'd caught my breath I stood up and began scanning the gleaming rows of cars and SUVs. There was one section I couldn't see from where I was.

As I stepped out to look, something dark ran across the floor and darted beneath a white Lexus SUV. It moved too fast to see what it was.

Then I saw another one, followed by three babies.

Raccoons.

They were smaller than me, so I didn't feel the instant urge to run away. But I wasn't going to hang around, either. Raccoons bit and carried rabies. One year they overran the dads' house in Portland, taking over the terrace—"like goddamn squatters!" Whitman complained. They were bold, stubborn animals, unafraid of humans, and it was like they expected you to feed them. If you didn't, they tried to get inside to feed themselves.

Keeping my eye on the shadow cast by the white Lexus, I quickly slipped off my ragged nylons and tossed them in the backseat of a nearby BMW convertible. I squeezed my swollen feet into my heels. I was afraid to walk barefoot past the animals.

I took a deep drag of my Marlboro for courage and then started slowly down the wide corridor between the cars, staying close to the opposite row. Nothing leaped out from beneath the white Lexus, but I had a sense of bright watching eyes.

Before I could get to the end of the corridor the biggest raccoon I'd ever seen came trundling down the ramp from outside, a rotten banana peel dangling from its mouth. It saw me and stopped. I stopped. It looked at me with those bandit-masked eyes, then sat back as if daring me to pass. I could see its paws with their weird, humanlike fingers.

Something growled behind me. I slowly turned my head. Saw sharp, beady eyes and sharp pointed teeth. The mother, maybe, thinking I was going to harm her young.

I did everything in slow motion, like a tai-chi routine. I stuck my cigarette in my mouth and quietly opened my purse, pulling out the box of red hots. I shook some out and flung them over my shoulder, as far behind me as I could. I heard a skittering, a scratching, as the baby raccoons darted out to get the red hots. The mother joined them.

The big one with the banana peel didn't budge until I threw

some candy off to one side of the ramp. Then he slowly walked over to sniff it.

That was my chance so I took it. But as I started toward the ramp, a piercing, pulsating siren suddenly went off. It was so loud that even the raccoons jumped. Mr. Banana Peel looked at me as if to say: "Now you've ruined our hideaway!"

It must have been my cigarette. It hadn't occurred to me that there'd be smoke detectors in the garage. I ground out the butt as fast as I could, then started toward the ramp. But now the heavy garage door was rolling down.

The big raccoon stood up and hissed as I scrambled up the ramp. I didn't have it in me to dive under the door. I was afraid I wouldn't make it and the force of it would chop off my legs or my head. Wouldn't that be cute?

I moaned and turned back around. And in that moment of super-adrenalated vision I saw the dads' Rodeo, parked back in a corner by a door.

An exit door. A door that must lead up to the lodge.

I started off, but realized to my horror that something in the descending door had caught on the big bow on the back of my dress. I was being dragged down to the concrete. Terrified, I let out a screech and lunged forward to escape. The movement triggered some sort of reversal mechanism in the door. It stopped and then started to rise, taking me with it.

"Oh my God!" I gasped as my feet left the driveway.

I was being, like, squashed to death in reverse. I could feel the tug of the bow and the fabric pulling tighter and tighter on my belly. The door strained and whirred and carried me upward. Then I heard a ripping sound.

I dropped back down and landed on the concrete driveway.

Bowless, I made for the exit door inside the garage.

Chapter

12

The door opened into a concrete stairwell. There was nothing to do but huff my way up the stairs to see where they led.

Three landings up I came to another metal security door. Excited voices were jabbering on the other side. I jumped back as the door swung open.

With a sharp snap of energy, like cops or firefighters, three men burst into the stairwell. The first was Geof Killingsworth. The second was a uniformed employee carrying a walkie-talkie and looking scared shitless. The third was my dad, John Gilroy. The three of them were so intent on getting downstairs that they didn't see me half-hidden behind the door.

"Why weren't the goddamn valets at their posts?" Geof Killingsworth raged as they clattered down the stairs toward the garage.

"Maybe it's that terrorist group," the uniformed employee said. "They could of set a trap. Knocked 'em out. And we don't have any guns."

"Probably just a cigarette," Daddy's voice echoed up the stairwell.

"If I find out someone's been sneaking smokes down there, his ass is grass," Geof Killingsworth shouted.

From the stairwell I slipped out into a large open gallery close to the reception desk and then ducked into the nearby ladies' room. Two women entered in a cloud of perfume just as I slipped into a toilet stall. I spied on them through a crack in the door as they primped in front of the mirror.

"Did you actually *see* her?" a young blonde woman wearing a black sheath with pearls asked her friend as she carefully remussed her Meg Ryan hair.

"I think so," said her friend, who was wearing a tight red Spandex minidress that looked like a gym costume. "I'm almost positive it was Godiva."

Godiva! They were talking about me! Unless, of course, the real Godiva was a guest at the lodge.

"What did she look like?" asked the woman in the black dress, leaning close to the mirror and examining her face.

"Kind of dumpy. Long dark hair."

"Why would she scream like that?" the black-dressed woman asked.

"She's a punk," her friend said. "That's her singing voice. What's left of it, anyway."

They straightened their dresses, appraised their perfect bodies and faces and hair and teeth one last time. "Did you see Tru Brant?" asked the woman in the red dress. "What a hunk!"

"I heard he wears platform shoes," said her friend as they joined the crowd buzzing outside in the gallery.

As I crept out of the ladies' room, trying to look inconspicuous, I felt like I was in one of those weird dreams where I'm stark naked in Daddy's busy office or on a crowded subway platform in New York. I was afraid more people would recognize me as Godiva, or, worse yet, that the real Godiva would make an appearance.

My goal was simple: to get through the lobby, into an elevator, and back up to our room without being noticed. If the dads' SUV was still here, so was Tremaynne. By now, I figured, he'd be back in our honeymoon suite, and maybe more in the mood for a honeymoon. We could drink wine and laugh over all I'd been through try-

ing to find him. He could apologize for being so hostile. I could for-
give him and try to put those phone calls out of my mind.

But we couldn't have sex. Not without a condom. Not if he had
herpes. No way. I'd have to come up with some safe erotic tricks
that avoided penetration.

People were scurrying back and forth across the lobby with worried looks on their faces. I could hear the distant hee-haw of the
siren in the garage.

"Everything's fine," a man at the concierge desk assured a knot
of wealthy guests. "It's a new alarm system, so it's jittery."

"Are you saying there isn't a fire?" a bald man with thick glasses
asked. "Yes or no?"

"We're checking on it now, sir."

"Should we evacuate?" another man snapped.

"My beautiful Mercedes!" moaned a thin blonde woman with a
lifted face and an English accent. "If anything should happen to
her—"

"Did anyone find out what that scream was?" the bald man
asked. "It sounded like someone being murdered out on the god-
damn terrace!"

"Someone said it was Godiva!" another woman standing by the
desk told him.

"Who the hell's Godiva?" the bald man asked.

"That famous Swedish rock star," someone else said.

"Whoever the creature is, she deliberately ruined Jane Bugler's
aria!" huffed the facelifted English lady. "These wretched celebrities
are all so hopelessly immature and self-centered. They'll do anything to get publicity."

I pulled my hair around my face, like a mask, and kept my head
averted as I slowly made my way toward the lobby, passing the
model of Pine Mountain Lodge. In miniature I could see exactly
where I'd been racing around like a crazy person for the last hour.

"Venus!" It was Marielle, wine in hand. "Did you find him?"

I shook my head. "I don't think it was Tremaynne you saw."

She squinted at me, a little drunk. "I'm certain it was." She let out a conspiratorial titter. "Anyway, you missed Jane Bugler. My God, was she pissed."

"Oh?" I said innocently. "Why?"

Marielle took a little step backward, lifted her wineglass, and started to laugh. "I shouldn't," she protested. "It was terrible. Right at the end of her big aria, someone screamed. Right outside." Her yellow diamonds glittered in the gallery lights. "Fokke was furious. He thinks some vulgar, childish American was making fun of Jane's singing."

"I wonder who it was," I said.

"Ya, I wonder. Someone told me it was Godiva, but I don't believe it."

"Yeah, I heard that rumor, too. But I've never heard of Godiva. Who is she?"

Marielle waved her hand dismissively. "Oh, I think she's some boring Irish pop star."

"Irish," I said. "I thought she was Icelandic. Or Swedish."

"No," Marielle said, shaking her head, "Irish. One of those untrained singers who can't read music but knows how to show off her naked body." She glanced appreciatively around the foyer. "You must be very proud of your father, eh?"

I nodded.

"I have never seen such a beautiful spa in my life," she said. "And believe me, I've been to all of them. Your father has an exquisite eye for materials and detail. And this setting!"

"The setting's cool," I agreed, adding silently, *If you have a husband or lover or domestic partner to share it with.*

"I *adore* the American wilderness. It is something we simply do not have in Europe."

"It's very pretty," I said politely, like a good girl, trying to extricate myself.

But Marielle wanted to talk.

I'd never really confided in her, but at a party she was always my safe haven. In fact, it was only at parties that I saw her. Through the dads, the glamorous Marielle with her exotic accent had been a part of my life for years. She was like a rich socialite aunt who took a kindly interest in my various sordid affairs.

"Dey're so cute, your dads," she sighed tenderly. "Half the women here are after them. And dere dey are, the poor dears, trying to have a honeymoon."

"They're always on a honeymoon," I said jealously.

"The management wants Whitman to write a good story, so they've packed his schedule from morning until night. And every time Geof Killingsworth gets nervous, he whisks your father away to look at something or other. Dey're both working! On dere honeymoon!"

"They're always working," I told her.

"Ya. So is Fokke." She cast a sad glance back towards the Great Hall. "Always working." She looked at me, head cocked. Her short auburn hair, fixed in a weird ultra-high-fashion style, stuck straight out from her head like a high-tech toilet brush. "You know," she said morosely, "I feel quite useless at times."

I didn't feel sorry for her. I'm not into the woes of the wealthy. "Marielle, you're rich and beautiful, for God's sake. You've got everything you want."

"Hah." She blinked back tears. "Money means nothing, Venus. Absolutely nothing."

"You wouldn't say that if you didn't have any."

"Once upon a time I was quite poor," she confessed.

"You?"

"Ya. My father ran off when I was ten. My mother supported us by working as a cleaning lady. To pay for music school, I had to win scholarships and work all the time. I never had a minute free, and if I did, I didn't have any money to do anything."

It was hard to believe. Marielle was so polished and sophisticated that I'd always assumed she was born rich.

"I was a student at the conservatoire when I first met your father," she said. "I mean, your other father. Whitman. He'd just broken with his family and was wandering around Europe after the Peace Corps."

"How did you meet?" I couldn't help being curious.

She smiled, remembering. "At the opera. In Paris. I knew him a little from the conservatoire. I mean, I'd seen him. Actually, I'd heard him."

"Heard him?"

"Didn't you know he studied to be an opera singer?"

I shook my head.

"My God, such a voice," said Marielle. "Anyway, there we both were. At the opera. Up in the highest part of the balcony. We were both as poor as church mice back then." She eyed me, maybe wondering how much she should reveal. "Being poor doesn't matter so much when you're in love," she said. "And being rich doesn't matter so much when you're not."

Scales fell from my eyes. It was like finally figuring out how sex worked. At that moment I realized that Marielle was in love with Whitman.

I had this sudden image of Whitman standing up on a stage singing an aria. I remembered how excited he used to get when we'd go to the opera in New York. "Why didn't Whitman become an opera singer?" I asked.

Marielle sadly shook her head. "To this day I don't know why."

We watched silently as a parade of employees carried covered trays and enormous wrought iron candelabras into the Great Hall. They were setting up for the candlelight dessert to be served at ten o'clock with chamber music accompaniment. The huge sliding glass walls on either side of the room were pulled shut.

"Luxury is very seductive," Marielle said quietly. A waiter passed and she exchanged her empty wineglass for a full one. "But it means nothing, Venus, unless you truly earn it."

I didn't say anything. What was she getting at? Was she implying that she hadn't really earned the right to be here? Or that I hadn't?

"Damn that Jane Bugler!" Marielle exclaimed suddenly. "She always reminds me of what I gave up."

I suppose she meant her career. The one she'd given up when she married a millionaire.

"I was a better singer than she was," Marielle said. "My top was brighter. I could trill."

She opened her mouth and let out a high fluttering noise, then stood there for a moment, silently staring out into space. I thought maybe she was going to cry. "You okay?" I asked.

She turned to me. "Come and have a mud wrap with me tomorrow morning."

"I think I'll—we'll—be sleeping in," I said evasively.

"Ah." She winked. "Is he a good lover, your new husband?"

I nodded, filled with a hot, sudden desire for Tremaynne's body.

"Very important," Marielle said. She stood there looking at me and smiling, like a kindly fairy godmother. "Let's go find Whitman, shall we?"

"Signorina?"

We turned. Marcello was standing behind us, holding out my shawl. He'd changed into a light black wool sweater and black trousers, his feet in elegant black leather sandals.

"You dropped this, signorina."

I took the dirty, wine-splattered shawl and quickly wrapped it around my waist, covering up my ripped dress. "Thanks," I muttered.

"*La donna,*" Marielle said to Marcello, "*non é una signorina. É una signora.*"

"Ah, *scusatami—signora.*" Marcello gave me a slight bow then said something in rapid-fire Italian to Marielle. She responded in Italian and they both laughed.

So did I. I didn't understand a word but forced out a fake, light-hearted party laugh, as if I were in the best of moods and having the time of my life.

But it was such a weird situation. There was this embarrassing tension between Marcello and me. We had to pretend that we didn't know one another, when, in fact, we were bound together by the secret sexual world we'd once shared.

"May I invite you in for dessert?" Marcello asked me.

"No thanks. I'm going up to my room. I mean our room. I mean, our honeymoon suite."

"The signora claims to be on her honeymoon," Marcello said with a shrug to Marielle, "but I have seen no honey."

"He's up there waiting for me," I insisted.

Before I could turn tail and run, I saw Daddy walking toward the front doors of the lodge. He was drawing shapes or diagrams in the air with one hand as he explained something to Geof Killingsworth. In his other hand Daddy held something that looked like a shiny, pale-pink sea creature. It took me a minute to figure out that it was the big satin bow from the back of my dress.

The minute they entered, Geof Killingsworth turned on his professional charm. He smiled and announced in a loud voice: "Ladies and gentlemen, I'm happy to report that there is no fire. It appears that a bit of stray smoke from a kitchen exhaust fan set off the smoke alarms."

Liar, I thought. I wondered if they'd found my cigarette butt, and what had happened to the raccoons.

"So now I'd like to invite everyone to relax," Geof Killingsworth said, "since that's what you're all here to do. Please enjoy some champagne from our fine wine cellar and one of the very special low-calorie no-fat desserts prepared by our dessert chef, Mary Mulrooney."

He gestured to someone and all the lights went off. There was a moment of surprised silence, then a subdued *aah* of appreciation. The room was beautifully lit by hundreds of flickering candles. A string trio started to play. Champagne corks popped. People moved toward the dessert table.

I was starving. Except for a tartlet and a roulade, I hadn't had anything to eat since that hot dog outside Boise. A dessert or two sounded pretty good. The sugar rush might help me stay awake. I'd had maybe two hours of sleep in the past forty-eight hours and was at that stage of exhaustion when you either collapse or start hallucinating.

Across the foyer, I saw Whitman join Daddy. They looked around, spotted us, and came over. Daddy held out the bow. "I found this stuck on the garage door," he said. "Isn't it part of your dress?"

"Yeah, the propeller." I took the bow and smiled dumbly. Everyone looked at me, as if expecting an explanation. I kept my mouth shut.

Of course the polite dads then had to thank Marcello for saving me from hurtling into a wall earlier in the evening. I was mortified.

"You are her fathers?" Marcello asked. "Both of you?"

"Yes," Whitman said. "John's her real pa, and I'm her faux pa."

"John was the architect here," Marielle said to Marcello.

Marcello nodded. "Yes, I know. We've been in several meetings together. But always by conference call." He took Daddy's hand and pressed it between his own. "A pleasure to meet you at last, John."

"So," Daddy said to him, "what do you think now that you're finally here?"

Marcello scanned the room. "What do I think? Of the building? *Bellissimo.* Tell me, were you at all influenced by Le Corbusier?"

Marcello glanced at me and then, to my horror, walked off arm-in-arm with my father.

Marielle and Whitman exchanged amused glances. "What do you think?" Whitman asked.

"I would have thought older," Marielle said. "Fokke always made him sound like an old man."

"*Molto hunkissimo,*" Whitman said. "Like Rossano Brazzi in *South Pacific.*"

"Alpha investor," Marielle said. "The entire region. Diversifying assets to United States."

"He's not mob, is he?" Whitman asked.

"Who are you talking about?" I asked. As if I didn't know.

Whitman turned me around, lifted my shawl, and tsked as he examined my ripped dress. "A mysterious rich man." He cocked an eyebrow at Marielle. "Gay-issimo?"

"No," I said. "Definitely not gay."

"How do you know?" Whitman asked.

"Radar."

"My gaydar says he's queer. Just molto closeted."

"Not hardly," I said. "The Italian guy? He was looking at Marielle."

"He was looking at *you*," Marielle laughed. "That's why I told him you were married. He's got quite a reputation in Europe."

"Well, it's *my* domestic partner he eloped with." Whitman took the bow and tried to reattach it. "Honestly, sweetheart, how do you manage to ruin every dress you put on? Every dress, since you were eight years old and I took you to Bloomingdale's for the first time."

Marielle brushed something off Whitman's shoulder. "How is it going for you?" She sounded like a concerned wife.

"Fine," Whitman said. "I've been doing my homework. Snooping around. General consensus is that Pine Mountain Lodge is a winner. Perfect alternative to Sun Valley. Investors seem quite happy. But of course there's a big fat fly in the ointment."

Marielle asked what it was.

"Earth Freedom." Whitman let out an incredulous laugh. "Here they are, out in the middle of the most pristine wilderness in North America, in a fantastic health spa meant to reduce stress, and they're worried that some gang of ecoterrorists is somehow going to break through the gates and set fire to the place. That's why everyone was so jittery when the smoke alarm went off in the garage."

"They did set a fire in Rancho Mirage," Marielle reminded him. "On Long Island, too. That place in the Hamptons."

"Being paranoid is part of being rich," Whitman said. "Ask anyone in my family."

"I want to try those desserts," I interrupted. "Then I'm going upstairs."

I didn't care if Whitman and Marielle followed me or not. What I really wanted to do was get Daddy away from Marcello. I'd been watching them. They looked like intimate friends. Marcello emphatically chopped the air with the side of his hand as he talked. Daddy stroked his chin as he listened.

"Daddy," I said, swooping in and tugging at his arm, "why don't you give me a tour of your building?"

"Not now, honey, I'm talking." Out of the side of his mouth he whispered, "May lead to more work."

"I, too, would love a personal tour from the architect," Marcello said.

Daddy brightened, immediately agreeable. "Okay, let's go."

The last thing I wanted was to traipse around with my father *and* Marcello. But, short of telling Marcello to fuck off, I couldn't figure out how to separate them. I shot him a few annoyed glances, but he didn't get the hint. Luckily Marielle and Whitman joined us just then, handing around plates of dessert.

It was deep purplish blue, like my hair color when I was sixteen. There were tiny BB-size berries in it. It was artistically splattered over a crispy crusted pastry with some kind of featherlight lemony cream inside. It was a pretty dessert, but not very well built. When I tried to cut the pastry, cream squished out the sides.

"*Squisito*, eh?" murmured Marcello, looking at me through thick black lashes as he ate.

We were standing there in the vast, candlelit Great Hall, eating our desserts, the string quartet playing, when a pulsing, high-pitched alarm went off.

Everyone jumped. There were groans. People looked at one another. Nobody moved. An annoyed voice said, "What is it *this* time?"

I looked at Daddy. He was turning around in an agitated circle. "That's the lobby-level smoke alarm," he said. Then he smacked his forehead as if something had just occurred to him. "The candles!" he exclaimed. "Blow out all the candles!"

There wasn't time to blow out the candles, because a sudden drenching downpour from the sprinkler system extinguished every last one of them. The giant glass-walled room went dark as a hundred high-pressure sprinklers sprayed water with the force of fire hoses.

People were too shocked to realize what was happening. In an instant everything and everyone was sopping wet. Pastries with purple dessert sauce shot off the plates. Women screamed and threw up their hands to protect their hairdos and faces. China crashed, glasses shattered, silver forks clattered on the flagstone floor.

Marcello shielded his eyes and squinted upward like a sea captain scanning stormy skies. Whitman, his mouth drawn up into a painful-looking grimace, turned in circles as the water shot out in every direction.

Daddy threw down his plate. "Turn on the lights!" he ordered. And when no one did, he hurried off through the gushing torrents to do it himself.

Marielle stood frozen, soaked dress clinging, avant-garde hairdo plastered flat against her skull, shoulders hunched, eyes squeezed tight. She held a plate in one hand and a fork in the other. "I lost my contacts," she cried. "Whitman, where are you?"

People gasped and wailed and shrieked as they held their hands out against the stinging force of the water. It was like being trapped in a giant car wash. I watched as an elegant woman in a tight dress slipped, threw up her hands, and fell to the floor. The musicians, scrambling to keep their priceless instruments dry, pulled open the heavy glass doors and escaped out to the terrace.

In a great surge the entire room followed them. Everyone flowed toward the open terrace doors, like they were being washed out. Whitman grabbed my arm and Marielle's wrist as we began to move forward with the others. The lights outside went off. I heard screams and the splash of bodies falling into the pool.

I tried to shake myself free from Whitman. "I've got to find Tremaynne!" I shouted.

"No!" Whitman held firmly onto my wrist, the way he used to in New York when we were in really crowded places. "Stay close to me!"

I tried to pull away, but when I turned I banged into Marcello.

"Laurie Ann," he said. "Let me help you."

I twirled back to Whitman's side.

It was all dark, drenching pandemonium. The crowd jostled us towards the terrace. A tuxedoed man in front of us slipped and grabbed for the long food table. He got the tablecloth instead, and brought half the candelabras and leftover desserts crashing to the floor. Marielle, her eyes clamped tight, tripped over him and fell in a squealing heap. Whitman and I tried to pull her upright. But the man she'd fallen on desperately grabbed at her dress as if he were going down on the *Titanic*. I heard a ripping noise, then a shriek. Marielle's form-fitting sheath ballooned out as water shot into a long tear down the back.

"Lights!" people called. "What happened to the lights?"

As Whitman and Marcello helped poor Marielle, I made my way back toward the lobby. The water was stingingly cold. My shoes were filled. I kicked them off and carefully made my way up Daddy's staircase. Each wet riser was as slick as cat shit.

By the time I got up to the second-floor landing, the sprinklers had stopped. The lights came on.

I looked down on the wet, dripping wreckage.

Too bad Tremaynne wasn't there to see it, too. I had a feeling he would have enjoyed the sight.

Chapter

13

I knocked first. Called his name. Put my ear to the door and knocked again. Finally dug out my plastic door card, swiped it, and went in.

The room was empty. I knew it the moment I entered.

Dripping and shivering, I made my way to the bathroom and peeled off my soaked dress and underwear. My skin was bright red and covered with prickles. I toweled off my hair, slipped into the thick white robe provided for guests, and made a futile circuit around the room and deck. The water in the stone hot tub steamed invitingly in the chilly night air. A steady rasp of agitated voices rose from the distant terraces. I hardly heard them. They could have been crickets for all I cared.

Where was my husband?

The only piece of luggage Tremaynne owned was his orange backpack. It was gone.

In my mind I played and replayed that glimpse I'd had of someone across the river. I tried to stop-frame the fragment of image, enlarge it, and zoom in. No good. Except for the dot of orange, which could have been Tremaynne's backpack, I hadn't seen enough to verify anything.

But what if he was in danger? Maybe he'd gone out for an inno-
cent hike and that terrorist group had . . .

When the phone rang I jumped for it, certain it was Tremaynne.

"Hello, sweetheart," my mother cooed on the other end. Her
voice was soft and caressing, as if she were talking to a baby. "Am I
interrupting anything? Just tell me if I am, sweetheart, and I'll say
good-bye immediately."

"No, Mom, you're not interrupting anything."

"Are you resting between sets?" she asked in a confidential tone.

"No, Mom, we're having sex while I talk to you."

She started to cough.

"Just kidding."

"Well, sweetheart, I just wanted to find out if everything's all
right," Carolee said. "The trip out there was uneventful, I take it?"

"Yeah, except for the elk that charged me, the restaurant that
wouldn't serve us, and the dead bear on top of a truck, it was completely uneventful."

"That sounds lovely, sweetheart."

She wanted to know if the room was pretty. Then she wanted me
to describe the furnishings and the setting and the lodge in general.
She sighed like she was having a little masturbatory orgasm when I
told her that a chilled bottle of wine and a huge basket of fruit were
waiting for us when we arrived.

"Any chocolates?" she asked. "I read that the most expensive
places leave little boxes of chocolates on your pillow or bedside
table."

"It's a health spa, Mom. No candy except what you smuggle in
yourself. Everything's low-fat and low-cal."

"What are the other guests like?" she wanted to know.

"Skinny and rich," I said, then gave her a thrill by dropping the
name of the movie star I'd seen.

"Tru Brant," mom gasped as I described my nonencounter. She
hadn't been so excited since I called her once from New York, when
I was twelve, to tell her I'd spotted Tony Randall eating a pastrami
sandwich in a deli on 57th Street. "Oh my Lord. Tru Brant. And you

didn't get in the elevator with him? You didn't ask him to bite his name into your arm?"

"The people here are way cool, Mom. They don't act that way."

She was hungry for more crumbs from the tables of the rich and famous. And it was up to me to throw them to her.

"Susan Sarandon!" she gasped when I told her who Daddy had seen. "Get her autograph," she pleaded. "Please, Venus. She's my favorite movie star after Bette Davis."

"Then Jane Bugler sang," I went on.

"Who's Jane Bugler?"

"Oh, you wouldn't know her," I said grandly. "She's a world-famous opera singer friend of Marielle and Fokke. The greatest Norma of her generation."

"Norma who?" Mom asked.

I didn't know either, so I ignored the question. "Fokke flew her over from Italy or someplace, just to sing," I said.

"Then you *know* she went first-class," Carolee said with certainty. "Not Business. First. She probably demanded it." She paused and regrouped. "So Marielle and Fucker are there with you?"

"It's Fah-kuh, Mom. That's how they pronounce it in Dutch."

"Whatever. You've mentioned them before. Friends of the dads."

"Millionaires. At least." I paused for effect. "Marielle's in love with Whitman."

"Oh?" It took her a moment to digest this juicy tidbit. "Does your father know?"

"I doubt it."

"Does Fucker know?"

"I doubt it."

"Is Whitman in love with Marielle?"

"I doubt it."

Carolee was silent for a moment. "Well, Whitman's a very handsome and personable man," she said generously of the person who'd stolen her husband. "I can see why a woman would fall in love with him."

I did the dutiful daughter routine and asked her how she was.

She prefaced her reply with a few deep coughs. "Well, I'm afraid I overdid it today and had a relapse. I cleaned up after your wedding party, and all the cigarette butts aggravated my sinuses. Then I started coughing." She honked a few more times to let me know how serious it was. "I felt terrible, but I forced myself to go out to my ecstatic dancing class. I told you about that, didn't I?"

"Yes," I lied, afraid to hear.

"It's a method of unleashing your inner ecstasy. Repetitive movements. Twirling, clapping. Sometimes we swoon."

"You don't wear your clown suit, do you?"

"You wear whatever makes you feel loose and free. I wear jeans and long white veils. Anyway, it's a huge class, about a hundred—"

"Mom, Tremaynne's waiting. I gotta go. "

"Oh!" She instantly reined in her impending story. "Well, sweetheart, it sounds like you're having a fabulous time on your honeymoon, in your beautiful suite with movie stars everywhere you turn."

"Mm-hm."

"You must be so glad you let the dads talk you into it."

"Mm-hm."

"Is Tremaynne having a good time?"

"I hope so."

"Well, give him my love, and kisses to the dads, and bring me a little bar of guest soap if you think of it."

I decided I was to blame for Tremaynne's disappearance. As I soaked in a hot lavender and sage bubble bath, and washed my hair with essence of green tea, I went through a list of all the things I must have done wrong.

√ When my husband wanted to take me away from all this meaningless glamour and go out to camp in the woods, I'd said no.
√ When he wanted to have sex, I'd said no.
√ I'd pestered him about those mysterious phone calls.
√ I'd voiced a suspicion that he was part of an ecoterrorist gang.

√ I'd annoyed him by wanting to take his made-up last name. Some of my unwifely sins Tremaynne didn't even know about:
√ I'd secretly eaten meat.
√ I'd wondered if he was gay when I saw him swimming naked with a hard-on with the dads.

The more I thought about it, the more furious I became. What a disappointment I'd been. Small wonder he'd taken off without me. I'd doubted and denied him, even listened to jokes at his expense. Was that what a wife was supposed to do on her honeymoon?

I'd probably looked repulsed and horrified when he told me he had venereal herpes. That wasn't very understanding of me. If he did have herpes, I was probably infected already, so what difference would it make if he wore a condom or not?

I should have fucked him on the spot.

I vowed that when he came back, I would make it all up to him. I'd go where he wanted to go and do what he wanted to do. I'd have sex at any time and in any position he wanted.

I could *not* let this marriage fail. As in baseball, so in marriage: Three strikes and you're out.

It was important, as usual, to hide my fears, confusion, and disappointment from the dads. I was in no mood for "We told you so."

Squatting down on top of a mirror, I examined myself for telltale signs of herpes, then pulled on the scratchy Patty Cakes' Baby Doll nightie with feather trim. The gauzy part was made out of some stiff synthetic material that wouldn't soften to the contours of my body. It stuck out like a pleated lampshade.

The peek-a-boo negligee brought back memories of being a lingerie model. Being half-naked and teasing a roomful of men. It occurred to me that those were the only times in my life when I felt powerful. Like I was in control. Seeing the deep hunger in men's eyes, complying with their secret sexual fantasies, that was life at its rawest and most real. No social etiquette was involved. No involvement of any kind was involved. They paid to fantasize about my nearly naked body; it was that simple.

As I sat there in bed, propped up on feather pillows, waiting for Tremaynne, I considered Marcello's offer. A thousand bucks to look at my breasts. Why not do it, right now, before Tremaynne got back? A thousand quick, tax-free dollars. One flash of my melon patch would cover two months rent and pay for a new carburetor.

No.

I couldn't.

I mustn't.

Not on my honeymoon.

It was too low.

I had a husband to think of.

Any moment now, I thought, he'll walk through that door. He'll see me waiting for him. I teased my body into a purring state of arousal. I imagined Tremaynne's busy hands all over me. His lips kissing me everywhere. Being compliant to his every wish. The hot steaminess of shared breaths, of naked flesh against naked flesh.

The minutes dragged on. I felt like I was going crazy. I was totally exhausted yet slithery with sexual energy. And my addictions were kicking in big time with no hope of release. I couldn't smoke in the room and I was afraid to smoke out on the deck for fear of triggering some new alarm. I was too restless to just lie there so I got out of bed and paced around the room. I opened the wine and drank it pretty fast. There was nothing with sugar or salt to eat, so I tore open and devoured all the low-cal fat-free snacks. Stuff I'd never heard of: organic rice cakes, dried seaweed chips, saltless wheatless eggless crackers. It was like eating air. None of it filled me up. I craved chocolate candy bars with gooey caramel fillings, hamburgers dripping with cheese, greasy french fries, giant glazed doughnuts.

And nicotine. That craving no nonsmoker can ever understand. That horrible sensation that you're going to jump out of your skin if you don't light up real soon.

Miserable, I crawled back into our giant queen-size bed, between the soft Egyptian cotton sheets, careful not to rip or injure my nightie. After ten minutes of twitching, scratching, and staring at the clock, I got out again.

I ended up spending the first night of my honeymoon with Tru Brant, the movie star, instead of Tremaynne Woods, my husband. *My Place or Yours*, one of Tru Brant's latest romantic-comedy hits, was available on the entertainment system.

It was really bad.

The sound woke me up. Sharp ticks on the big glass windows. Bits of tossed gravel.

My romantic instincts flared up immediately. Who else if not Tremaynne? He must have gotten locked out or lost his door card. My nightmare was over. Relief turned my heart giddy with desire.

I dashed excitedly out to the deck. It was like plunging into a dark unheated pool. The mountain air was sharp and stunningly cold. My nipples stiffened; the soles of my feet danced on the dew-slick flagstones. I could see my breath.

At first I just ran along the balcony railing, back and forth, like an excited animal in a cage, smiling dumbly and peering down into the darkness. Below me was an open meadow and a giant stand of trees. Beyond the trees I could hear the impatient rush of the river.

It took my urbanized senses a minute to remember that this wasn't a Portland park ringed with houses. Wilderness spread out for hundreds of miles around me. The vast black sky was smeared with stars, so many and so clear that it made me dizzy to look at them.

I leaned over the balcony, my tits hanging down like the water balloons I used to drop on cars from freeway bridges, and quoted the only Shakespeare I could remember: "Romeo, Romeo, whenceforth art thou, Romeo?"

From deep within the trees I heard what sounded like a suppressed giggly laugh. I couldn't be sure. As I now knew, animals made all kinds of weird noises.

"Tremaynne?" I stage-whispered.

Silence. I heard a rustle. From far back in the darkness of the trees a low urgent voice whispered: "Come down."

It had to be Tremaynne.

"I'll be right there," I called softly.

* * *

There were fire doors off the corridor, but if I used them to get outside I'd set off alarms and create another panic. So I decided to leave by the front door of the lodge and from there make my way around back, to where our suites were located at the end of a wing.

For this secret tryst it was important to look romantic and unforgettable. I wanted Tremaynne to see me and think he'd never seen anyone so soft, beautiful, and alluring in his entire life. I wanted to stir his poetic and protective instincts.

So I wore my long, crushed-velvet dress the color of midnight. Face hidden in the shadowy confines of its soft, cowl-like hood, I hurried along the dark stone corridors. A mysterious woman, in love.

A cleaning crew was busy downstairs. It looked like every employee in the lodge had been pressed into service under Commander Geof Killingsworth. All the furniture had been cleared out of the Great Hall. Guys perched on enormous ladders were busy squeegeeing all the interior glass and wiping dry all the wood finishes. The glass doors were open and a broom brigade methodically swept water out onto the terraces. Enormous fans were blowing to dry the place out.

I took the elevator down and hurried toward the lobby doors. I don't know why I felt like I was doing something sneaky. I was a guest. I could do any damn thing I wanted.

In my long velvet gown, I felt like a princess. What was this velvet-clad princess doing? Escaping from a castle? No, running to meet her lover. I lifted the hem of my gown as I made a swift, graceful descent down the broad flagstone entrance stairs and along the path in front of the lodge. I stopped for a moment to light a Marlboro, then excitedly rushed on to my mysterious assignation.

It was very late or very early, depending on how you looked at it. The hour before dawn, that crossroads hour when magic drifts through the air like pollen and extraordinary things happen to ordinary people. At the end of this adventure, I would find sanctuary in the strong, loving arms of my prince. I could rejoice in his body and my own.

A warning flashed through my thoughts, interrupting the flow of the fantasy. Something about birth control. I waved it aside. I didn't want warnings. I didn't want caution. I wanted life served steaming hot and beautiful.

As the princess rushed to meet her secret lover, I mentally wrote, *her full, eager breasts strained against the bodice of her tight velvet gown.*

Behind darkened windows the thin rich people slumbered and dreamed of suing the hotel for damages or trauma. Outside, it was nothing but stars and trees and a vast yearning silence. Living in the city, I'd never heard the kind of immense natural quiet that engulfed me now.

Behind the building it was darker still. One narrow path threaded across the meadow and through the giant trees to the river. Shadows were heaped upon shadows. The river sang its urgent rushing tune.

More and more space opened up around me as my eyes adjusted to the dark. True wilderness began just a few hundred yards from where I stood. It was so mysterious, quiet but deeply alive, a huge, breathing, completely unknown world.

I stopped in the middle of the meadow, expecting Tremaynne to emerge from the trees and claim me. I was all his. My heart was beating fast. I knew he could see me. I didn't want to speak. I didn't want to call his name. I was there. I was his. That was enough.

A shape appeared from the pool of nocturnal shadow and slowly approached me.

It was not Tremaynne.

Unless my husband had been transformed into an enormous white horse.

For that's what approached me in the star-spangled darkness. A giant white horse led by Kristin, the girl who'd mistaken me for Godiva.

She smiled and put a finger to her lips. Then she brought the giant creature right up next to me.

I moved away, skittish of its massive weight, its animal unknowability. The horse shook its head and snuffled, silvery vapor shooting from its nostrils.

I just stood there, staring in surprise. I didn't know what to say.

Kristin held out the reins. "Your horse, oh my queen," she whispered.

"I don't have a horse," I whispered back.

"The one you ride naked," she said. "In the video."

"Oh. That."

Kristin kept her voice low. "That song you sang about naked passions? I could have written that song."

"Listen," I said, finally coming to my senses, "did you see anyone else down there? In the trees?"

"There wasn't anyone else. Just me and him."

"Him who?"

"Him the horse. Chiron. I snuck him out of the stable. We've been waiting for you."

She was a fan so I tried not to sound disappointed. "Why?"

"Well, *look* at him." She stroked Chiron's shoulder. "He's the strongest, handsomest horse in the West."

I looked, still wary. Chiron was beautiful, I had to admit. He was perfect, like an illustration in a fairytale. A thick golden mane fell across his strong white neck. The silvery-gold cascade of his tail was so long that it swept the ground. The horse looked rare, noble, and incredibly strong.

"I thought you might like to ride him," Kristin said. "Like you do in the video."

"That was just a video," I said.

"It changed my life," Kristin said solemnly.

"It did?" I felt a thrill of pride but didn't know what for.

"You made me realize. *Finally.*"

"Realize what?"

"Who I am," she whispered, eyes shining, voice husky with emotion. "What I am." She stepped closer.

Her intensity was pretty intense. She looked vulnerable and predatory at the same time. I knew I could have her if I wanted to. I could induct her into the sisterhood right then and there. I wasn't totally unresponsive: Her need brought out my own. She wanted comfort, and so did I.

But she looked so young.

And I was married.

"They'd fire me if they knew what I did," Kristin confessed. "This is, like, the most expensive horse in the world. Andalusian. Mr. Brunelli just bought it."

"Marcello Brunelli?"

"He's going to breed it. So if anything ever happened to this horse—"

"Well, thanks for showing it to me."

"You don't want to ride him?" She sounded incredulous, as if she couldn't believe I would refuse her extraordinary offer.

I smiled meaninglessly.

"How about just sit on him for a minute? I wouldn't dare, but you—well, it's kind of like he belongs to you." She stared at me with that disconcerting blend of hope and hunger. "And I'd never forget it."

"It doesn't have a saddle," I said.

"Mr. Brunelli keeps the saddle in his cabin."

"Where's that?"

"His cabin? Way out in the woods. On the river. It's huge. A palace. But you don't need a saddle with this horse," Kristin insisted. "I'll help you up. I'll lead you around the meadow. Very slow. Like a queen. Like in the video."

"I can't sit on a horse wearing this dress," I protested.

"Sideways!" she said eagerly. "I'll help you. I used to raise horses. You don't have to be afraid."

I eyed the massive white creature looming above her. Chiron eyed me. I didn't know if it was me or Godiva who finally gave the fatal nod.

*   *   *

I used to dream about horses when I was a girl, but I'd never been on one in my life.

Chiron seemed perfectly docile when Kristin helped me up, but then nodded his head and stepped back and forth like he was having second thoughts.

"He's just getting used to your weight," Kristin reassured me. "Whoa, boy."

"What am I supposed to hold onto?"

"Just balance yourself so you don't fall. You have to turn more sideways, almost like you're riding sidesaddle."

How the hell did those women do it, I wondered. How did they manage to look poised and beautiful while corkscrewed sideways wearing heavy riding habits and hats with veils?

"Go really slow," I said when I was settled on the horse's broad white back.

"Here," Kristin said, "take the reins."

It was like being handed the keys to a powerful new car. "Stay close," I ordered.

"Don't worry. I'm right here." She made a clucking sound and softly patted Chiron's rump, then my thigh.

We started off. It was more about trusting myself, and my sense of balance, than it was about trusting the horse. My confidence grew as we slowly made our way across the meadow.

Kristin gazed up at me with rapturous eyes, like a besotted valet accompanying a queen. I straightened my back and tried to look noble. Queen Godiva on horseback in the River of No Return Wilderness Area.

"This is like my dream come true," Kristin said. "I don't want to wake up."

I respected her fantasy and didn't object when she pulled out a small camera and begged for a few snaps. I did my best to look memorable, smiling with my mouth shut.

"Oh, Godiva. I'd do anything for you." Kristin laid her head against my thigh, then began to kiss and caress it.

To keep her, or me, from going any further, I flicked the reins. Kristin looked up at me, her eyes drowning with desire, as Chiron strode deeper into the trees and toward the river. The air was cold and sweet on my face and hands, but the heat emanating from the animal warmed me. Veils of silvery mist swirled along the surface of the river and trailed up its banks. The horizon blushed pink and a pale light seeped into the sky. A bird began to call out a sequence of tender liquid notes.

"He must be thirsty," Kristin said as Chiron moved steadily toward the river. His hooves crunched on the pebbly rocks heaped along the shore. I stiffened as he splashed into the water and lowered his head to drink.

"Get me back on land," I said.

"Pull back on the reins," Kristin said from the bank.

The moment I did so, the horse gave its head an obstinate shake and stepped deeper into the rushing current. The water was fast but still pretty shallow along the shore. A few feet farther out it was so deep I couldn't see the bottom. It looked like maybe there was a sudden drop-off.

"Pull his tail or something," I called to Kristin.

"No, you have to rein him back," she said. "Get his head up and turn him back around."

I pulled on the reins. Chiron resisted. I gave a sharp tug. That seemed to piss him off. He let out an annoyed snuffle, shook his head, and plunged another few steps into the river. His long golden tail swished up a spray of cold water.

My perch suddenly felt extremely precarious. The rushing sound of the river filled my ears. I could feel the force of the current. If I looked down, all I saw was a dizzying sheet of moving water brightly freckled with morning light. I didn't want to freak and do anything to further annoy the horse, but I was starting to feel prickles of panic.

"Help me," I called to Kristin. "Do something."

"I'm coming out there." Kristin tugged off her boots and jeans. She was wearing boy's underpants. Her legs were strong and shapely. She let out a gasp as she waded into the river. "It's freez-ing!" She lost her balance but caught herself before toppling back-wards. "The rocks are really slippery!"

The horse looked at her with its big black eyes.

"Come on, boy," Kristin coaxed. Chiron ignored her. He turned to stare at the far bank. "Throw me the reins," Kristin said, hobbling closer.

I was afraid I'd slip off Chiron's back if I made one hasty move. So when I tossed the reins it wasn't far enough, and Kristin wasn't able to catch them. The current took the leather straps and carried them downstream.

Chiron shifted uneasily. He let out a soft whinny and stretched his long white neck.

As I leaned forward to retrieve the reins, he took another step for-ward. The pebbly rocks gave way under his weight. I let out a squawk of terror as he started to slide down into the water. Sensing the danger, he tried to back up and regain solid footing.

"Come on, boy, come on, come on," Kristin pleaded.

I scrunched forward, clinging to his neck. Beneath me I could feel the giant muscles and machinery of his flesh working to regain his balance.

"Venus!"

Just as the horse was wheeling around I heard someone shout my name from the opposite shore. It took a second before I dared to turn my head and look in the direction of the shout.

I couldn't see anyone. But I knew it was Tremaynne.

I was certain of it.

The minute Kristin was able to grab Chiron's reins and lead the horse onto dry land, I jumped off and scanned the far side of the river. "Tremaynne!" I called, cupping my hands like a bullhorn.

"Shhh!" A wet, shivering Kristin tied Chiron to a tree and scram-bled to get her pants back on. "Please! If anyone hears you—"

"Tremaynne!" I called.

"They'll hear you and come down to investigate. Security will."

"Where are you?" I yelled.

"Please. Shhh. If they find out I took the horse . . . *Please.*"

Her panic finally registered with me. "Is there any way to get across this river?" I asked.

"Canoe," she said, staring at me with a mixture of fear and longing as she jammed her feet into socks and boots.

"Do you know how to canoe?"

She nodded. "But I gotta go. Gotta get him back. Gotta dry him off."

"You said you'd do anything for me."

"I'm a coward," she cried. "I'm not like you. My naked passions won't ever become real."

I stared at her, dumbfounded. "Sure they will."

I reached out to stroke her hair, but she pulled away and refused to meet my eyes. "If he's not back when the stable opens . . . It's almost morning . . . Security."

She untied Chiron and quickly led him away.

Chapter

14

Daddy was standing in the lobby, staring moodily at his model of the lodge, when I walked in. He looked at me like I was a ghost come back from the dead.

"Venus. Honey. Are you all right?"

I wasn't, but I nodded.

"Where've you been?" He glanced at his watch.

"Went out to have a smoke."

He smiled in amused disbelief. "You can smoke on the balcony of your room, silly."

"I was afraid I might accidentally set off an alarm."

"That was very considerate of you." He put an arm around my shoulder and kissed my cheek. "All these alarms and detectors and sensors and monitors. They're a complete pain in the ass."

"Did the sprinklers go off because of the candles?" I asked.

"Probably. The smoke detector wasn't properly calibrated."

"Could have been worse, Daddy."

"I'm not so sure," he sighed. "Of course they want to blame me, but it's the manufacturer who's at fault. And the installer." He scratched his jaw, fingernails rasping on the stubble, then nervously turned back to his model, like a bird protecting its nest. "Everyone demands heightened security systems. But if they don't know how to properly install or operate them, what good are they?"

"It was an adventure, Daddy. Nobody got hurt. It'll give them something to talk about."

"That's what the management's worried about." He spied a smudge on the Plexiglas covering his model and rubbed it with his shirt sleeve.

It was one of the few times in my life that I'd seen him unshaven, his face covered with the dark sexy shadow of a beard. He hadn't been to bed at all, he said. After the "sprinkler event," Geof Killingsworth asked Daddy if he'd accompany him on a complete inspection of the hotel to make sure there was no additional water damage. Then Daddy had voluntarily helped to coordinate the cleanup effort. He wanted to make sure that the staff didn't use any abrasive solvents or tools that might damage the fresh new surfaces of his building. Daddy couldn't bear it when people moved into his buildings and didn't take care of them properly.

Now, at 5:30 A.M., he was waiting for Geof Killingsworth again. This time Geof needed his help to deactivate the computerized smoke alarm and sprinkler systems. Lumina International, the company that owned and managed Pine Mountain Lodge, didn't want to risk any more unpleasant surprises that might make their rich and famous guests bolt and spread horror stories to the media. From a public relations standpoint, this gala opening was crucial. So the highest-ups had decided to switch off the fire systems until they could get the installer back to recalibrate.

"It hasn't been much of a honeymoon for you," I said sympathetically, clasping Daddy around the waist from behind, the way I used to when I was a little girl and wanted to keep him from going off to work.

"Things happen," he said, stroking my cold hands. His hands were big and warm and calming. "Whitman understands."

I put my cheek against his back, like a papoose. "I wish I did."

"What?" He stroked my arms.

"Understand."

"Understand what, baby?"

"Why things happen the way they do." It was puzzling to me. "I mean, do we make things happen to ourselves? Or do they just happen, and there's nothing we can do about it?"

"Both," Daddy said.

"So how's a person supposed to know what to do?" I asked.

"Depends on the person and the situation," he answered.

"Okay, let's say someone's missing. *Maybe.* You aren't sure. I mean they could be missing, or they could just be pissed off at you and staying away."

"Who is it?" Daddy asked. "Child, lover, husband, parent, who?"

"Let's say husband."

"Tremaynne?"

I pulled away from him, trying to hide a sudden squall of weepiness. "Let's say my husband is missing. *Maybe.* Let's say I can't be sure."

Daddy smiled and took me in his arms again. His breath smelled of coffee. "You'd have to be a pretty careless wife to lose your husband on your honeymoon."

It came out before I could stop it. "That's when Mom lost you, wasn't it?"

Daddy let go of me and stepped back with a cool, disapproving look. "What's that supposed to mean?"

"Well, you didn't want to have sex with her, did you?"

"Yes," he said, "I did."

"But you didn't. Or couldn't."

He frowned at me.

"So that's when she knew she'd lost you. Women know when they're not wanted."

"Venus," Daddy said, "what's this about? Whatever it is, it's not about your mother and me."

I turned away and sucked in a ragged breath as my eyes filled with tears. I could barely choke out the words, but it was a question that I really needed to ask. "How do you know when someone loves you? How do you know that?"

My sudden burst of weepy emotion drew a look of bewildered concern. "I suppose you can tell from the way a person behaves toward you," Daddy offered.

I sniffed and cleared my throat.

"Venus?" He lifted my chin and made me look at him. "Do you want to tell me what's wrong? You haven't looked happy once on this trip."

I wanted to tell him. Oh man, I wanted to scream out my frustration and doubts and worries. But I couldn't bear to admit, even to myself, that I was a loser in the sweepstakes of love. I wanted my life to be fun and glamorously romantic, the way Daddy's life was with Whitman. And what was it, so far, my life? One big messy mistake after another.

"Sorry, Daddy. It's nothing." I blew out a deep Buddha breath, the way Whitman had taught me years ago when I was painfully constipated and needed enemas all the time. "I'm just really tired."

Daddy kissed me again, this time on the lips. "This is your honeymoon, baby. It's supposed to be fun. Unforgettable."

I nodded. "Well, so far it's been pretty unforgettable."

Daddy suddenly looked amused, like he was keeping a funny secret to himself. "What do you think of Geof Killingsworth?" he asked.

I shrugged. "Really handsome and really tight-assed. Why?"

Daddy looked at me, then away, like he was embarrassed. "He made a pass at me."

"Oh my god. When?"

Daddy didn't seem to hear me. "I was stunned. No one's made a pass at me in twenty years."

His naïveté was mind-boggling. "Daddy, people make passes at you all the time. Men *and* woman. You just don't see them. It doesn't register. Because you're always so tuned in to Whitman."

"This one registered," he said.

"Well? What happened?"

"Swear you won't tell Whitman Whittlesley the Fourth?"

I raised my hand for the solemn oath. "I swear."

Daddy thrust his hands in his pockets and began to jingle his change. "Well, we were going around the building and suddenly he just stopped. We were standing in a hallway. Right about here." He tapped on the Plexiglas, above a wing of the lodge. "He just stopped and turned around to face me. And he said, 'John Gilroy, you are the hottest man I've ever known. I'd do anything to have a lover like you.'"

"Wow." My pulse was racing. "What did you say?"

"Nothing. I was too embarrassed."

"So what happened?"

Daddy scratched his chin again. "Well, I just sort of nodded and said thanks. And he nodded and we started off again."

"And now you're going off with him again?" I couldn't help thinking that maybe Daddy was secretly attracted to Geof Killingsworth. If he was, it was the first time his attention had ever strayed from Whitman—at least that I knew about. Maybe the dads weren't as happy as they seemed.

"John?"

We both turned. There was Geof Killingsworth hurrying down Daddy's signature staircase. He was graceful as a dancer and carried what looked like a thick manual.

My presence hardly registered with the manager of Pine Mountain Lodge. He couldn't peel his eyes away from Daddy. "I think between us we can figure out how to disengage the system," he said.

"We can give it a try," Daddy agreed.

"I really appreciate all your time, John. There's no one else around who's smart enough to help me with all this."

Daddy thrust his hands back into his pockets and jingled some more change, rocking back and forth on his heels. "You don't want the system turned off for more than a day or two," he said. "In case there's a real fire."

"I know," Geof said. "But we can't afford to have another sprinkler event." He turned to me with a big disarming smile. "You're not going to write about that in *Travel,* are you?"

I shook my head.

"It's the sort of glitch that can happen with any new computerized security system." Geof Killingsworth looked at my dad again. "Okay, John, should we go?"

Daddy nodded and the two of them hurried off, heads together, discussing the sprinkler system.

Or were they?

When I got back to my suite I fell onto the bed and wept until my eyes burned. But crying didn't provide any relief.

I had to *do* something.

But what?

I couldn't just sit back and passively wait for Tremaynne's return. I had to get across that goddamned river and find him. Without letting the dads or anyone else know what I was doing.

I had to let him know that I loved him. That I wanted him back. That I'd do whatever he wanted.

So how?

That cold, swift river scared me.

And so did the realization that my brand-new husband, still under warranty, had up and left me without so much as a word of explanation.

I hated him for that.

Between bouts of sobbing I looked up and saw that the telephone message light was blinking. My heart leapt. Then crashed when I didn't hear Tremaynne's voice.

"Venus, this is Whitman. I don't want to disturb you so I'm leaving this message without having the phone ring. Listen, I think you've still got my cell phone. I gave it to you yesterday when we were driving here. In Hell's Canyon. At least that's what I remember. Anyway, sweetheart, I can't find it anywhere and I've got a lot of important numbers and things programmed into it. So please be a darling and bring it over to our room when you're up and about. Just leave it on top of my briefcase if I'm not here. Looks like both your dads are going to be busy all day. But sometime later this afternoon we're going to sneak away and try to find that secret hot springs my source told me about. We'll need the four-wheel drive, so leave the keys on my briefcase with the cell phone. Okay, darling, that's it. Bye-bye. I hope you're enjoying your honeymoon. Everything's free, so take advantage of all the spa services."

Whitman's cell phone. I ransacked my purse and luggage to make sure it wasn't there. Then I sat on the edge of the bed, panting and chewing my lips.

I'd given the phone to Tremaynne. He'd made that first call on it. He'd never given it back to me. He still had it.

I picked up the room phone and dialed Whitman's cell number.

It rang four times, then I got a message that the call was being forwarded to a voice messaging system. Whitman's voice came on, asking callers to leave a message. I hung up. Then redialed. Again it rang four times before clicking over to the message.

I did this for an hour. I figured if Tremaynne had the phone he'd eventually answer it. If your cell phone rang steadily for an hour wouldn't you assume someone needed to talk to you really bad?

But maybe Tremaynne didn't have the phone. Maybe he'd lost it or someone had stolen it or he'd turned it off. It was my responsibility to find out. Otherwise, Whitman might find himself with a ten-thousand dollar phone bill and it would be my fault because I was the one who handed the phone over to Tremaynne in the first place.

Finally it happened. Someone answered.

But nothing was said.

I thought I could hear birds chirping and maybe a distant voice on the other end.

My heart started to hammer. I walked out to the balcony. "Tremaynne? Can you hear me? It's Venus."

"Yeah," he finally whispered. His voice sounded frightened.

"Where are you?"

"Hot springs."

"When are you coming back?"

"Can't. Big fuck-up."

"What're you talking about."

"Can't talk!" he hissed.

"Are you hurt?" Silence. "Tremaynne, are you hurt? What's the matter?"

"Don't tell anyone where I am."

"Are you okay?"

Silence.

"I'm coming to get you," I said.

"Hurry!" he said.

The phone went dead.

I didn't have any practical outdoor clothes with me. The lodge boutique sold expensive "casual wear," but I didn't have enough cash to buy anything and all my credit cards had been revoked. Besides, the boutique didn't open until ten o'clock.

I called the switchboard and asked to be connected to Marielle and Fokke Van der Zout. I prayed Marielle would answer.

She did, but obviously I awakened her from a deep sleep. It took her a moment to register who I was and what I wanted. She told me the room number and said, "Come over."

I had a quick morning wake-up smoke out on the balcony, tossed the butt into the hot tub, and moved into action. I was completely focused on what I had to do. There was no time for hesitation or procrastination.

Tremaynne was in danger. I was sure of it.

I had to rescue him.

As I hurried down the corridors, the lodge was coming to life. A hand reached out from one of the rooms and snatched up the *New York Times* lying in front of the door. Room service was busy delivering breakfast. Service carts laden with fresh sheets and towels and rolls of toilet paper appeared in the hallways.

Marielle opened the door. I almost gasped when I saw her. I had no idea how much work went into how she looked.

She'd pulled on a long purple silk kimono. Above it, her scrubbed face looked as shiny as a waxed apple. Her skin was blotchy, her eyes puffy, and she didn't seem to have any eyelashes. She fussed self-consciously with her stiff tufts of hair, trying to smooth them down. "Come in, Venus," she murmured politely, still half-asleep, unable to stifle a yawn.

"Marielle! Call down for some coffee!" Fokke shouted from the bedroom. He stared at me as I entered, looking me up and down. He was sitting in bed, naked, with the sheet pulled up to his waist, pointing a remote wand at the television. He looked like a chubby little boy with soft hairy tits. "Been up all night, party girl?"

I nodded.

"Marielle," he called again, turning back to CNN, "did you hear me?"

"Ya, I heard you," she grumbled. "I have to pee first."

"Call down for some coffee. And rolls. While you're pissing. See if they have those fig and anise rolls. And some good Gouda cheese."

Marielle obeyed. It was the first time I heard someone peeing and ordering breakfast at the same time. While she was on the phone, I stood as still as a statue, surveying their hotel living habits. The room was messy. Wineglasses and an empty bottle. Plates with orange peels and banana skins. Newspapers, magazines, and thick hardcover books scattered about. Towels thrown outside next to the hot tub. Fokke's laptop open, with a stack of documents beside it.

But the bed had a warm, mussed, slept-in look that made my heart ache.

"No fig and anise rolls," Marielle reported from the bathroom. "How about spelt and raisin?"

"Ya, okay." Fokke's attention was riveted on a news story about a group of anarchists clashing with police at some economic conference in Brussels. He laughed excitedly and shook his head in disbelief. "Idiots! How can anyone be an anarchist in this day and age?" He shot me a glance and shifted on the bed so that the sheet fell down to just above his dick. "Tell me, Venus. What kind of world would it be if anarchists were in charge? Hey? Hey?"

"I hate politics," I said.

"I'll tell you what kind of world," he said. "One no one wants to live in! Ya! Because if everyting's anarchy, dere-dere-dere's no system but a non-system. And people need systems to live by. Hey?"

"I guess so."

"Your generation just wants to have a good party, right? Make love and have orgasms all over the place."

"Yeah, that's all we want."

The toilet flushed and the bathroom door opened. Marielle motioned me in. Through another door, which she had to unlock with her room card, there was a large, private dressing room. The first thing I saw was her yellow diamonds, laid out in a long box with a black velvet lining.

Marielle yawned again. "Ya. So. What do you need? You can have anything except my diamonds."

Funny how you never really know what you're capable of, or who your friends are, until there's a crisis.

Marielle, it turned out, was a friend.

Wearing her blue jeans, a little tight in the rump and thighs, and her wilderness hiking boots, about a size too large, and a thick knitted wool sweater, shaped to her ample breasts, and an all-weather jacket, I clomped down to the reception desk.

"Good morning!" It was Mike, the same red-haired desk clerk who'd checked us in. His smile looked completely fake. "How can I help you this morning?"

"I'm told you sell maps down here. Really detailed maps that show logging roads and hiking trails and stuff like that."

He pulled a map out and said, "Eight ninety-five. It's the most detailed map you'll find."

I smiled and moved closer. "I'm not very good at reading maps. I wonder if you could help me with it."

"I can try," he said, trying not to stare at my tits.

"Someone told me there's a wonderful hot springs. Somewhere out in the woods."

"Devil's Spring?"

"Yeah, I think that's it. Sort of a secret place."

Mike looked down at the map. "Lumina International says we're not supposed to give directions to Devil's Spring. Forest Service, too. People have gotten lost trying to find it."

"Okay," I said calmly. "I understand. But just tell me, is Devil's Spring marked on this map?"

"Yes, ma'am," he said.

I laughed, trying to put him at his ease and turn him on. It was awfully early in the morning to be seducing someone, but I had a job to do.

"Ma'am?" I said, leaning closer to him over the counter. "Come on, Mike. Do I really look like a ma'am?"

"No, ma'am," he said, his eyes darting around the lobby to see if anyone was looking.

"Don't you know who I am?" I asked.

"You're John Gilroy's daughter," he whispered. "You work for *Travel* magazine."

"That's just a front," I whispered back. "Don't you know who I really am?"

"No," he gulped, "who?"

"Godiva."

"Really? Honest to God?" His eyes were round as saucers.

"I have to protect my identity." I let out a little conspiratorial titter. "Those men I came with? They're just friends. Helping me out. So I can have a little vacation."

"Oh," he said.

Finally I was able to lean far enough across to actually touch his hand with my right breast. "Couldn't you just show me on the map about where it is? Devil's Spring. Without actually telling me?"

He straightened up, unfolded the map, turned it, peered at it, pointed.

I studied the map, staying close to him. "Looks like the best way to go is up the river here, and then follow this dotted line."

"That's an old logging road," he said.

"Is this a bridge across the river?" I asked.

"Very primitive. A single log with guide ropes. The smoke jumpers use it for training exercises."

He confirmed my fear that the log was the only way to get across the river for several miles. There was one route you could take with a four-wheel drive vehicle. I couldn't do that because Tremaynne still had Whitman's car keys, and I didn't want to ask Daddy for his set. The other option was to canoe across. Pine Mountain Lodge rented canoes, but beginners weren't allowed to go out alone because of the whitewater rapids.

"Looks like it'll have to be the log," I said.

"Ma'am," he whispered nervously, "you have to be really careful if you go up there."

"Why?"

"Bears. Maybe even grizzly. This is their foraging season."

"Okay, I'll be careful."

"If you run into a bear, you know what to do?"

I licked my parched lips. "Scream?"

"No. Talk soft. Move slow. Avoid eye contact because they see that as aggression. And pray that it runs away. It will unless it's got cubs, or it's a male establishing territory."

"Do you sell guns?" I whispered.

"No, ma'am, and I wish we did. I'd feel a lot better about you going to Devil's Spring if I knew you had a gun with you. You've got to be careful up there. They say there's—" He popped up like a jack-in-the-box as a guest came over to ask when the spa opened.

Then he turned back to me, getting as cozy as he dared. I didn't flinch when the side of his arm brushed against my breasts. The information he had was too valuable.

"They say there's what?" I prompted.

"Goings-on. You know. Weird people hanging out there and that type of thing."

"What weird people?"

"I don't know. It's just rumors. The forest service calls it a cult."

"What kind of a cult?"

"That's all I know," he whispered confidentially, smiling and nodding at another passing guest. "If you're going up there, get your friends to go with you. Or wait until next Tuesday when I'm off."

Chapter
15

I didn't give myself any alternative. It was just something I had to do. I couldn't afford to freak out or be scared. I had to keep moving forward, into the unknown, until I found him.

I'd used maps before, but never one that showed roadless terrain. Instead of streets and highways, this map showed trails and topographical features with names like Dead Horse Canyon, Rattlesnake Creek, Moccasin Lake, and Smartypants Peak.

Under the watchful eye of Mike, the desk clerk, I traced the entire route to Devil's Spring in ink before I left the lodge. Mike told me to be prepared for some climbing. He also insisted that I take his sterling-silver bear whistle. (Sweet of him, since these whistles sold for $29.95 in the gift shop.) Bears had poor eyesight, he said, and didn't always see humans until the humans literally stumbled upon them. If I blew the whistle at regular intervals, it would alert any bears to my presence and give them time to run away.

That was reassuring.

"Keep an eye out for rattlers, too," Mike told me. "Seems like there's a bumper crop of 'em this year."

My knees went weak. "Will the whistle scare snakes away, too?"

He laughed. "Nah. Snakes don't have ears. All you can do with snakes is keep an eye glued to the trail. Rattlers like hot, sunny spots. Big flat stones, that type of thing."

Once for a lit class in junior college, I had to read this book of ancient myths. There was this one myth about a lovely maiden who was bitten by a serpent and sent to the Underworld. Her adoring husband loved her so much that he entered Hell and confronted all its horrors in order to see her again. This dude loved his wife so much that the gods in Hell took pity. They said his wife could follow him back up to the world of the living. But if he looked back at her even once during the journey, he'd lose her forever.

And that's what he did, of course. Tormented by doubt or curiosity, he looked back. And the poor wife, I think she turned into a pillar of salt or something weird.

As I left the lodge, I was thinking a lot about that myth. What I was doing was like a version in reverse. The wife going after her husband. A woman risking Hell for the love of a man.

A flat, easy trail covered with bark dust threaded east from the lodge along the river. A pair of joggers nodded as they huffed by. The trail led past tennis courts, an archery range, and another stable and horse paddock. I wondered if this was where Marcello housed his valuable stud Chiron. Beyond the meadow used as a private landing strip, the trail plunged into the dark forest.

Here the path was still maintained, and there were signs pointing off to various other trails. I stayed close to the river, which cascaded down an increasingly steep and rocky course. The rushing waters filled the air with a cool, effervescent mist that sparkled in the soft morning light. The air smelled so sweet and clean it tickled my nose and tingled around the roots of my hair.

Wheezing lungs and aching thighs soon told me the trail was getting steeper. Natural steps had been created from the exposed roots of giant riverside trees. The sight of those gnarled, fingerlike roots reminded me of something I'd read as a kid. Was it *Peter Pan?* Whitman had given me a beautifully illustrated copy for my tenth birthday. In the book, someone or something lived beneath a tree, and the entrance was through a vaginal opening at the base.

I continued to climb until the trail leveled out again and I entered, as if by magic, a huge open meadow. In the bright, clear light everything looked freshly created. Soft silvery-green grasses grew in clumps along the banks of the river. The meadow was dappled with wildflowers blossoming in bright shades of red, yellow, purple, white, and blue. Butterflies popped up from the thick carpet of meadowgrass, skated along the top of it, and disappeared again. I'd seen moths before but never real live butterflies. Every few seconds a gust of wind swept over the scene, like a hairbrush, making everything twitch and tremble. The crystalline air was filled with the chirruping songs and sudden piercing cries of unseen birds.

It looked like a safe place for a quick rest. I found a dry log on a pebbly curve of the river and pulled out my smokes. The air was so fresh it made me yawn. My eyes were watering. I closed them and raised my face to the morning sun. It was like being caressed by soft warm hands.

As I sat there, eyes closed, soaking up the warmth, I heard a soft whirring noise. I opened one eye. A hummingbird was hovering just inches from my head, so close I could feel the vibration of its wings. When I moved, it let out a faint *tsking* click and zipped away.

I followed its progress to a nearby bush covered with a froth of reddish-purple flowers. And when I saw what was happening, I just sat there in a kind of delighted shock, staring with wonder, like a kid in front of a department store window at Christmas.

The bush was covered with hummingbirds. Dozens of the tiny iridescent creatures, their rosy feathers gleaming in the sunlight, were zooming in to sip nectar. I'd never seen anything like it. In and out, up and down, backward and forward, darting, clicking, their wings a vibrational blur, they probed the heart of every flower, hovering effortlessly in midair as they stuck their needle-thin beaks in like nozzles to suck up high-octane sugar. They were tiny but plucky and didn't fly away when I slowly approached for a closer look.

But I couldn't be sidetracked. I had my own work to do.

I studied the map, trying to pick out topographical features. I'd come to a place called Sleepy Meadow. The jagged line of trees on a rise at the far end of the meadow must be Lightning Ridge. I couldn't see it, but nearby was Rheumatiz Gulch. So many creeks fed into the river that the map looked like it had a bad case of varicose veins.

I had to keep following the river until I came to the log bridge in Dead Horse Canyon. I couldn't tell how far that was, but I suddenly realized that I hadn't brought anything to eat or drink with me. Also, I had to go to the bathroom really bad.

I looked around for someplace to go. Which was pretty ridiculous, since I was the only person up there. If I wanted to, I could just walk along and poop wherever I pleased, like an animal.

I wondered what Sacagawea used for toilet paper.

Marielle's hiking boots seemed to weigh a hundred pounds each. The hot beginnings of a blister throbbed on my right big toe and left heel.

As I started off again, my mind nervously played out various disaster scenarios. From my brief phone contact with Tremaynne, I didn't know what to expect. He'd sounded like he was trying not to be overheard. He'd said "Hurry." Did that mean, *Hurry up, say what you have to say, and get off the phone?* Or, *Hurry up and get your ass to the hot springs because I'm in deep-shit trouble and I need your help?* He'd said he couldn't come back because of some big fuck-up. It all added up to ominous.

Maybe he'd been kidnapped by the weird cult that hung around Devil's Spring.

Maybe the cult was involved with the underworld of drugs. Drug people were dangerous, as I knew from my brief introduction to them in middle school. A girl I knew was shot and killed on the playground because she turned her crack-selling brother in to the police.

Or maybe when Mike said "cult," it was code for "terrorists."

That was what all the rich people at Pine Mountain Lodge were so nervous about. It had crossed my mind that Tremaynne might somehow be tied up with Earth Freedom. But if he was with them, why had he been so tight-lipped on the phone? Because they were on a secret mission? Or because he'd somehow run afoul of them? I felt instinctively that he was in danger, but I didn't know how or from what. One horrible possibility after another presented itself for inspection. Images tumbled through my agitated brain. Completely unsuspecting, Tremaynne goes out for a hike, crosses the river, and gets nabbed by the terrorist group or some weird cult hiding in the forest. They force him to the hot springs . . .

If that was the case, why didn't he want me to tell anyone where he was?

Because he'd escaped and was hiding from them? Or because one of them had a gun pointed at his head as he spoke?

I kept walking. My mouth was dry as a bone, but I didn't dare to drink the river water. I couldn't believe there was a river anywhere in the world that was clean.

I thought about it as my thirst grew. What could possibly pollute this water, way up here in the wilderness, away from factories and sewage? It looked absolutely pristine. But, of course, it was teeming with micro-organisms.

And fish.

It would be like drinking from an aquarium.

The river cut a wide, deep, curving trench through the meadow. The water didn't look more than waist deep, but it was running fast. Golden flecks of light shimmered on its surface. I walked along the bank, boots crunching on gray gravely rocks.

As I moved farther and farther away from the lodge, the map was all I had to find my way back. I held it tight, like a talisman. If I lost the map, I was a goner.

It was beautiful, what I was seeing, but it was frightening, too. It didn't make a lot of sense to me. Without people, it was just an empty landscape. I was more comfortable with concrete and asphalt and being indoors. Rooms with stale air and tinted windows and machines were more my style.

But thinking about that world, my world, as I trudged through this landscape, was like remembering an agitated dream. Out here, on Sleepy Meadow, my cramped concept of space was stretched beyond recognition. There was nothing around me but open land. I didn't signify in this place. I didn't matter. Who I was, or thought I was, or wanted to be, meant nothing. The only creatures that lived out here were the ones that knew how to adapt and survive. Even the fragile hummingbirds knew how to stay alive. But I didn't.

I figured I could go for at least one whole day without food. Water was more important.

I wondered what it must have been like for the Indians, riding through this vastness on their horses, and for the pioneers on the Oregon Trail, hauling all their worldly belongings across it in creaky covered wagons. Those people had no city consciousness, the way I did. Their way of life was incomprehensibly inconvenient. They'd never once torn open a bag of potato chips, for instance, or popped the tab on a can of cold Dr. Pepper.

At the next bend of the river, I came upon a thicket of berries. A thorny green tangle of vines cascaded down from the meadow above the riverbank. Ripe berries dangled like luscious black jewels among the treacherous thorns.

Blackberries. I was almost positive. But what if I was wrong, and they were poisonous?

A thorn pricked my finger as I reached in. The berry slid free. I carefully withdrew my hand and studied my prize.

It had to be a blackberry. Carolee made a fruit tart with blackberries. Every summer, the dads went out blackberry picking and served them with lemon sorbet or crème fraîche. I'd seen blackberries all my life, but I'd never picked one.

I couldn't be sure unless I tasted it. And even then . . .

I drew back my lips and took a tiny bite. A familiar sweet tartness exploded into my mouth.

Soon my hands were sticky, scratched and bleeding as I stripped berry after berry from the thick ripe clusters and stuffed them in my mouth. I wished I had some half-melted vanilla ice cream to go with them. I was starving and must have eaten a hundred.

Then, feeling bold, I decided I would drink some of the river water. Just a few sips, to slake the worst of my thirst.

I crouched by the shore and dabbled my stained hands in water so cold that it burned. I washed off the blackberry juice and then dipped up some water and looked at it. It was clearer than the water from my tap at home.

I scooped up another handful. At first I just put my lips in it. The ice-cold water took away the sting from raw blackberries and hot sun. Then, half-expecting to keel over as some *Alien*-like organism slid down my throat, colonized my gut, and exploded out through my chest, I closed my eyes and took a sip. Then another. The river water entered my system.

It tasted sweet, dense, unlike any water I'd ever drunk before. But I couldn't shake the notion that it was like drinking from an aquarium. What I really wanted was a super-size Dr. Pepper with tons of chewable ice chips, or a latte grandissimo with raspberry syrup and plenty of sugar.

Just upstream, some scrubby-looking bushes had taken root in the pebbly shore of the river. It was like seeing "Ladies" on a rest-room door. I could crouch between the bushes and do my business in private.

Flies buzzed around big splatters of what looked like dried black-berry puke caked on rocks near the shoreline. The river had thrown up smooth, broken branches. Leaves. Strings of plant debris. I passed the skeleton of a fish, its cloudy gray eye staring up at the blinding blue heavens.

Once inside my powder room I peeled Marielle's tight jeans down to my ankles, squatted over a weatherbeaten log, and let it gush. What a relief. The wind tickled my bare ass, blew through my crotch hair. Those Indian and pioneer women must have known the exact same feeling.

As I crouched there, relieving myself, I idly looked through the leafy branches.

That's when I saw the bear.

It was slowly ambling along the riverbank, stopping often to sniff the air. It was still quite a way off, but definitely heading in my direction. I looked for cubs but couldn't see any. A male, then?

I clamped down in mid-pee, stood straight up, and quickly yanked up my underpants and jeans. My head was light with fear. I looked across the meadow to see if there was any sort of protection.

And that's when I saw, far in the distance, almost at the base of Lightning Ridge, a house. Or a cabin. But it was hardly more than a speck; if I left the bushes, the bear might see me or smell me and give chase.

I stood there in a rising tide of panic, not knowing what to do. The bear stopped and stuck its snout into the blackberry thicket. Then it pulled back and looked in both directions. As if to say, *Who's been eating my blackberries?*

It was brown. Maybe six feet long.

The bear seemed to be hesitating. It lifted its nose and took a couple of pigeon-toed steps in my direction.

The glint of the sterling-silver bear whistle hanging around my neck brought me to my senses. It seemed like a dangerous thing to do. Wouldn't the sound identify my whereabouts, anger the bear, and bring him running?

In college, Daddy washed dishes at a lodge somewhere in the mountains of Montana. I suddenly remembered the stories he'd told me about bear attacks. The woman who came in carrying her own ripped-off arm.

At first I blew softly because I couldn't quite catch my breath. The bear didn't respond. When it began walking in my direction I blew as hard and loud as I could. The sound was high, sharp, piercing. I stayed in the bushes, shaking the branches. I blew until I was light-headed.

The bear stopped. Looked all around. Stood up on its hind legs and sniffed. Then turned tail and lumbered up the bank and across the meadow.

In a sweat, weak-limbed and gasping, I slowly crawled out from the bushes. I kept the whistle in my mouth, like a traffic cop. My eyes were as sharply focused as an eagle's.

The bear was loping toward Lightning Ridge, in the general direction of the house or cabin or whatever the distant building was. I lost sight of it in the long waving grasses of the meadow.

I stood up. My hands were trembling and I could barely concentrate on the map. It indicated that I'd find Dead Horse Canyon by following the river. I couldn't miss it.

I set off again.

The sky gleamed like hard blue enamel. I felt like I was high up and walking very close to the sun. The light flowed down in a bright golden sheet. It was getting hot. I shucked off Marielle's jacket. The heavy knitted sweater weighed on me like soft armor. I held it open for the breeze as I trudged along the riverbank.

Moving at a snail's pace through a gigantic landscape is a strange experience. Things you'd never bother to look at become charged with mysterious importance. You realize that everything's alive in its own way. "It's so quiet," I said to myself, but it wasn't quiet at all. The liquid rush of moving water was always there. Dry grasses hissed softly in the wind. Leaves rattled on shrubs and on the tall lanky trees growing on the opposite shore. Birds hidden in the meadow sang the same sweet-sad notes over and over again. Big fat flies buzzed. Every once in a while a fish jumped.

It made me sad that I knew so little about this world. I didn't know the names of the trees, or the shrubs, or the fish in the river, or the birds in the trees. I couldn't identify the wildflowers in the meadow, or the butterflies, or the stones on the shore, or even the kind of bear that had scared me half to death. I could identify things only by the coarsest terms: tree, shrub, rock. It was humbling and frustrating.

Tremaynne would have known what everything was. This was the kind of world he knew and wanted to be in all the time.

Any future we had together would have to include this world, and that scared me. Because it took work to live in this world. There were no conveniences, no short cuts, no ways to distract the mind. Tremaynne's goal was to be outside, in a vast unspoiled landscape, as much as possible. His goal was to save this, and the forests, and the free-flowing rivers, and even the bears and elk. Things I'd never thought about, or that I'd only seen on TV.

I remembered how he'd ignite in fiery rage when talking about developers and developments, about "sprawl," about the endless assaults made on land and water and sky, so that the animals were forced into smaller and smaller habitats. "All humans do is confiscate," he'd shouted once. "All we do is take and destroy."

I wondered, trudging along, where his rage came from. You had to have really strong beliefs to do the kinds of things he did. That's why I admired him so much. He was out of the ordinary. Above the ordinary. In his own world.

What about my own beliefs? What did I believe in? Did I have any beliefs at all? Or was my life about nothing more than seeking love, sex, and comfort?

Instead of feeling like a strong, confident, responsible woman, I felt like a silly little girl.

A silly little girl on her way to becoming a silly big girl.

Sweating and light-headed, I stood as close to the precipice as I dared and looked down into Dead Horse Canyon.

Horses walking along the narrow trail must have slipped and plunged down the steep rocky slope to their deaths. Or maybe they drowned trying to cross the river, which boiled and leapt through the canyon in whitewater rapids and waterfalls.

The air roared from the gigantic force of the water. The river came pouring down fast and furious to the canyon, where it was cinched tight like a thick waist in a whalebone corset. The water didn't seem to flow so much as explode, hurtling past boulders and spraying out from rock ledges.

I'd been following the trail, climbing up Smartypants Peak, for almost half an hour. I was burning and freezing at the same time. I shivered violently as the sweat dried on my skin. Marielle's sweater was soaked.

My mouth was parched, but there was no way to get down to the river and back up the canyon walls again. Or maybe there was, but I couldn't envision myself doing it.

I panted on until the log bridge materialized like a nightmare before my eyes.

I was supposed to cross that?

It was nothing more than a tree that had either fallen or been cut to span the chasm at its narrowest point. It was maybe twenty-five feet long. Ferns had sprouted on its sides and underbelly, kept damp by the constant mist rising from a waterfall roaring forty feet below. The log was unsecured. But someone had rigged two guide ropes from giant trees on either side of the canyon, so there was something to hold onto as you crossed.

"No," I said out loud. "I can't." I almost peed in my pants one time when the dads took me to Cirque du Soleil in New York and I watched the tightrope walkers.

I weighed my options. I didn't trust my footing, or my sense of balance. Instead of standing, maybe I could straddle the log and inch across that way. Still, my greatest fear was that I'd get halfway across, freak out, lose my balance, and plunge into the rapids and be swept into the waterfall.

I tugged on the guide ropes, checking how tight they were. Pretty tight.

I edged closer to the precipice. Even if I got down to the river by sliding down the slope, I'd still have to cross over to the other side. And given the belligerent force of the water, that was impossible.

It was either cross the log bridge or give up. The choice was that simple.

I could be a lazy coward and give in to my fears, as I always did. Or I could test myself . . . repudiate the helpless Venus who thought only and eternally of herself and her narrow comfort zone.

Faced with this choice, my thoughts turned brutally honest. Did I really want to risk my life for someone who'd maybe given me genital herpes? A husband who didn't want me to take his name in marriage? A man who'd probably deliberately stolen Whitman's cell phone for some purpose I couldn't fathom? A groom who'd inexplicably left his bride on their wedding night?

The choice was really about Tremaynne. It was about trusting him. Accepting him. Loving him. *Saving* him. If I turned back at this point, it meant the end of us and the little we'd had. Because it meant that I really had no faith in the power of our love. It meant that I didn't believe our love was worth the effort.

All my fears chimed in like a chorus of boogeymen. If he'd been kidnapped by a cult or the terrorists, what could I do? They'd get me, too. What if guns were involved? I had no weapon. I might be walking into a trap.

It would be easier to continue my search for Tremaynne back at the lodge, enlisting the police. It was the coward's way out, but it would save me from having to cross Dead Horse Canyon balanced on a log.

I remembered Kristin's hopeless declaration: "I'm a coward. I'm not like you."

She said that because she thought I was Godiva. And Godiva was not a coward.

I looked at the map for the hundredth time. Devil's Spring was so close. The trail on the other side of the canyon was even called Devil's Spring Trail. The trail left the river and wound up past Moccasin Lake to the hot springs. It was impossible to judge distance or gauge time, but it looked like it wouldn't take more than an hour if I was able to keep up my pace.

Oh, why couldn't I be Wonder Woman? She had no fears. She'd be able to leap over this canyon.

I was standing there, smoking my last cigarette, when I looked down the trail and saw someone on horseback far in the distance. The horse was white. It was moving slowly, picking its way up the rocky track beside the river.

Suddenly I wanted to move fast. I wanted to cross Dead Horse Canyon and disappear into the forest on the other side before Marcello reached me.

I got down on all fours and crawled to the edge. The sound, smell and moisture of the racing water rose up the canyon walls. I grabbed the log bridge with both hands. It was wet. I closed my eyes, steadying myself, and straddled it. My body was shaking, my heart pounding.

Keeping low, like a jockey on a racehorse, I inched forward. I was still on the earth. It was now or never. I sucked in a breath and moved forward until I was grasping the log where it left the cliff. It was like holding onto a shaggy beast with a wet coat, only instead of hair it was covered with ferns. My jaws were clenched so tight I thought my teeth might snap.

I couldn't bring myself to rise up and grasp the guide ropes. Instead, I intended to creep along like a blind inchworm. I kept my face so close to the log that I could smell its wet woody odor.

I commanded myself not to open my eyes. There was no reason to. If I held tight to the log and kept moving slowly forward, I could cross the span without once looking down into the raging torrents below.

But of course it was like the gods telling what's-his-name not to look back at his wife. The second you know what it is you're not supposed to do, you want to tempt fate by doing it. That had always been my way.

I tried to compare what I was doing to one of those really scary adventure-park rides that give you a wee-wee tickle just looking at them. The difference was that on a ride you were never the one in control. Someone else was at the switch. And no matter how much you screamed in fear, some part of you knew that you'd come out safe and that it would soon be over.

This was way worse than any ride. I knew that the moment I actually shinnied out far enough so that I wasn't on land anymore.

I squeezed that log like it was my lover. I kept my cheek clasped to its coarse, peeling bark. I wanted to look but I didn't dare. I could feel the airy nothingness of empty space all around me, and the force of the river vibrating up the canyon walls and thrumming through the bridge like current in an electrical wire.

It was like dying. That's how scared I was.

There was no such thing as time. There was only the next inch of forward movement. As I crept farther out, toward the center, I could feel the tension of the log, its slight bounce. I was soaked by the mist rising up in a cold wet breath from the waterfall.

"Laurie Ann!"

The sound was very faint, almost drowned out by the thundering roar of the river.

"Laurie Ann, stop!"

I tried to look back over my shoulder. But the moment I opened my eyes, I was aware of only one thing: the watery jaws of the river snapping and snarling forty feet below me. The disorienting perspective threw me off balance internally.

"Laurie Ann! Stop! I am coming out for you!" Marcello called.

"No!"

"I will save you!"

"I don't want to be saved!" But screaming was pointless. My voice was sucked out of my mouth and dissipated in the deafening roar of the water.

I felt the log tremble as he stepped onto it. That really freaked me out. "Stay off!" I cried. I inched forward until I could feel the upward heft of the log. It was so long that it sagged in the middle. I'd been going down, now I had to go up. It altered my sense of balance and I had to recalibrate every inch of my body.

I heard a terrifying cry and felt the log bounce. I looked back and saw Marcello frozen in a very weird pose. He looked like a mime taking a giant stride in midair. One foot had slipped, but he'd managed to hook the toe of his other boot around the log. He was clutching the guide ropes, actually pushing them away, as his foot dangled and scrabbled for the log.

His face betrayed no fear. He was intensely focused on saving himself.

I clung there in my jockey position until I saw him regain his foothold. Then I closed my eyes and inched forward as fast as I could. The log was bouncing as Marcello tried to steady himself.

"You must stop!" he called angrily.

Why must I stop? I'd come this far. I couldn't believe how much I'd survived already. It gave me a jolt of pride. For once in my life I felt lucky, even though I didn't know what for.

With a final spurt of determination, I reached the other side. I crept onto land.

I had crossed the river. I'd done it.

I looked back. Marcello was no longer standing on the log bridge. He was sitting on it, holding tight to the guide ropes, eyes clamped shut, as if he were praying. That was my last view of him before I headed up Devil's Spring Trail and back into the forest.

Chapter

16

Crossing the river shot me full of confidence. I was radiantly proud of myself for not succumbing to my fears. I had actually conquered my age-old panic about heights.

I felt as though I'd entered a new world.

I strode into the forest, fearless as Wonder Woman, and began to clamber up a rocky spur of Smartypants Peak, following the next segment of the trail.

Pain and discomfort didn't signify in this new world. The blister on my left heel was worse and my clothes were soaked, but it didn't bother me.

I was on a mission.

Finding my husband, rescuing him if necessary, was all that mattered. I couldn't just leave him to an unknown fate.

When we met again, it would be the beginning of our life together. I would prove to him how much I loved him, how much I was willing to sacrifice. He'd see just how wrong he was to doubt my love and my allegiance.

I moved fast, determined to elude Marcello. I didn't want to give him the satisfaction of stopping me from carrying out my mission.

No doubt like all rich men Marcello was accustomed to getting what he wanted. I figured he wanted me the way sportsmen want a moose or a bear or a duck. If he wanted to chase after me, fine. I didn't care. But he'd have to move fast because I was determined to reach Tremaynne within an hour.

I doubted Marcello would come after me, though. If Chiron was as valuable as Kristin said he was, Marcello wouldn't leave the horse alone on an isolated mountainside in the middle of nowhere. That's one thing I do know about the rich: they take good care of their status symbols.

I climbed higher, exhilarated by my lack of fear. I gulped the thin, sharp mountain air as deeply into my lungs as I could. Pretty soon I was hawking up mouthful after mouthful of slimy green phlegm.

Spitting was a new experience. It was kind of disgusting, but I liked shooting my firm snotty wads like soft green bullets through the air. Spitting made more sense than reswallowing that gunk.

The trail was little more than a narrow track following the steep, rocky contours of Windy Ridge. The trees here were enormous. Their crowns, towering a hundred feet above me, nodded and swayed to the chorus of winds that must have given Windy Ridge its name. Scattered along the side of the ridge were giant boulders and jagged rock formations. The colossal scale of everything was enhanced by the view, which swept down to a vast high valley densely packed with pine trees and veined with glittering silver streams.

It was completely quiet except for the soft scouring sound of winds sweeping through this huge natural arena.

As I reached the top of the spur, the track I'd been following vanished. The map indicated that Devil's Spring Trail hooked up with a logging road on the opposite side of the ridge. To reach it I had to go down into a scoop of forest, cross a stream, and climb up to a still higher plateau. It looked pretty strenuous, but I didn't cut myself any slack. I was in this to win.

* * *

On one of my trips to New York, the dads took me to see St. Patrick's Cathedral and another cathedral that Whitman called "St. John Too Divine." The sense of awe that came over me as I entered those gigantic buildings, one hand in Daddy's, the other in Whitman's, swept over me again as I made my way into the forest.

It looked like nothing had been disturbed on this protected shelf of land for thousands of years. The trees grew and the stream ran and the wind blew high overhead. It gave off the weirdest feeling, one that was hard for me, a city girl who knew nada about nature, to describe to myself. Without knowing what "holy" really means, I'd say it was holy. Or sacred, maybe. There was a sense of the eternal about it, a sense of something immortal, undying. It existed outside the realm of human anguish.

The stream was swift-flowing but shallow and easy to cross. I crouched down on a big stone in the middle of it, scooped water into the bowl of my hands, and splashed it into my face. Then I drank, greedily slurping down the sweet cold water until I was full.

That strange inner glow, as if I'd successfully passed some major test, came over me again. Something was different. I wasn't used to having this much physical energy or this much confidence.

If I'd read the map correctly, the logging-road segment of Devil's Spring Trail was on the plateau above me. I eyed the hillside, figuring out my route, and started up.

The map showed Moccasin Lake on top of the plateau. I envisioned pristine waters shimmering like a fat blue diamond in the green folds of the forest. But as I climbed towards the top, huffing and sweating, I started to get a strange feeling that something was wrong.

The upper hillside showed serious signs of erosion. There'd been landslides, and the earth felt unstable beneath my heavy boots. The wind blew harder and harsher up there. It didn't sing and hum, like in the forest. It sounded for all the world like a faint keening scream.

When I reached the top of the plateau, and saw it with my own eyes, I knew why it was screaming.

The whole plateau looked blank-faced with shock.

Every last tree had been cut. A massacred wasteland was all that was left. Moccasin Lake stared up at the sky like the cloudy-gray eye of a dead fish.

The plateau was like a battlefield where bombs had been dropped. Whole areas were gouged up and cratered out. All that was left of the trees were giant, overturned stumps that stuck up from the ground like corpses ripped from their graves.

A sense of dread clutched at the pit of my stomach. I wanted to get out of there as fast as I could.

The logging road wound through the devastation, past the lake, and into what appeared to be untouched forest. Devil's Spring wasn't far. But all my newfound confidence suddenly vanished, whisked away as if it had been nothing more than a magician's trick with smoke and mirrors.

A shadow passed over the decimated landscape like the wing of a huge dark bird. The sky lightened, then grew dark again. I looked up. Thick gray clouds were churning across the sky. When the sun disappeared, the temperature immediately dropped about fifteen degrees. Everything looked cold and desolate. That faint scream in the wind grew louder.

I forced myself to move ahead, to keep my feet going in what I hoped was the right direction.

I wondered what I was getting myself into.

It was like walking through a nightmare. The landscape was eerie and oppressive. What had been a teeming forest was now a huge, scarred absence, a nothingness. It was weird, but it was like I could sense the faint ghostly vibration of the forest still clinging to the battered earth.

There was no cover. Walking along the gouged and rutted logging road, I was completely exposed.

The sky grew darker. Sharp, bitter winds slapped up clouds of dust. I felt like I was the only living thing in a dead world. It was haunted, shunned by all creatures.

I hurried toward the forest rising up like a giant palisade in the

distance. According to the map, Devil's Spring was about a mile farther. First, I had to locate Devil's Spit Creek. I could follow that up
to the spring.

The air was buzzing with electricity. I could feel it crackling in
my hair, a current that seemed to be sucking energy straight up
through my body. A flicker of lightning, swift as a viper's tongue,
forked through the dark sky. It was followed by a crack of thunder so
loud that I cried out, like a scared kid. I felt like I was caught in the
crossfire of gigantic forces that spit fire and crushed the bones of
puny humans like me.

I began to run as more lightning bolts streaked through the air
above nearby peaks and ridges. The sky swelled and glowed like a
fresh bruise, all black and green and reddish purple. The winds that
started to blow were unlike any gust or gale I'd experienced on the
sidewalks of Portland or New York. All I could do was tuck my
hands under my armpits and keep moving, hunkered down, as they
swept over me. I thought my hair would be torn from my scalp. If I
straightened up, I was afraid that the wind would catch me like a sail
and blow me up and off Smartypants Peak. I could hardly catch my
breath. The wind sucked it out of my mouth.

I couldn't see any kind of shelter on the clear-cut plateau. I'd be
better off in the forest, surrounded by trees. I could hear them creaking, like the floorboards in the big old house I used to live in with
Daddy and Carolee. I thought of that big comfortable house where
once, for a short period, I'd felt safe and protected. The world around
me howled, screamed, shook with terrific cracks and rumbles. I kept
my head down and plowed into the wind like a linebacker.

The rain started just as I reached the perimeter of the forest. It
came in a sudden drenching sheet, not falling straight down but
blown horizontally by the winds that raged up and over the sides of
the mountain. The drops smacked my face like cold BBs. I moaned
but kept moving, moving, moving until I reached the perimeter wall
of forest and darted in like a wet, shivering cat.

The forest was full of rushing movement as the wind bellowed its way in from the naked plateau. Branches flopped and swayed; tree trunks groaned. But as I penetrated deeper, it became quieter, like a sturdy house in a raging gale. The canopy was so dense that it kept out the worst of the rain.

I had the sense that everything—trees, animals, and anything else that lived or lurked here—was alert and watching, silently waiting for the storm to pass.

And it did pass, departing as suddenly as it arrived. The last of the black billowing clouds swept by like the ragged hem of a witch's robe. A moment later sunlight pierced through the branches high overhead, needling down into an understory steamy with floating mists. The forest filled with a soft dense light. Birds called out their relief. The air swelled with a wet earthy fragrance.

I followed a well-worn trail, climbing over and ducking under fallen trees along the path. The hard red droppings of hunters littered the edge of every open glade. Some of the discarded shell cartridges looked new.

Cardboard signs had been tacked high on some of the trees. *No Trespassing. Private Property. Parcel T-341. Leased by Lumina International.* The signs were riddled with bullet holes.

Like victims awaiting execution, the biggest trees were marked with stripes of fluorescent orange paint.

I wondered if any of the trees had been spiked. Tremaynne had told me about this tactic. In disputed old-growth areas about to be logged, radical environmentalists would sometimes hammer iron spikes into the trees at the point where loggers would cut. If a chainsaw bit into one of the spikes, the chain would snap in two. It might even fly back and rip open the face of the logger.

It was hard for me to picture forests as war zones, but that's what Tremaynne said they were. This was his battle terrain.

A hissing sound carried through the silence of the forest. When I got to Devil's Spit Creek, I saw that the water was actually steaming. It must have been heated by the hot springs higher up the narrow gorge. The air had a sulphurous edge to it.

* * *

The moment I heard voices I stopped in my tracks and hardly breathed. As quietly as I could, I inched over to slide down and hide behind a tree. The voices were too low to be heard clearly over the hissing splash of the creek.

I sat as still and wide-eyed as an animal hiding from a predator. What next? I had to get closer. I had to see if it was Tremaynne. I had to be smart and careful.

The warmth of the water as it ran down its narrow rocky gorge heated the surrounding air and created a green belt of foliage around the creek. Beyond that, the forest trees were dense and enormous, and the underbrush thick. The steamy air cut down on visibility. Moving slowly and carefully, I made my way closer to the voices.

Six tents were pitched in a small clearing. Camping gear and a bunch of other equipment was scattered around the tents. I could see coils of rope, boards, and what looked like fish nets. Large plastic canisters were stacked on one side of the tents. Buckets and plastic containers were strung high on a rope between two trees. The air was charred from a recent campfire.

Beyond the tents was Devil's Spring. My view of it was partially blocked by trees and rocks. From what I could see, it was a series of wide stone pools. The water steamed out from a rocky shelf, dripped down from one pool to the next, and ran into Devil's Spit Creek.

The voices were coming from the hot springs.

I crept closer, on my hands and knees, alert to every snapping twig.

I got so close that I could clearly see them and hear what they were saying.

There were two of them. One was burly, bearded, and potbellied, his body covered with a mat of thick black hair. The other one was skinny with pale skin and long hair hanging down in dripping strands from a bald crown. The two of them lolled in the shallow, steaming pools of water, taking deep gulps from pint-size bottles.

I was certain I'd seen them before and racked my brain to remember where.

"That dumb fuck," Blackbeard was saying. "If he screws up—"

"Then fuckin' do it yourself, man," Skinny said.

"The point is, can he do it and get outta there fast enough?"

"Kind of late to be worrying about that shit now," Skinny said. He lifted his pint and chug-a-lugged. Then he popped open his eyes and shook his head and cried, "Shee-it! That shit's got one fuckin' mean kick when you ain't had none for three years."

"Cap was never one of us commandos," Blackbeard was fretting. "He never trained in the woods with us. His fucking wife wouldn't let him join."

"He ain't fuckin' got her to deal with no more," Skinny said. "He's fuckin' ready."

"I told him where the shit was hid. I made him repeat it to me."

"He'll find it."

"Gibbs did a good job with the sprinklers. That fucker's smarter'n he looks. They'll never suspect him."

"Always better to work from the inside," Skinny agreed.

Blackbeard tilted his head back and scratched his wooly throat. Suddenly he laughed, a high, whinnying sound. "I wish I could see it. I wish I could fuckin' be there."

"We done enough," Skinny told him.

"I'd like to see it, though. See the looks on those rich fuckers' faces." His own face suddenly contracted with anger. "Who the fuck do they think they are?" He gulped the last dregs from his bottle and hurled it in my direction. It smashed on a nearby boulder.

Skinny stood up and pissed handless from a long red dick into the basin below. "Who the fuck do any of 'em think they are? Rich Jews or rich college kids, none of 'em belongs out here. This land ain't theirs. They don't fuckin' own us. They can't fuckin' come out here and tell us what to do with our fuckin' trees and our fuckin' land."

"They're gonna find that out soon enough," Blackbeard laughed.

Skinny stepped unsteadily out of the pool and disappeared from sight. I heard snapping branches. A minute later he was back, still naked but wearing a red hunting cap and carrying a mean-looking automatic rifle. "Where the hell are those fuckers, anyway?"

"Out spikin' trees and building platforms. The cut starts next week unless they get a court order to stop it."

"You signed up with Lumina?" Skinny asked.

"Hell yes. It's the only work there's been around here for two years. Unless those fuckers stop it again."

Skinny raised the rifle to his shoulder. "We should just wait here and mow 'em down when they get back." He narrowed his eyes and fired six shots, aiming in all directions. "Nobody'd ever know."

"Then who the fuck would get blamed for setting the fire at Pine Mountain Lodge?" Blackbeard asked.

"Sweet," Skinny smiled. "Very sweet."

"Let's go have a look in the tents," Blackbeard suggested. "Might find something we like." Water sloshed over the side of the stone pool as he hoisted himself up. Flesh steaming, belly hanging like a heavy sack, he moved slowly toward his clothes. "Shit. That water made me dizzy." He blew out a breath and sat down on a rock.

"It's not the water, dude," Skinny said. "It's the hundred and twenty proof and that shit we smoked."

"Shit. I shouldn't of—" Blackbeard leaned over, opened his mouth, and spewed out a gush of vomit.

Skinny looked at him with amused disgust. "Shit, man. What kind of pussy are you?"

"It's the water," Blackbeard groaned. He retched again, then slowly got to his feet and wobbled back to splash his face. He stood for a moment, head bowed, then lifted it and let out a terrific belch.

"Where's the towels, man?" Skinny asked.

"Ain't they here?" Blackbeard's voice was weak. "You must of left 'em in the truck."

"*You* left 'em in the fuckin' truck," Skinny said accusingly.

"Just fuckin' stand there for one minute," Blackbeard yelled, "and you'll be dry."

"My hair won't," Skinny said.

"Fuck your fuckin' hair. Your fuckin' hair looks like a fuckin' monk in the middle of a fuckin' sex-change operation."

Skinny took off his hat and threw it aside. He didn't say anything but his face tightened, like he was ready to explode. It was the way Sean, my first ex, used to look when the mean side of the booze kicked in.

Skinny started hopping around on one leg as he tried to pull on his underpants. When he fell over, Blackbeard laughed.

"Shut up, you fuckin' son of a bitch," Skinny shouted irritably. When Blackbeard didn't stop, Skinny lurched over, grabbed his rifle, and pointed it at the laughing man's head. "I said shut up!" he screamed.

Blackbeard stopped laughing. "Don't fucking point your gun at me, you stupid fuckin' cocksucker."

Skinny didn't respond. He kept the rifle pointed at Blackbeard's head.

"Hey, we're buddies, man." Blackbeard's voice quavered. "We're fuckin' commandos!"

Skinny lowered the rifle. Then, just as quickly, he swung it up and let off a volley of shots. I closed my eyes and hunkered closer to the big rock I was hiding behind.

A frightened "Oo!" came out of a nearby tree.

It got really quiet. Skinny obviously heard the sound and was listening for more.

I looked up, trying to locate where it had come from.

"You hear that?" Skinny asked.

Blackbeard shook his head.

"Is someone the fuck up there?" Skinny yelled.

Blackbeard picked up his shotgun.

"Up in that tree." Skinny didn't aim, he just shot in the general direction of the sound. Then waited.

"Maybe it was a owl," Blackbeard said.

"Wasn't no fuckin' owl," Skinny said irritably. He fired again.

This time the tree said, "Uh!" like it was sucking in a scared breath.

Skinny, wearing his baggy underpants, and Blackbeard, naked, stepped unsteadily through the woods until they were at the base of the suspected tree. They passed so close to me I could smell the reek of the liquor they'd been drinking.

"Tell me if someone's up there," Skinny called, "or I'm gonna shoot your ass down."

As Skinny and Blackbeard were looking up, a thick slosh of fluorescent orange paint came hurtling down from the tree and splashed over their heads and shoulders.

"What the fuck? Shit!" The two of them danced in wet, confused circles, shaking their arms. Furious, half-blinded by the paint, swearing unlike I've ever heard anyone swear, Skinny fired up into the crown of the tree. I could hear the bullets pinging through the branches. He must have run out of ammunition because he screamed, "Fuckshit cocksucker!" and slammed his rifle into the side of the tree. Then he grabbed for Blackbeard's shotgun, but Blackbeard wouldn't give it up. The gun was covered with paint and so slippery that neither one of them could hold on to it.

I heard creakings, shakings and crackings up in the tree, as if some really large animal was jumping down from branch to branch in a frenzied effort to escape. Or maybe it had been wounded and was crashing down, unable to hold on.

I crouched there in a sweaty panic, watching from behind my rock, not daring to show myself. I couldn't run away. I was terrified the gun was going to go off and kill Skinny. Or that if I ran they'd shoot me, like an animal. Or that whatever was in the tree had been shot and would momentarily plummet down to earth.

Then I saw him. Tremaynne. Using a rope, he swung and jumped down to a lower branch of the tree. The branch bounced up and down. I was certain it was going to crack under his weight. He'd fall to his death, or they'd see him and shoot. I screamed his name and stupidly ran out into the clearing.

Blackbeard finally wrenched the shotgun away from Skinny. He fell backward and the gun went off. I screamed again.

Skinny, eyes glaring, spun around in my direction. Blackbeard scrambled onto his knees and took aim. I stopped in my tracks, frozen like a deer in headlights.

This is it, I thought. *If there's one bullet left, it's got my name on it.*

"I'll take care of her," Skinny said. "I want some Sierra Club pussy real bad." He made grunting, guttural sounds and pretended to be an animal stalking me. He made a sudden lunge and laughed when I darted away.

I didn't know where to go. I was afraid to run deeper into the woods. I didn't want him attacking me there, out of Tremaynne's sight. And I didn't want to run closer to the tree where Tremaynne had been hiding. They hadn't seen him yet, and the best thing would be to decoy their attention away from him.

"Save some of that pussy for me," Blackbeard said.

"You wanna shoot it first?"

"No, man. I want it live."

"Yeah," Skinny said, "we can fuck it live and skin it afterwards."

Help me, help me, help me, I prayed. *Someone come. Someone please come.* Then I saw what Skinny and Blackbeard couldn't see because they were so hung up on me. Tremaynne was lowering himself down from the tree. He was silently hanging there on a rope, in midair, and if they turned they'd see him and use him for target practice. I had to keep their attention away from him long enough for him to reach the ground.

My mind was racing. I had to come up with a plan of action. I had to disable two grown men who had a gun.

"I'll get her," Skinny vowed. "You keep watch on the tree."

Skinny started after me, and I ran. I had so much adrenaline racing through my veins that I could almost fly. I ran back to Devil's Spring, snatched up their shoes and clothes, and threw them down into the lowest pool. Now they'd have to carry on naked or take the time to fetch out their soaked clothes.

It wasn't easy racing through a dense forest without shoes or clothing. Skinny was forced to slow down to a hobbling sprint. When he saw what I'd done, his face contorted with rage. "Fuckin' cunt! Now I'm really going to slam your ass!"

I ran back toward the tents in the clearing. There was no place to hide. The tents offered no protection. I dashed back and forth, my eyes scouring for a weapon, for someplace safe. I ducked down behind the stacked canisters and carefully peered out.

Blackbeard had turned his attention back to the tree. He saw the rope. He moved closer and aimed his shotgun up into the tree. That's when Tremaynne leapt out and smashed Skinny's discarded rifle into the back of Blackbeard's knees. Blackbeard let out a startled cry and dropped as if his legs had been chopped off. Tremaynne used that moment of surprise to whack the butt of Skinny's rifle against Blackbeard's head. Blackbeard toppled forward but held on to his old shotgun.

I saw Tremaynne trying to pry the gun away. Blackbeard was at least twice Tremaynne's size. He suddenly reared up, teeth bared, like an enraged beast, and tried to knock Tremaynne down. Tremaynne pestered him like a fly so that Blackbeard couldn't get a solid grip on his gun or take aim. His ponderous belly swayed and shook.

I was so engrossed in watching them that I didn't see Skinny until he sprang out with a roar from behind a nearby tent. His sticky orange skin was covered with leaves and debris. He'd obviously been crawling to escape my detection.

Plunging forward, out of his reach, I knocked down the wall of plastic containers. It was harder for him to maneuver, shoeless, but he looked like he was at the point where physical pain no longer mattered. Trapping me was his sole concern.

I made a frantic circuit up and down and between the tents, like a ball trapped in a pinball machine, trying to keep him at a distance. But Marielle's big boots weren't exactly made for pirouetting in tight spaces. My toe caught in one of the taut ropes at a corner of a tent. Arms flailing, I crashed down on top of the tent, which collapsed under my weight.

As I scrabbled to get free of the nylon, I felt a hand tighten around my ankle. I didn't know what I was doing by then. Everything was blind instinct. Before he had time to bear down on me, I pulled my leg up and kicked it back with all my might, like a furious horse.

The sole of Marielle's boot landed right in Skinny's face. He let out a moan and reared back, covering his face. Blood spurted out of his nose and gushed between his fingers.

His shocked surprise gave me time to scramble to my feet and jump away from the collapsed tent. I looked back to see what was happening with Tremaynne and Blackbeard.

It was horrifying. As I watched, Blackbeard managed to swing around from his kneeling position, whack Tremaynne's jaw with his gun, and pull him down. Given Blackbeard's size, I could see that Tremaynne, once down, didn't have a chance.

Skinny took his hands away from his face, revealing a thick wet mustache of blood. Blood was mixed with the orange paint. His eyes were red, his hair hanging in sticky coils. The look he gave me was so terrifying that I didn't allow it to register on my emotions. Chest heaving, panting for breath, he slowly stood up and started for me again, slower this time but with even more determination.

I snatched up a board lying beside the tents and raced toward Tremaynne and Blackbeard. Skinny shouted, "Behind you!" When Blackbeard turned, I slammed the board as hard as I could into his face. I used it like a baseball bat.

Blackbeard let out a short, strange, high-pitched grunt and pitched forward. Tremaynne wriggled free, jumped up, and started kicking the squirming, moaning Blackbeard. He kicked him once right in the balls. Blackbeard shrieked.

"Stop, stop, oh my God, stop," I whimpered. "Don't kill him."

"Get the gun," Tremaynne panted, slamming his booted foot down on Blackbeard's back.

I looked down. Blackbeard was lying on top of the gun. I turned
back to Tremaynne, but it was Skinny that I saw. He was plowing toward us with a long heavy net. I saw what was coming and cried out
"No!" But by the time Tremaynne turned, Skinny had already
hurled the net and we were caught.

Chapter
17

Once they had us netted and tied up, Skinny and Blackbeard pondered our fates. It was payback time for the painful indignities we'd inflicted on them. Whatever their ultimate decision, Skinny made it clear that raping me was part of the plan.

Tremaynne and I were face to face, molded together under the heavy net. I searched his eyes, trying to anchor myself, as Skinny and Blackbeard weighed various options. Should they drag us behind their truck? Douse us with gasoline and set us on fire? Scalp us with the hunting knives back in the truck?

My mind was in a panic. I started to cry. I tried to keep it quiet, so they wouldn't hear me, but tears flooded my eyes and I couldn't brush them away because our limbs were bound with rope tied outside the net. I started to shake, my body spasming uncontrollably.

Tremaynne brushed his lips back and forth across my face. I think he even licked up some of my tears. "Don't give up," he whispered. "Breathe."

I pulled in a raw, snuffly, uneven breath. I felt like I'd been stripped naked in front of him. There was no room for fantasy. I wasn't Godiva, or Wonder Woman. All I was was me, Venus Gilroy, who'd stumbled into a really dangerous situation. Thinking to rescue him,

I'd done just the opposite. I'd fucked up big time. I'd put both our lives on a roulette table spun by a couple of stoned, gun-happy freaks.

"You know they're going to come back and find you," Tremaynne suddenly said in a loud voice.

Skinny kicked him in the back. "Who said you could talk?"

"Just leave us," Tremaynne pleaded, "just leave us and get the hell out of here and we won't do a thing."

Skinny kicked him again. "Dude, you ain't in no position to make no deals."

Tremaynne grunted with the blow but refused to shut up. "They're going to be back any minute. There's ten of them. They'll see what's going on and stop you."

"No they won't," Skinny said, "'cause we got a gun."

"Yeah, but you don't have any shells left," Tremaynne said.

The statement seemed to enrage Skinny. He held out his hand. Blackbeard handed him the gun. Skinny circled around us, stopped, took aim. "Didn't nobody ever tell you what we do to shitfaced kikes who come out here and spike our trees and keep us from working?"

I whimpered and squeezed my eyes tight.

"I'm telling you," Tremaynne persisted, his voice quavering. "They're gonna be here. Any minute." He was so scared that he had to gulp in a breath about every three words. "That was the plan. I'm not shitting you. That was the plan. They're gonna be here. Ten guys. Big guys. Get out of here now. While you can. Leave us and go."

Skinny and Blackbeard were silent. Tremaynne took advantage of their silence to keep talking. "Look, we're on your side," he argued. "You don't get that, but we are."

Skinny let out a high dry laugh.

"We are," Tremaynne insisted. "We're on your side. We're not against you."

Skinny hawked and spat. I opened my eyes and saw a wad of bloody snot running down Tremaynne's cheek.

"Let's go get our shit," Skinny said. "These pussies ain't going no-where."

"Venus," Tremaynne groaned. "Why did you come?"

"I thought you were in trouble."

"I didn't expect you to come."

"I had to find you."

"You shouldn't have come."

"You just disappeared."

But there was no time for any personal, emotional stuff. No love scenes between reunited lovers. We had to act quick.

"Listen," Tremaynne said, "there are no bullets in that gun. Okay? You don't have to worry about the gun. He's bluffing with it, and the other gun's broken."

"I got the hairy one pretty good with that board," I said. "He still looks out of it."

"They're both out of it. They've been drinking all day. But they're pissed off, really pissed off, and that gives people weird energy."

"What do we do?" I sucked in a ragged breath, trying to hold back the panic I could feel plucking at me.

"We've got to stall for time," Tremaynne said.

"Where are those ten men?"

"What ten men?"

"You said ten men would be here any minute."

"It's five, and they're scattered all over the forest."

"Who are they?" I asked.

He turned his face away and wouldn't answer.

"Are they Earth Freedom?"

He didn't answer.

"Did you come out here to be with them? Tell me the truth, god-damn it!"

He nodded.

"Oh God," I said.

"But they've set us up," he whispered, his voice hoarse and urgent. "This paramilitary group. They're going to set the fire. Because they know we'll be the fall guys."

I wanted him to say he was sorry. But that was stupid. It was pointless to be mad or hurt or upset. Right now we had to work together. Our survival depended on mutual cooperation. Coming up with a plan and sticking to it.

It was impossible to stand because the net had been bunched and tied beneath our feet. But within the net we could use each other for leverage and roll sideways.

Our bodies were sticky with orange paint and dripping with sweat. Our breath came in grunts and gasps. Sharp sticks pierced our clothes and jabbed our faces as we clumsily hauled ourselves across the forest floor. The goal was to reach the trailhead that cut in from the logging road. Tremaynne said if we could get to the parking area, maybe someone in the Earth Freedom group would be there, hiding out in the vicinity, waiting for the two hunters to leave.

I was a very obedient wife and did what my husband told me to do. I didn't trust *him*, but I trusted his strength and his ability to remain clearheaded in extreme situations. I admired him for that.

And I cursed myself for being so goddamned secretive. Nobody except the desk clerk at Pine Mountain Lodge knew where I'd gone, and he thought I was Godiva. All I'd told Marielle was that I was going out hiking with Tremaynne. I hadn't told the dads zip. If the dads wanted to find me, they wouldn't think to ask the desk clerk, and the desk clerk had no reason to tell them, unless I didn't come back.

I had a vision of them—the dads, Marielle and Fokke, Geof Killingsworth, Kristin, Mike, Marcello, everyone trapped and screaming as a homemade bomb exploded and flames engulfed the lodge. A surprise attack. Even if everyone escaped, Daddy's beautiful building would be destroyed. And the ecoterrorist Earth Freedom movement, of which my husband was a member, would be blamed for the work of a right-wing paramilitary organization.

This wasn't the sort of honeymoon I'd been counting on.

* * *

Moving by inches, like some monstrous larva, we finally reached the trailhead. There were no other vehicles parked there, just Skinny and Blackbeard's metallic blue pickup. The minute I saw the big cage in back I knew where I'd seen them.

They were the hunters who'd killed the bear. We'd run into them in Snakebite, the day before. They'd draped the dripping bear carcass over the cage to enrage the blood-lust in their dogs. Tremaynne had shouted at them in front of the Snakebite Café, and they'd laughed.

Thank God there weren't any dogs now. Maybe they came later . . .

"Shit," Tremaynne whispered, "here they come."

I listened. It sounded like they were thwacking their way through the brush.

"What now?" My heart was booming. So was Tremaynne's. I could feel it through all my clothes. Once upon a time our hearts had beat together like that when we were making love. Now they were beating from fear.

"Where could they of got to?" It was Skinny, sounding like a parent hunting his children in a game of hide 'n seek. "You see 'em? They can't of got far."

Tremaynne wrenched his body. This was my signal to roll on top of him and pull him down on the other side. We started our routine, trying to move away from the truck. But then I saw where he was headed and my body froze.

"I can't," I wheezed. "Tremaynne, I can't."

We were about a yard from the edge of a steep precipice. The wind roared up over the lip of it.

"We'd never make it," I cried. "We couldn't control our fall."

Tremaynne looked at me. His breath had a hard metallic smell. I know now that's the smell of terror. His eyes were sharp and glittering. "What choice do we have?"

My teeth were chattering and my breath wouldn't come right.

"No sign of 'em anywhere." Skinny's boots crunched out on the gravel near his truck. They crunched over to where we were. *"Mm, must of got away. Guess we may as well go."*

What were they up to? We were right in the road. They had to see us.

They got into the pickup. The motor roared. The truck slowly started to back up.

Straight toward us.

We stiffened. Then, frantic, we rolled, once, twice, until we were at the very brink of the chasm. And still those huge wheels slowly kept moving, until they were no more than a foot from our heads and we could smell the exhaust and the rubber of the tires.

The truck kept inching backward. It would either crush us or force us off the cliff.

I thought I'd conquered my fear of heights. I hadn't. I looked once and saw what would happen. The drop was a vertical plunge down a steep cliff face to a river far far below. Our fall would be broken by a rock ledge about thirty feet below. Maybe we'd land there and stop, all our bones broken. But more likely we'd glance off the side of the ledge and plummet down like a dislodged boulder.

Skinny maneuvered the truck until the wheels were actually touching us. Another inch and we'd be over. That's when I screamed. I had to. I screamed as loud as I could. I screamed until my throat was raw. I screamed so loud that the sound echoed in the canyon below.

"Venus." Tremaynne tried to calm me but I wouldn't be calmed. "Venus. Venus."

I screamed until the truck stopped and I heard the emergency brake being pulled up. The two doors opened. I heard the crunch of boots.

"You hear a sound?" Skinny said, looking right at me.

"Didn't hear nothin'." Blackbeard's voice was subdued, like he still wasn't feeling so hot but had to play along.

I was trying to catch my breath but afraid to breathe because the exhaust was making me sick to my stomach.

And then, in the distance, I heard strange music. I thought maybe this was what you heard when you were dying. I was light-headed from the exhaust. My eyes were so heavy I could barely keep them open, and my whole body started to go limp.

What I heard was an opera aria. I didn't know the name. I didn't know the opera. It was one of those things I'd heard a hundred times but never paid any attention to. It was an aria that Whitman was always playing.

Tremaynne tried to rouse me. "Venus!" He brushed his face against mine.

"Pretty music," I babbled.

"Venus, stay awake. Someone's coming."

"Tell the dads I love them."

I was vaguely aware of fast-talking voices and sudden movement. Skinny and Blackbeard jumped back in the cab and the truck shot forward. A rush of fresh air revived me. The truck stopped, and they leapt out again and ran around to the back. Skinny slammed down the tailgate and fumbled to open the door of the kennel.

"Get 'em in there, fast," he ordered.

They dragged us toward the truck. Once we were away from the cliff edge, Tremaynne started to struggle. He squirmed and wiggled like a powerful fish and his manic energy infected me so I squirmed and wiggled, too. The only way we could resist them was to slow them down.

The opera aria was louder. It was coming closer. Someone was loudly singing along with it. There was only one person who sang opera like that.

"My dads are coming!" I cried.

It was true, wasn't it? The dads had saved me countless times before. In New York, Daddy saved me when a man suddenly grabbed me on Broadway and tried to jam his hand into my underpants. Daddy knocked the man out, and the man later sued Daddy for assault. And once, I remembered very clearly, Whitman saved me from drowning at Jones Beach. We got caught in a swell and were being sucked out to sea, but he somehow managed to get hold of me and shoot me forward out of the deep water until I could stand up again. Every time someone or something tried to harm me in New York, the dads had been there, fearless.

We squirmed and thrashed, banging against the wire as Skinny and Blackbeard tried to stuff us into the cage. Even fighting as hard as I was, I could see and smell how filthy it was back there.

"Fuckin' stuff 'em in!" Skinny screamed. He tried to jam our heads in as we flopped and hurled ourselves around on the tailgate. "We'll cover 'em with the tarp."

"There's no time, man," Blackbeard panted. "Let's just get the fuck out of here." He was starting to panic. "They catch us, man, you go back to the pen."

"We can't leave 'em. They know too much. Let's fuckin' throw 'em."

Then the joyous sound of a motor, of wheels on a dirt road, of that aria and Whitman singing at the top of his lungs as the dads rounded the last hairpin and started up the long steep incline toward us.

The goal was to be heard. We had to be heard over the music, over Whitman's voice. I screamed "Daddy! Daddy! Help!" and Tremaynne screamed along with me.

"Shut the fuck up!" Skinny bellowed. They were working fast now. They picked us up and hurled us into the kennel, slammed the door, flipped up the tailgate, and hopped back into the cab. The truck hurtled forward, spitting gravel, backed up, and sped down the road. The tailgate fell open as we lurched over a hump in the logging road.

We were sprawled on the floor of the cage and being jolted around so much I thought all my bones would be broken. A terrible stench, like rotten meat, rose up from the bed of the cab. The side panels on the truck were so high I was afraid the dads might not even see us. Our only chance was to make ourselves heard.

The road was so narrow that two vehicles could pass only with difficulty. Skinny was driving at breakneck speed, but he had to slow down to get past the dads. When he did that, I screamed until my jaws locked and I thought my eyes would explode. Tremaynne screamed. We screamed louder than the orchestra that was carrying the voice of the opera singer and Whitman.

Once he got past the dads, Skinny sped up again. Behind us, through the open tailgate, we saw the dads' battered SUV sitting motionless on the road. The music stopped. We screamed again. The SUV started to maneuver into a U-turn.

Desperate people do desperate things. That's the only way to explain it.

You have to be desperate to drive that fast along a dirt road with hairpin curves and no side barriers. A dirt road so worn and rutted that we bounced into the air and fell back to the floor of the cage like a heap of clothes in a dryer.

And you have to be desperate to give chase on a road like that.

And we were desperate, too, because all the bumping and jolting loosened the cage from the bed of the pickup. We could feel ourselves sliding off by inches, and we were powerless to do anything about it. Every time the truck squealed around a curve, I was certain we'd be flung out into the canyon.

At one point the cage bounced sharply, and when it crashed down again, we found ourselves wedged up in a half-sitting position against the back. That's when I had my first glimpse of the dads. The minute I saw them, I just started to bawl my head off. I didn't see how they could do what it looked like they were trying to do.

In that moment I knew that they were risking their lives for me.

Whitman was driving. His face was sharp and totally focused on the back of the pickup, reading and responding to every move. He was inching up and trying to get alongside. But the dads were on the outside of the road. One misjudged moment and they'd plunge off. That was obviously what Skinny wanted them to do. He swerved out and shimmied back in.

Daddy was shouting out the window for us to hold on.

But we couldn't hold on. That was the problem. There was no way we could keep the cage from fishtailing off the tailgate.

At the next sharp curve, Whitman slowed and the SUV fell behind the pickup. He followed just inches behind. If the cage flew out now, we'd smash into their windshield and go careening off the edge of the road.

Once he was around the curve, Skinny accelerated. He was now going faster than before. This stretch of the road felt relatively smooth, until his left rear tire blew. There was a loud pop and a sudden lurch as that side of the truck collapsed. The kennel hopped forward another couple of inches.

But even with the blowout, Skinny didn't stop. He slowed down for a few seconds, but then it felt like he actually speeded up. The back of the truck, sunk down on its left side, began to shudder and vibrate. Something was being ground up. I could smell it burning. Major damage was being done, probably to the axle. If he didn't stop, the whole chassis could be ripped out.

Whitman took advantage of the momentary slowdown to roar up alongside us. I couldn't believe my eyes. The passenger door opened. Daddy squeezed out between the door and the seat. When he yelled, "Now!" Whitman veered away from the truck, giving Daddy enough space to squeeze out the door and grab the side panel of the truck. He hauled himself in just as Skinny hit another curve and the cage went sliding. Daddy held onto it as we squealed around the curve.

Whitman fell back behind us as the pickup started to skitter and shake. It was hard to tell if Skinny was deliberately swerving close to the edge before swinging back in again, or if he was losing control of the truck. The blown tire and collapsed rear were throwing the whole thing out of alignment. If he kept up this speed, the axle would snap.

We roared around another hairpin curve. Daddy could barely keep his grip on the cage and hold himself upright. "Hold on, baby, hold on!" he shouted.

But we couldn't. Daddy was the only one who could hold on. When the truck hit a huge pothole, he lost his footing and crashed forward onto the cage. We all slid toward oblivion. I saw the edge of the road and then nothing, just a vast distance across the canyon.

I screamed. Tremaynne clenched his eyes tight. Daddy swore. We were about halfway off the tailgate. One more major rut or pothole and we'd be tipped out. If we crashed down to the road we might survive, provided Whitman could stop fast enough. But if the truck was juddering along next to the precipice when it hit the hole, that was it. We'd be flipped out into eternity.

At some point I just gave up. I realized there was nothing I could do. I turned my life over to whatever weird forces were in charge of the universe.

Then Whitman started to lay on his horn. He kept at it and kept at it, signaling something. Daddy managed to turn and snatch a look over the cab.

"Another truck!" he shouted. "He'll have to slow down."

No, I thought, *he doesn't have to do anything. Desperate people like Skinny don't do what you want them to do.*

"When he slows, I'm going to push you off," Daddy said. "So be prepared."

I wanted one last look at him. A snapshot to take with me to whatever place came next. To see him, I had to crane my neck and roll my eyes back. There he was. The dad I'd loved and hated for twenty-five years. I don't know how he was holding on. I could feel the incredible strain of his body as he tried to keep me safe. His face was beet red, his lips pulled back in agony, veins popping from his neck and the side of his head. Legs spread wide, feet jammed up against built-in toolboxes on either side of the bed, he grasped the metal cage with his bare bleeding hands and kept his eyes focused right on me.

I couldn't speak. I had no sound left. I mouthed the words. *Love you.*

Then I looked away from Daddy and turned my attention to Tremaynne. What message could I give him? In the end, all you want to leave behind is love. You realize that when you get there.

Love—

I'd just started to mouth the word when the truck rounded another curve, hit another hole, and we were flung up and over the broken tailgate. Daddy, still clinging to the cage, went with us.

I felt the impact as we hit and flipped and skidded toward the edge of the canyon. I heard *"Oof"* and *"aah"* but didn't know who the sounds belonged to. Maybe to me. I heard the squeal of brakes and the skidding of tires.

Then I was dizzily aware that we'd stopped moving.

I felt like a rag doll, battered and flung into a corner.

A car door slammed. Whitman was racing toward us.

Daddy slowly stood up. He motioned toward us.

Whitman got the door of the cage open and untied the ropes. The release of pressure was like a huge orgasm. Tremaynne and I flopped back, panting with relief. Tremaynne was a mess. I shuddered to think what I looked like. Whitman helped us crawl out of the cage. My legs wobbled like a calf just out of the womb.

We all just stood there holding and hugging one another and crying our eyes out. The two of them held Tremaynne and me in a tight four-way embrace.

Daddy lifted his head, wiped his nose, and pointed down the road. "Look."

The pickup had stopped. It was blocked by a large white vehicle parked at an angle in the middle of the road. The pickup sat there, broken-down and smoking, as worn-out and sad-looking as the guys inside it.

It was suddenly so quiet. My buzzing ears picked up the sound of the wind flowing through the great canyon below us.

"What's he doing?" Whitman said.

The pickup gunned its motor. It careened backward. The passenger door flew open and Blackbeard clumsily leapt out.

We watched in a kind of silent awe as Skinny turned the wheels, stepped on the gas, and removed himself from the scene.

Chapter
18

"Oh my God," one of us said. I think it was me.

Without another word we piled into the dads' SUV and raced down the road.

My attention was focused on Blackbeard. He was standing in the middle of the road, frozen, his arms thrown up in shock or disbelief. And we all knew why. He'd just watched his buddy deliberately run his car off the cliff and plunge to his death.

An ashen-faced passenger in a white Chevy Suburban got out and walked stiffly toward the precipice. He was a young guy, no more than twenty, but his movements were so slow that it looked like he was struggling under the weight of heavy armor. He wore a green maintenance uniform with *Lumina* stitched across the breast pocket.

"Jesus Christ," he said, peering over the edge. He looked back at Blackbeard. "Why'd he do that?"

Blackbeard couldn't speak. He stood there, mouth open, making little choking sounds.

The man looked at us, huddled together in stunned silence, as if we were his accusers. "Wasn't our fault!" He pointed nervously toward the Suburban. "Prince Brunelli there, he thought there might be trouble up at the Lumina parcel. He thought we should go up there to check it out."

No one said anything. I stared at the tracks of the pickup in the dusty road. They were clear as a diagram. You could see them right up to the edge, and then nothing.

"We seen the pickup tearing down the road in this direction," the Lumina guy continued, "and the prince thought something was wrong, thought he'd better stop. Thought he could force the pickup to slow down."

Now the driver climbed out. It was Marcello. Face grim, he approached us. Approached me, I should say. The look in his deep dark eyes was so intense that for a moment I thought he was going to take me in his arms and kiss me. His voice was husky when he spoke. "You are—all right?" When I nodded, his attention widened to take in the others. "All of you?"

We heard a gagging noise and turned to look. Blackbeard appeared to be choking. He gasped and grabbed his throat, mouth gaping, eyes bulging, tongue protruding, face red as a poisonous mushroom. His hands shot out and clawed at the air, and then he turned and took a couple of tottering steps, his eyes imploring us to help him, before collapsing into an epileptic seizure.

It was horrible to watch, but I wasn't wasting too much sympathy on him.

"Give me your belt!" Whitman snapped his fingers at Marcello. I thought he was going to strap Blackbeard's huge, hairy hands together. Instead Whitman straddled the convulsing body, bunched up the belt, and managed to insert it between Blackbeard's gnashing teeth. Daddy, the driver, and Marcello helped to hold Blackbeard down. His body arched as if he were being electrocuted; his eyes bulged and rolled.

My hand found Tremaynne's, clasped it, and squeezed. He squeezed back. We stood there, silently watching.

Tremaynne nodded toward Marcello. "Prince Brunelli. He's the one who owns Lumina International."

Tremaynne was being oddly quiet. I was the one who did all the talking. I told the dads, Marcello, and Marcello's assistant everything I'd overheard about the plan to destroy Pine Mountain Lodge.

Marcello whipped out his cell phone and made three quick phone calls. He called Geof Killingsworth at the lodge, the police chief in McCall, and someone at the Bureau of Land Management. It was obvious that he wielded a lot of clout locally.

Was he really a prince? I'd never seen a prince before. The title made him into a completely different person in my eyes.

Blackbeard finally stopped his frantic thrashing and lay panting on the road like an injured animal. Marcello said he and his assistant would stay with him until the police and ambulance arrived. It was impossible to reach Skinny except by helicopter. His car was flipped upside down like a squashed bug on the canyon floor. No one could have survived that kind of impact.

By the time we returned to Pine Mountain Lodge, the county police had arrived and a couple of officers were combing the grounds. Geof Killingsworth was waiting on the front steps when we pulled up. He hurried over and asked Dad Two if he'd mind driving around to a back entrance.

"Yes, I would mind," Whitman said obstinately. "We've just been through hell, and we all need to sit down and decompress. *Immediately.*"

Geof K looked over his shoulder. Curious guests were peering out from the reception hall. "I was hoping that we might avoid any further negative impact on our guests."

Whitman turned off the SUV and we all got out.

"Holy Christ," Geof K said when he saw Daddy's ripped shirt and scraped arm. "John. Do you need an ambulance?" Then he saw Tremaynne and me. "Holy Christ. Should I call for an emergency helicopter?"

"We're all right," Daddy said, putting one arm around me and one around Whitman. I fished my hand behind me hoping Tremaynne would take it and not feel left out.

He didn't.

* * *

Geof Killingsworth ushered us through the lobby, past the staring guests, toward his office.

"What happened?" someone called out.

"Just a little car accident," Geof Killingsworth lied.

"Whitman!" Marielle rushed over, a stricken look on her face. She clasped Whitman tightly in her arms.

"We're okay," Whitman assured her. He gently peeled himself free. "I'll talk to you later."

Geof Killingsworth herded us into his office and closed the door. "Please," he said. "Someone tell me exactly what happened up there."

They all looked at me. So I repeated the entire story. Only this time I left out a few small details pertaining to the Earth Freedom group that I now knew was hiding out in the forest.

"The Commandos," Geof K said when I told him about Skinny and Blackbeard. "Shit." He looked at Whitman. "I know you won't mention this in *Travel*," he said. "It would be a public-relations nightmare."

"It certainly would," Whitman agreed.

"This isn't the only state with right-wing paramilitary groups," Geof K said defensively. He paced around his office. "They're everywhere. All over the country. Half of them are fronts for methamphetamine labs."

"This guy Gibbs," I said. "The one who screwed up your sprinklers. Who is he?"

"*They* sent him out," Geof insisted. "The sprinkler company sent him out to do the calibration."

"He must have known if the sprinklers went haywire this opening weekend, you'd turn them off," Daddy One said.

"Perfect setup," Daddy Two agreed.

Geof K smacked his big fist into his palm. "We're going to sue their asses. Big time."

"You need to find the one called Cap," I said, "and stop him before he can do anything."

"I've doubled security," Geof K said. "If he's out there we'll find him."

"It might be a good idea to get people out of the building," Whitman said.

Geof K clasped his hands together, almost like he was praying. "I don't feel comfortable evacuating everyone."

"It's a good way to test if all your emergency systems are working," Daddy said.

"It's a good way to scare off every rich fucking asshole we've got staying here!" Geof snapped. "Shit. Prince Brunelli's got so much invested in this place. If we go belly up—" He suddenly looked very haggard. "The local economy's already's so shaky. All those fucking eco-freaks have practically shut down the logging industry. Tourism's all that's left."

I looked over at Tremaynne. He slowly chewed on his lips and stared at me with wary eyes. His expression was, like, *Are you going to tell them about Earth Freedom?*

The door opened and a wide-eyed Kristin entered. "I thought maybe you could use some advanced hydration delivery systems." She put down a tray of bottled waters. "And a first-aid kit." Her eyes swam with tears when she saw me. "Oh my God. Godiva. Are you like okay?"

"I'm okay," I said.

Whitman said, "Godiva?"

"We all know," Kristin said. "You don't have to pretend anymore."

Everyone looked at me. The room was totally silent.

"I'm not who you think I am," I said to Kristin.

"Yes, you are," she insisted. Her eyes darted back and forth. "Did you tell them?" she whispered, close to tears. "About the horse?"

She was terrified that I'd tattled about Marcello's horse. When, in fact, I'd completely forgotten about it. "Everything's okay," I reassured her.

"Kristin, you can *go*," Geof said.

She practically bowed and walked out backward, like we were royalty.

"I don't think any of us wants an advanced hydration delivery system," Daddy said. "I think we all need a strong shot of whiskey."

Geof K had a private bar. He was pouring out whiskies when a middle-aged police officer wearing an ill-fitting black wig and aviator glasses was shown in. The color drained from Geof's tanned face when the officer told him they'd found a cache of explosives hidden in one of the maintenance sheds.

Incredulous, Geof turned to Daddy. "Why would they want to blow up our beautiful resort?"

I was about to blurt out, "So Earth Freedom would be blamed and the timber sale could go ahead." But I didn't. I looked at Tremaynne and bit my tongue. He sat there with his head bowed, gnawing on his lips, peering up occasionally at the other men. In this male power clique, he was the one with no power. Nobody knew who he really was, or the real reason he'd come out here, so he was ignored. But if they ever found out . . .

Maybe he's done with Earth Freedom, I thought selfishly. *Maybe now he'll be mine.*

"Why would someone want to blow up my beautiful building?" Daddy shrugged and shook his head, wincing as Whitman dabbed hydrogen peroxide on his lacerated arm. "Resentment?"

So Daddy and Whitman didn't remember about Earth Freedom either. I was babbling a mile a minute when I first told them about the plot I'd overheard at Devil's Spring. Maybe I hadn't even mentioned Earth Freedom.

"Resentment?" Geof Killingsworth couldn't fathom such a concept. "This is going to be one of the world's great resorts. It's going to spur development all over this region. Why should anyone resent it?"

We couldn't go back to our suites until we'd given statements to the police.

With Tremaynne at my side, I gave my name, age, date of birth, social-security number, and then told our story for the third time. How the two of us had gone out for a hike, hoping to find Devil's Spring. How we hid from the two armed men at the hot springs and overheard their plan to destroy Pine Mountain Lodge. How the men discovered us and assaulted us and how we'd fought back and tried to escape and been captured and thrown into the cage in their truck and how the dads had saved us.

"And Prince Brunelli," the officer added. "If he hadn't stopped in the middle of the road, blocking their escape, God only knows where you'd be right now."

When it was Tremaynne's turn, he gave his name as Phillip Klunk. He spoke so softly that the dads, sitting on the other side of the room, couldn't hear him. But I heard him.

He kept his eyes on me. I understood that I wasn't supposed to contradict anything he said.

I didn't gasp or object when he gave an address in Sacramento as his place of residence. He obviously had his reasons. I'd just assumed he'd say his home was with me, in my apartment in Portland. He told the officer my story was exactly what happened. He had nothing else to add.

We couldn't get into our suite because I'd lost the security card. Rather than go back downstairs to get a new one, Daddy said we should go through their room.

"We're going to leave you absolutely alone," Whitman promised. "Order room service. Order a massage. Order anything you want. You still have one day left on your honeymoon."

"So do you," I said.

"And we're going to make the most of it." Whitman turned to Daddy. "If Geof Killingsworth pesters you one more time, I'm going to bust the caps off his perfect teeth."

The phone started to ring. "And what about Marielle?" Daddy said.

"I'll talk to Marielle tomorrow."

And then, having settled that, it was like they couldn't wait a second longer. With a loud groan of delayed passion, they embraced and kissed right there in front of us.

The sight made me feel weak in the knees.

I turned to go but Tremaynne just stood there, staring. Finally the dads realized that we hadn't left. They turned and looked questioningly at my husband.

Tremaynne nodded and cleared his throat. "I uh—I just uh—I wanted to uh—to say uh—well—." He walked over to them with his hand extended. "She's lucky to have dads like you."

I closed the door. We were finally alone.

We turned to look at one another. It was the queerest feeling. Like, *we're alive. We made it. We're safe.*

But also, *we're in this together now.* Because I now knew that my husband was a member of Earth Freedom, a radical group that had claimed responsibility for destroying buildings worth millions of dollars. Earth Freedom had never killed anyone, that wasn't their intention, but they were considered terrorists.

Enemies of the capitalist system.

I didn't know what to say. What could I say? Tremaynne didn't say anything either.

He brushed his dirty hand along my paint-smeared face. I caught it, held it to my sticky cheek.

Then with a gasp we were locked in one another's arms, kissing and crying and tearing off one another's filthy clothes.

"Ow!"

"Aah!"

Pain was part of the pleasure. It meant we were alive. Our flesh was covered with scrapes, cuts, bruises. We kissed each other's wounds. We were hot as fire. We were alive and together.

"Awh!"

"Careful!"

We both smelled, but I inhaled the stink like it was perfume because it was our odor, our conjoined stink, and it told the story of what we'd just been through and what we'd escaped. Together.

"Ouch!"

"Ooh!"

We kicked our clothes aside and stood locked together in a naked embrace. I could feel his cock, full and hard, pressed against my thigh. He stroked my breasts, then lifted them to his hungry mouth, all the while pushing me back toward the bed.

We fell back onto softness. Softness now, instead of hard earth. He climbed on top of me. Then he rolled over and roughly pulled me on top of him.

"Oh, Venus, Venus," he moaned. "Why the fuck did I ever marry you?"

Husband. Hot tub. Champagne and Dr. Pepper. Caesar salad for two. Cheese platter with double-fat French Bries and Camemberts. Huge musky Italian grapes. Warm focaccia with peanut butter and jelly. Sliced papaya, mango, and kiwi. Dunhill cigarettes in a fancy red box.

I had everything I wanted except money, power, and a huge juicy cheeseburger with dill pickles and french fries. I didn't want to offend Tremaynne by giving in to my carnivorous desires. I'd have to change my eating habits big time to make them compatible with his vegetarian ways.

Our meatless feast must have cost over a hundred bucks, but it was all paid for so I didn't care. We had it laid out on the terrace beside the hot tub.

We ate and soaked and for the longest time just sat there, naked, Tremaynne holding me in his arms. The steaming water was like liquid balm.

A luminous midsummer moon hung bright and clear in the star-washed sky, pouring its silvery light over the distant folds of forested mountains. It was so quiet that we could hear the river singing. The air was sweet and chill, perfumed with scents that were now familiar to me.

A feeling of security spread through me as I lay in Tremaynne's arms. It was the first time I'd ever had this sensation. It was like the calm after a storm. A feeling of being safe with someone who was stronger and calmer and surer.

I've finally found the right one, I thought. *Different as we are, we are destined to be together.* The thought made me light-headed with joy.

I'd finally found a love to equal the dads' love for one another. I could now live in that same mysterious place they lived in, that secret sacred spot where two became one and no one else could ever hope to intrude.

I felt like our bodies were permanently bonded. Working together, as one, under the most extreme circumstances, we'd forged a physical partnership that would last forever. After what we'd been through there could never be any barriers between us.

"I have to go," Tremaynne whispered in my ear.

I thought he meant, go to the bathroom, so I slid to one side and said, "I'll wait out here."

He stroked my chin. "No. I mean go. Leave."

I stared at him. I heard the words, but they went dead in my ears. He said, "You knew that, didn't you?"

I shook my head. I could feel the blood draining from my face.

"It'll all disappear, Venus, unless we do something about it."

"Do what?" My voice was harsh. "Spike trees? Burn buildings?"

"You saw it with your own eyes," he said calmly. "You saw it, Venus."

I turned away, curling up like a silent fetus in the hot broth of a mother's womb.

"You walked through it," he said. "You drank the water. You saw the trees. It isn't a fantasy, Venus. It's real."

"They're just trees," I cried miserably.

Tremaynne hoisted himself out of the tub and sat on the edge, his flesh steaming. "I'm not going to get into an argument with you about it."

"Why not? We're married! We're supposed to argue."

"You said you wouldn't stand in the way of my personal fulfillment."

"What about my fulfillment?"

"File for a divorce," he said. "It's better to do it now rather than later."

"No," I said.

"It was a mistake, Venus. I'm sorry, but it was a mistake."

"It wasn't a mistake. I love you."

"A mistake on my part," he said quietly. "I should have known it wouldn't work. We're just too different. I'm too different." He hugged himself. "You said once that you could accept me as I really am. Well, this is how I really am."

"We can work through the differences," I said. "I'll change. I'll totally change."

"For me?"

"Yes, for you."

"That's not a good reason to change," he said.

I couldn't bear what I was hearing. I almost wished we were back in the forest, tied up, struggling to survive. "You used me," I sobbed. "You used me to get out here. That's all it was."

He reached out to touch me, but I slapped his hand away. We didn't speak for a few moments. In those moments my entire life flashed before my eyes. I saw clearly what I had now and what I'd done with my life: nothing.

"I'll come with you," I said finally. "I'll join. I'll help you."

"Venus."

"I'll sit in a tree. I can do it. I know I can do it. After today I can do anything."

"Venus. This isn't play-time. This is what we believe in. It's our lives. We'll die for it if we have to." He tilted his head, trying to get me to look at him. "It's more important than any—relationship. I didn't know that until I got out here. Until I saw what's here, and what they're doing."

I lunged out of the tub and took him in my arms, squeezing and sobbing. "You can't go. You don't have anything. No clothes. No food. Nothing."

He tried to make light of it. "Hey, that's how I came into the world."

"Don't leave me," I cried. "Please don't leave me."

An owl hooted far in the distance. Tremaynne, instantly alert, peered in that direction. I realized it wasn't an owl at all, but one of them, calling him away.

He stood up, leaving me half in the tub, and went into the room.

I looked up at the bright silver moon, at the sparkling stars, at the vast mysterious forest rolling away as far as the eye could see. It wasn't asleep. I knew that. Under the soft white blanket of moonlight it was alive. Every inch of it. Breathing. Watching.

The owl hooted again. My heart felt like broken glass. I looked in and saw Tremaynne pulling on his clothes. Getting ready to go.

Chapter
19

Wearing dark glasses to hide my puffy eyes and some of the scratches on my face, I waited for the dads down in the lobby. I felt weirdly fragile, ghostlike, transparent, as if the light pouring in through the glass wall in the reception area could pass right through me.

An empty vessel. A drained glass. A sponged blackboard. A blank page.

A nothing.

Maybe it was delayed shock. Or the fact that I hadn't slept or stopped crying for the past ten hours. I was all cried out. Any more tears and I'd be weeping blood.

The dads were taking care of last-minute details. A valet had gone to fetch the SUV from the garage. Our luggage was sitting on a cart out by the front steps. In less than fifteen minutes, I'd be leaving Pine Mountain Lodge. And my husband.

The honeymoon was over.

So was my marriage.

I wandered over to look at Daddy's model of Pine Mountain Lodge. A meticulous world in miniature, it was perfect down to the last detail. You could almost see tiny people hurrying through the rooms, living tiny, thumb-size lives.

Daddy was big on order. Whitman, too. Life for the dads was about organization.

Mine was about chaos.

I remembered the look on their faces when I burst into their room early that morning. Burst in with a keening wail, running blindly for their bed, for their comfort. I crawled in right between them and clung desperately to Daddy. I told them everything. That Tremaynne was a member of Earth Freedom, everything. I put his future in their hands.

A tanned couple in white tennis clothes, carrying tennis rackets, eyed me as they crossed the lobby. Did they think I was Godiva, the wild European rocker? Their eyes had that hungry, searching look, as if they thought I might be somebody.

What a joke. I was nobody. I felt like I had no identity at all.

And I didn't want to be seen. I was certain that people could look right through me. See the nothing I was. So I crouched down beside the model, found our suite, and peered in. There was the very room where we'd made love with an intensity that I would remember the rest of my life.

As I was examining the tiny room, replaying the scene of our lovemaking, I remembered that I hadn't taken my birth control pills.

I'd missed two days.

My body went hot. I stood up very slowly.

I saw Kristin walking toward me and I turned away, not wanting to smile or talk.

"I was afraid you'd left already," she whispered.

I shook my head.

"Are you waiting for your handlers?"

I nodded. "Only they're not my handlers," I confessed. "They're my dads."

Kristin didn't hear me. She didn't want to. She didn't want the truth to spoil her fantasy. "I wanted to give you something," she said. "Something special, to remember me by." She thrust a small polished piece of wood into my hands.

Cut into the wood, in a flowery script, were the words "Eternal Love." A rawhide thong was poked through holes at either end.

I looked at her, unable to speak.

"I made it myself," she said. "In shop class. Three years ago. It's a necklace. See?" She took it from my hand and placed it over my head. "The words glow in the dark."

I nodded and sucked in a really deep breath.

"You probably meet thousands of girls," Kristin said. "On your tours and stuff. So you probably won't remember me. But maybe you will. Maybe I'll come visit you in Iceland. Or you'll come back here, to Pine Mountain Lodge."

I stroked her bare arm and quickly walked away, using the butt of my hand to wipe away a new flood of saline. Outside, on the front steps, I dug in my purse for a cigarette. My hands were shaking so bad I must have looked like a drug addict, or like I'd just chug-a-lugged six double espressos in a row.

Sniffing and clearing my throat, I made my way over to the luggage cart and sat down. I was weary beyond exhaustion.

Two days of missed contraception.

Was it too late?

Was it already growing?

How could I stop it?

Did I want to stop it?

When would I know?

I'd have to quit smoking.

The dads' SUV pulled up beside me, dented but sparkling clean, and the valet hopped out. "Well, here she is." He gave the hood an affectionate pat. "This baby's taken quite a beating, but Prince Brunelli had our mechanic check out the engine and everything's cool. They gave her a wash, too."

I nodded and stood so he could get the luggage.

Where were the dads?

Where was Tremaynne? Was he back in the Earth Freedom

camp? I retraced my journey up the river, over Dead Horse Canyon, through the forest and the clear-cut plateau to Devil's Spring. From now on that would be my inner geography. My secret universe. In my thoughts and fantasies, Tremaynne would live somewhere in that magical and terrifying stretch of forest.

I touched Kristin's necklace. Love might be eternal, but fate was heartless. I'd fallen in love with Tremaynne because he had ideals, because he was dedicated to something larger than himself. I hadn't known that his demanding ideals would ultimately take him away from me for good.

He'd been mine only when we were in bed. I knew that now.

Where was he at this very moment? How would he live? What if the police or Bureau of Land Management found the camp and confiscated all the tents and supplies and arrested the members of Earth Freedom?

"They'll never find us," Tremaynne laughed when I voiced this concern the night before. "They never have and they never will. We move fast."

If anyone ever came to me seeking information, I was to disavow all knowledge of his activities.

But what if there was a baby?

I moaned and turned to climb into the SUV. I'd just sit there until the dads came. I couldn't understand what was taking them so long. I wanted to get the hell out of there as much as I wanted to stay. If I'd had a wedding ring, I would have anxiously twiddled it, turning it around and around on my finger like a talisman to help me in my hour of need. But I didn't have a ring. All I had was the tattoo permanently etched at the root of my ring finger. I stroked it and felt my face go all quivery, like I was going to start bawling again.

The other passenger door opened. A deep voice said, "Some coffee for you."

Marcello handed me a large stainless-steel travel mug with *Pine Mountain Lodge* printed on the side.

"I added some cream and sugar," he said. "I hope it is satisfactory." He snapped his fingers and someone darted forward with a cardboard box. "Some sandwiches," Marcello said. "Fruit. For your journey."

"Thank you." My voice was so low even I could hardly hear it.

Marcello suddenly slid in beside me. He reached out for me but quickly caught himself and pulled back. "If you tell me it is impossible," he said, "it will only make me work harder."

I couldn't speak. All I could do was look at him.

"I can arrange things," he said. "You could live here."

I touched his hand. Just a touch, then drew it away. I was grateful to him, but I didn't want to give him any ideas.

"I will take that as a beginning," he said.

"What?" I whispered.

"It is the first time you have touched me."

I gave him a wan smile. "Listen," I said, my voice low, "I'm not Laurie Ann, okay? That person's dead."

Marcello moved an inch closer, staring at me. "Then who are you?" he asked.

I thought about it. "Venus," I said. "Just plain old Venus."

"Venus." He smiled and gently took my hand. "Pleased to meet you."

"Are you really a prince?" I asked.

He nodded. "But, in America, I try not to be."

We sat there like two kids on a first date who didn't know what to say to each other. Finally Marcello fished in his pocket and pulled out a business card. On the back, he scribbled a number. "This will always reach me. Direct." He patted his breast pocket. "I keep this phone right next to my heart."

I took the card and managed a faint smile.

Marcello stuck his hand out the door, snapped his fingers again, and this time was handed a beautiful bouquet of wildflowers. "These are for you. So you will remember me and Pine Mountain Lodge."

I nodded.

He raised his hand and gently stroked my hair, then slid out and was gone.

*   *   *

We were all pretty quiet. Daddy and Whitman took turns driving. We'd travel for, like, fifty miles before one of them would say something.

"I canceled my cell phone number," Whitman informed me. "He won't be able to use that phone."

The phone. I'd completely forgotten about it. And now it didn't matter. It was no longer a lifeline, merely a dead gadget.

At one point Daddy looked at me in the rearview mirror and said, "Were *they* planning to burn down my building, too? Earth Freedom?"

"I think they're trying to stop a timber sale," I said.

"Because they've destroyed other buildings," Daddy said. "We did a search on the computer this morning. We checked all the newspaper stories about Earth Freedom."

"Daddy, I don't know."

"It's a very shadowy group," Daddy said.

My faux pa turned around to look at me. "The next time you say you're getting married, we're going to run an FBI background check on the guy."

"I'm never getting married again."

I don't think Whitman heard me. "This must be the shortest marriage on record," he said. "No, I think there's one even shorter. I read about it in *Ripley's Believe It or Not.* The couple drove directly from the church to the lawyer's office and filed for divorce."

He was probably trying to cheer me up. But he was also reminding me of my tendency to leap before I look. I think the dads thought I was mad at Tremaynne. Hated him for betraying me. And I did, of course. But I didn't see him as a criminal or a dangerous terrorist. Those were words used by the other side.

I stared vacantly out the window as we sped along the blacktop, past mile after mile of tall pines. It was hypnotically monotonous. Unless you got off the road and out of your car, you'd never have a clue as to what was really out there, in those deep canyons and high plateaus and mountain peaks already dusted with snow. You had to feel the earth beneath your feet. Hear it with clean ears. Smell its powerful but elusive scents. You had to put yourself right in the middle of it, without any of your daily props, and accept it as something that existed in and of itself, for itself, beyond your grasp. It was a home for creatures that didn't obey human laws. For whom humans were the enemies.

The bouquet of flowers Marcello had given me sat on my lap, along with his card. *Marcello Brunelli. Lumina International.* That's all it said. There were two telephone numbers, a fax number, and an e-mail address. I turned it over and studied his handwriting, the way he formed numbers. Figures were important to him. Each numeral was very clear. The sevens had lines drawn through them, the European way.

All I had to do was pick up a phone and dial.

The afternoon sun beat down on the speeding SUV, releasing the scents of the wildflowers and sandwiches and fruit supplied by Pine Mountain Lodge. We'd decided we'd stop only for gas and toilets. If we kept up our pace, we'd be back in Portland by ten that night.

Every mile took me farther and farther from Tremaynne.

Every mile brought me closer and closer to Portland, where I'd have to resume a life that suddenly seemed terrifyingly meaningless. I'd have to go back to work at Phantastic Phantasy. Stand behind the counter in that stuffy, smelly porn shop with tinted windows and cum stains on the carpet and help men check out their sexual fantasies. Or rap sharply on the doors of the video booths to remind them that they had to spend money. Run the barcodes for *D Cups* and *Rump Roast* and *Manmeat* and other magazines across the scanner. Order new dildos and buttplugs.

And go back to my tiny apartment and deal with things like what I'd microwave for supper.

Go over to my mom's and hear about her latest self-esteem serum.

Unless I made some changes in my life, big changes, humongous changes, I was headed nowhere fast.

School? Maybe.

Possibly.

A baby? Maybe.

Possibly.

All I knew was that I couldn't go back to being what I was. Something in me had changed. I didn't know what it was or how, ultimately, it would affect me. I had followed the river and crossed Dead Horse Canyon and traveled to places most mortals don't even know exist. I'd been Venus, Godiva, and Laurie Ann.

I'd done it, and I'd come back, and if I didn't find some new way to keep moving ahead, I would never find fulfillment.

Maybe there was no such thing as fulfillment. Maybe it was all in the doing.

I looked at the dads. They were holding hands. They were in love. In their own way, they had followed the river and crossed the canyon.

I saw a sign for Hell's Canyon.

I waited until Daddy was just about to head down the first stretch of the narrow, hairpin canyon road.

"Let me drive," I said.

The dads looked at each other.

"What?" Daddy sounded alarmed. "Why?"

"I just—want to."

"It's not an easy road," Whitman said. "Remember what happened on the way out?"

"Please," I said. "It's important. It's something I need to do."

They looked at each other again. Daddy pulled over. "I'm putting it into four-wheel drive."

"I want both of you to sit in the back," I said. "You'll make me too nervous up front."

Whitman made the sign of the cross and got out. Daddy got out. I got out. The wind was blowing up the canyon. A mile down, the Snake River wriggled along the canyon floor. The sky was completely clear, the hot sun scouring down from the western sky.

The dads climbed in back. I got in the driver's seat. We all buck-led up.

"Are you sure you know what you're doing?" Whitman said.

"I'm taking you guys for a little honeymoon tour." I adjusted the rearview mirror and caught a glimpse of their tense faces. They were clutching each other's knees. "Trust me?"

Daddy said, "We trust you, Venus. We know you can do it."

"Just keep it slow," Whitman said, "so we can admire the view."

I turned around and said, "I love you guys." Then I released the brake, slipped the gear into Drive, and started forward with the sun in my eyes.